After Midnight

By Teresa Medeiros

AFTER MIDNIGHT
YOURS UNTIL DAWN
ONE NIGHT OF SCANDAL

TERESA
MEDEIROS

After Midnight

AVON BOOKS
An Imprint of HarperCollinsPublishers

AVON BOOKS
An Imprint of HarperCollins*Publishers*
10 East 53rd Street
New York, New York 10022-5299

To the memory of Hellen Chism.
It was an honor, a privilege,
and a blessing from God to call you "Granma."
I will keep you in my heart
until we meet again.

For my darling Michael,
for being generous enough
to share his love, his life,
and his "granma" with me.

Acknowledgments

I want to thank my amazing editor, Carrie Feron, whose keen insight and discernment turned this book from a dream into a reality, and my extraordinary agent, Andrea Cirillo, for being a dream to work with for the last fifteen years.

I want to thank Richard and Eleanor Morris, wherever they are. Drayton and Linda Hatcher would also like to thank you for opening up your hearts and your home to their little girl when she needed you the most.

I want to thank my Axis of Angels, for always making me laugh when I wanted to cry.

After Midnight

Prologue

London, 1820

He prowled the fog-shrouded alleys, searching for prey. His footfalls were mere whispers on the cobblestones as he slipped from shadow to shadow, his cloak rippling behind him. Although his passing drew more than one hungry, sidelong look from the cutpurses and whores slouched in the doorways, he didn't spare them so much as a glance. For him, the night held no terrors. At least none that the living could provide.

Of late, the darkness had become both his lover and his enemy, the thing he craved and the thing he most longed to escape. When a gust of wind whipped through the narrow alley, driving both the mist and the clouds before it, he turned his face to the moon, his senses starved for light. But even its pale, silvery rays were no longer any balm for the bloodlust that had infected his soul. Perhaps it was too late. Perhaps he was already becoming the very thing he was hunting. A predator without mercy or remorse.

He heard it then—a soft ripple of feminine laughter followed by a man's low murmur, smoky with promises and lies. Drawing back into the shadows, he slipped a hand into his cloak and waited for his prey to come into view.

The man could have been any young buck, fresh from a recent triumph at some Covent Garden gambling hell or brothel. His beaver top hat was set at a cocky angle on his fashionably trimmed curls. The woman stumbling along in his possessive embrace was little more than a girl, her shabby finery and rouged cheeks marking her as one of the lightskirts who lingered outside of the seedier gambling hells, hoping to find a protector for more than just one night.

Humming a snatch of drunken song, the man swung her around in a clumsy parody of a waltz before pinning her against the nearest lamppost. Her shrill giggle held a note of both desperation and defiance. Even as the rogue slipped a hand into her bodice to cup her naked breast, he wound her thick auburn hair around his other fist and tipped her head back, baring the pale curve of her throat to the moonlight.

The sight of that throat—so tender, so graceful, so pitiably vulnerable—stirred an unnatural hunger in his own belly.

Striding out of the shadows, he grabbed the man by the shoulder and spun him around. When she saw the feral gleam in his eye, the girl's pretty face went slack with fear. She stumbled a few feet away and dropped to her knees, clutching at her gaping bodice.

Closing his hand around his prey's throat, he slammed him up against the lamppost. He lifted him effortlessly, tightening his grip until the man's booted feet flailed at the air and his icy blue eyes began to bulge. In those eyes, he saw both fear and fury. But most gratifying of all was the bleak recognition that came a moment too late for it to matter.

"Pardon me, mate," he growled, an affable smile curving his lips. "I hate to trouble you, but I do believe the lady promised this dance to me."

One

"Our sister is marrying a vampire," Portia announced.

"That's nice, dear," Caroline murmured, making another neat notation in the open ledger on the writing desk.

She'd long ago learned to ignore her seventeen-year-old sister's rioting imagination and penchant for drama. She couldn't afford to abandon her responsibilities every time Portia spotted a werewolf sniffing around the trash heap or fell back upon the sofa in a semiswoon and announced that she was coming down with the Black Plague.

"You must write Aunt Marietta immediately and insist that she send Vivienne home to us before it's too late. We're her only hope, Caro!"

Caroline glanced up from the column of numbers, surprised to find her baby sister looking genuinely distressed. Portia stood in the middle of the dusty parlor, clutching a letter in one trembling hand. Her dark blue eyes looked stricken and her normally rosy cheeks were as pale as if some cloaked fiend had already sucked all the blood from her tender young heart.

"What on earth are you going on about now?" Her concern growing, Caroline laid aside her pen and slipped off the stool. She'd been hunched over the writing desk for nearly three hours, struggling to find some creative way to subtract the monthly expenses from their household accounts without making the final tally add up to less than zero. Shrugging the tension from her shoulders, she pried the letter from her sister's hand. "Surely it can't be as grim as all that. Let me have a look."

Caroline immediately recognized their middle sister's flowery scrawl. Brushing a pesky strand of pale blond hair from her eyes, she quickly scanned the letter, skipping over the endless descriptions of tulle-draped ball gowns and sprightly curricle rides down Rotten Row in Hyde Park. It didn't take her long to hone in on the passage that had drained all the color from Portia's face.

"My my," she murmured, arching one eyebrow. "After only a month in London it appears our Vivienne has already acquired a suitor."

Caroline refused to recognize the familiar pang in her heart as envy. When their aunt Marietta had offered to sponsor Vivienne's debut, it had never occurred to Caroline to point out that her own Season had been indefinitely postponed when their parents had perished in a carriage accident on the very eve of her introduction to court. And Caroline had soundly dismissed those same pangs when Vivienne departed for London with a trunk packed with all of the beautiful things their mother had chosen for her own postponed debut. It was a waste of valuable time to mourn a past that could never be changed, a dream that could never be realized. Besides, at four-and-twenty, Caroline was now so firmly entrenched on the shelf that it would take an earthquake to dislodge her.

"A suitor? A monster, you mean!" Portia peered over Caroline's shoulder, one of her sable ringlets tickling Caroline's cheek. "Did you fail to note the blackguard's name?"

"On the contrary. Vivienne has transcribed it in her boldest hand with a number of lovingly lavish embellishments." Caroline grimaced at the second page. "Good heavens, did she actually dot the *i* with a heart?"

"If the mere whisper of his name doesn't strike terror in

your own heart, then you must be unaware of his reputation."

"I am now." Caroline continued to scan the letter. "Our sister has thoughtfully provided a most extensive catalogue of his charms. From her glowing recitation, one can assume the gentleman's list of virtues is rivaled only by the Archbishop of Canterbury's."

"While she was extolling the fine cut of his neckcloth and his many kindnesses to widows and orphans, I don't suppose she bothered to mention the fact that he's a vampire."

Caroline rounded on her sister, her scant patience evaporating. "Oh, come now, Portia. Ever since you read that ridiculous tale by Dr. Polidori, you've been seeing vampires lurking behind every curtain and potted shrub. Had I known 'The Vampyre' would seize your imagination in such a ruthless grip, I'd have tossed the magazine on the trash heap as soon as it arrived. Maybe one of the werewolves you've spotted digging through the refuse would have carried it off and buried it."

Drawing herself up to her full five feet and two inches, Portia sniffed. "Everyone knows that Dr. Polidori didn't write that story. Why, he himself admitted to publishing it on behalf of his most famous patient—one George Gordon, Lord Byron himself!"

"A claim which Byron staunchly denied, I should remind you."

"Can you blame him? How could he do otherwise when the ruthless and brooding character of Ruthven was only a thinly disguised version of himself? He can deny it all he likes, but 'The Vampyre' revealed his true nature for all the world to see."

Caroline sighed, a vein in her temple beginning to throb. "His true nature being that of a bloodsucking creature of the night, I presume?"

"How can anyone doubt it after reading *The Giaour*?" Portia's eyes took on a distant sheen Caroline knew only too well. Lifting a hand and striking a suitably dramatic stance, Portia intoned:

> *"But first, on earth as Vampire sent,*
> *Thy corpse shall fall from its tomb be rent:*
> *Then ghastly haunt thy native place,*
> *And suck the blood of all thy race:*
> *There from the daughter, sister, wife,*
> *At midnight drain the stream of life."*

As Portia's voice faded on a suitably ominous note, Caroline massaged her throbbing temple with two fingers. "That doesn't prove Byron is a vampire. It only proves that he, like every other great poet, is on occasion capable of spouting momentous drivel. I can only hope you have more substantial evidence to convict Vivienne's new suitor. If not, I shall have to assume this is just like the time you shook me awake before dawn and insisted that a family of fairies was living beneath one of the toadstools in the garden. You can imagine my keen disappointment when I stumbled barefoot through the morning dew only to discover your family of fairies was nothing but a family of grubs with not a gossamer wing or a sprinkling of fairy dust to be found among them."

Portia's blush did little to temper the sulky jut of her bottom lip. "I was only ten at the time. And I can assure you that this isn't a fancy of my own making. Don't you remember the scandal sheet gossip during his last visit to London? Not once during all those months in Town was Vivienne's suitor *ever* seen abroad during daylight hours."

Caroline let out an unladylike snort. "That's hardly a habit reserved for the undead. Most of the young bucks in Town spend their days sleeping off the excesses of the previous night. They only emerge after the sun has set so they can start the cycle of drinking, gambling, and wenching all over again."

Portia clutched at her arm. "But don't you find it the least bit odd that he arrived at his town house under the cover of darkness and took his leave the very same way? That he insisted that every curtain in the house be kept drawn throughout the day and that every mirror be draped with black crepe?"

Caroline shrugged. "He could have simply been in mourning. Perhaps he had recently lost someone very dear to him."

"Or *something* very dear to him. Like his immortal soul."

"I should think that such a reputation wouldn't make him a very desirable dinner guest."

"On the contrary," Portia informed her, "the *ton* love nothing more than a delicious hint of scandal and mystery. Just last week in the *Tatler*, I read that he is to host a masquerade ball at his family seat this Season, and half of London is vying for invitations. From what I've read, he's one of the most sought after bachelors in the city. Which is precisely why we have to get Vivienne out of his clutches before it's too late."

Caroline shook off Portia's clawlike grip. She could hardly afford to give in to her sister's dark flights of fancy. She was the eldest, the sensible one, the one forced to step firmly into both her mother's slippers and her father's boots after their untimely death eight years before. The one left to comfort two sobbing, grief-stricken little girls when her own heart still lay in broken shards in her aching breast.

"I'm not trying to be cruel, Portia, but you really must rein in that imagination of yours. After all, it's not every day that a viscount pays court to a dowerless girl."

"So you don't mind if Vivienne weds a vampire, as long as he also happens to be a viscount? You don't care that he's probably just prowling the *ton* looking for some innocent soul to steal?"

Caroline gently tweaked her sister's cheek, restoring its rosy hue. "As far as I'm concerned, he'll not take possession of Vivienne's soul for anything less than a thousand pounds a year."

Portia gasped. "Have we become such a terrible burden to you? Are you so eager to be rid of us?"

Caroline's teasing smile faded. "Of course not. But you know as well as I that we can't depend on Cousin Cecil's largesse forever."

After their father's death, his second cousin had wasted no time in claiming his rightful inheritance. Cousin Cecil had considered it the very height of Christian charity to move the girls out of Edgeleaf Manor and into the ramshackle old cottage tucked away in the dampest, dreariest corner of the estate. They'd spent the last eight years there, with only a sparse monthly allowance and a pair of elderly servants to look after them.

"When he called on us last week," Caroline reminded her sister, "he spent most of his time hemming and hawing and strutting about the parlor, muttering about his plans to turn the cottage into a hunting lodge."

"You know, he might be more charitable to us if you hadn't so soundly spurned his suit all those years ago."

Remembering the night the fifty-eight-year-old bachelor had graciously invited them to move back into the manor—on the condition that she, at seventeen, become his bride—Caroline shuddered. "I'd surrender my own soul to a vampire before I'd wed that gouty old lech."

Portia sank down on a faded chintz ottoman that had been hemorrhaging cotton batting long before they'd moved into the cottage, rested her chin on one hand and shot Caroline a reproachful glance. "Well, you could have refused nicely. You didn't have to shove him out the door and into that snow bank."

"It cooled his ardor, didn't it? Among other things," Caroline muttered beneath her breath. After striving to convince her of what an *attentive* husband he would be, Cousin Cecil had snatched her against him with his thick, fleshy hands, thinking to sway her with a kiss. Needless to say, the hot, greedy press of his tongue against her tightly clamped lips had inspired revulsion, not devotion. The memory still made her want to scrub her mouth with lye.

She sank down heavily next to Portia on the ottoman. "I didn't want to alarm either you or Vivienne, but when Cousin Cecil came calling last week, he also hinted that we might have strained the limits of his charity. He implied that unless I grant him certain . . ." She swallowed and glanced away, unable to meet Portia's innocent gaze. ". . . *favors* without benefit of matrimony, we might be forced to look for another situation."

"Why, that miserable wretch," Portia breathed. "Hunting lodge indeed! You should have mounted *his* fat head on our parlor wall!"

"Even if he allows us to stay on at Edgeleaf, I don't know how much longer I can go on squeezing every pound of our allowance down to the last halfpenny. Only last week I had to choose between buying a goose for supper and a pair of new leather soles for your boots. Our winter cloaks are all growing threadbare and we're running out of pots to put under the leaks in this moldy old roof." Caroline's helpless gaze drifted from her sister's outraged profile to her gown. The faded white poplin had been handed down from herself to Vivienne, then finally to Portia. Its ruched bodice was stretched taut over Portia's plump breasts, and the thread-bare hem dragged the top of her scuffed boots. "Don't you ever miss the little luxuries you and Vivienne used to love so well when Mama and Papa were alive—the pots of water-colors, the pianoforte music, the silk ribbons and pearl combs for your pretty hair?"

"I guess I never minded giving them up as long as the three of us could stay together." Portia rested her head against Caroline's shoulder. "But I have noticed that your portions at supper keep getting smaller while ours stay the same size."

Caroline stroked a hand through Portia's soft curls. "You're going to be a prize yourself someday, my pet, but we all know that Vivienne is the True Beauty of the family, the one most likely to make an advantageous match that will rid us of Cousin Cecil's bullying and assure both her future and our own."

Portia tilted her head to gaze up at her, unspilled tears clinging to her thick, dark lashes. "But don't you see, Caro? If Vivienne falls beneath this devil's spell, she may not *have* a future. If she surrenders her heart to him, she'll be lost to us forever!"

Caroline could see a shadow of her own fears reflected in Portia's pleading eyes. If Vivienne was successful in landing a husband, it would only be a matter of time before he found a suitor for Portia among his eligible friends. He might even be charitable enough to invite his spinster sister-in-law to come live with them. But if not, she would spend the rest of her days rattling around this drafty old cottage at Cousin Cecil's capricious mercy. The thought sent a fresh shudder down her spine. She was old enough to know that there were some men who could be far more terrifying than monsters.

Before she could attempt to soothe either of their fears, Anna came shuffling into the room, her white head bowed. "What is it?" Caroline asked the elderly maidservant, rising from the ottoman.

"This just came for ye, miss."

Caroline took the missive from Anna's palsied hand without bothering to ask her what it was. The maid's rheumy eyes were fogged with age.

Caroline ran her fingertips over the ivory vellum, admiring its expensive weave. The folded missive had been sealed with a single dab of ruby wax that glistened like a drop of fresh blood against the fine paper. She frowned. "I thought the morning post had already run?"

"Indeed it has, miss," Anna confirmed. "A private messenger brung it. Some great strappin' lad in scarlet livery."

As Caroline broke the seal with her fingernail and unfolded the letter, Portia scrambled to her feet. "What is it? Is it from Aunt Marietta? Has Vivienne taken ill? Gone into a sudden and unexplained decline?"

Caroline shook her head. "It's not from Aunt Marietta. It's from *him*."

Portia raised an eyebrow, urging her to continue.

"Adrian Kane—Viscount Trevelyan." As Caroline's lips shaped the name for the first time, she would have sworn she felt a shiver ripple through her soul.

"What does he want from us? Is he demanding some sort of ransom for Vivienne's soul?"

"Oh, for pity's sake, Portia, stop being such a silly goose! It's not a ransom demand," she said, scanning the message. "It's an invitation to come to London and make his acquaintance. That should allay your ridiculous suspicions, should it not? If this viscount was harboring less than noble intentions toward Vivienne, he wouldn't bother to secure our blessing before pursuing her, would he?"

"Why doesn't he call on us right here at Edgeleaf, as any proper young gentleman would do? Oh, wait, I forgot! A vampire can't enter his victim's home unless he receives an invitation." Portia cocked her head to the side, looking for an elusive moment both older and wiser than her seventeen years. "Just what exactly has the viscount invited us to?"

Caroline studied the bold masculine scrawl for several seconds, then lifted her head to meet her sister's eyes, already dreading the triumphant gleam she was soon to find there.

"A midnight supper."

Two

"What if it's not an invitation, but a trap?" Portia whispered in Caroline's ear as their aunt Marietta's rickety carriage wended its way through the deserted London streets.

"Then I suppose we'll soon find ourselves manacled to a dungeon wall, at the mercy of some fiend's dark desires," Caroline whispered back. Caught off guard by the curious heat her own words stirred in her, she snapped open her fan and used it to cool her flushed cheeks.

Portia went back to gazing sullenly out the carriage window. Her younger sister was the only person of Caroline's acquaintance who could *flounce* without so much as batting an eyelash. Caroline knew that Portia was still nursing a sulk because she had sworn Portia to silence regarding the rumors swirling around the mysterious Viscount Trevelyan. If Vivienne wasn't aware of them, Caroline didn't see any point in letting such nonsense cast a cloud over her sister's happiness or put all of their futures in jeopardy.

Aunt Marietta shot Caroline and Portia a disapproving glance. "Wasn't it the very height of kindness for Lord Trevelyan to extend your sisters an invitation, Vivienne?" She drew a handkerchief out of her bodice and dabbed at her plump cheeks. They were already beginning to glisten beneath their thick layer of rice powder. With her blond froth of curls and powdered rolls of flesh, Aunt Marietta had always reminded Caroline, rather unkindly, of an underdone pastry. "It's just another shining example of the gentleman's generosity. If you continue to engage his fancy, dear, I'm hoping we might even be able to snag an invitation to the masquerade ball he is to host at his ancestral estate."

Aunt Marietta did not have to point out that the *we* did not include Caroline or Portia. Her mother's flighty sister had always considered Portia tiresome and Caroline far too dull and bookish to be good company. She'd never breathed one word about taking them in after their parents' death, and if not for the viscount's invitation, she would have never invited them to share the Shrewsbury lodgings her late husband had bequeathed to her, not even for a miserly week.

Her aunt droned on, extolling more of the viscount's apparently endless list of virtues. Caroline was already growing heartily sick of the man, and she'd yet to meet him.

She glanced across the carriage at Vivienne. A serene smile hovered around her sister's lips as she dutifully listened to Aunt Marietta's shrill chatter. It would take more than a mere cloud to dim Vivienne's radiance, Caroline thought ruefully, her expression softening as she studied her sister.

With her upswept golden hair and the fair, creamy skin so prized by the *ton*, Vivienne positively glowed. Even as a child, it had been nearly impossible to ruffle her composure. When she was barely five, Vivienne had come tugging at their mother's skirts while she was cutting roses in the garden at Edgeleaf.

"Not right now, Vivi," Mama had scolded without turning from her task. "Can't you see that I'm busy?"

"Very well, Mama. I'll just come back later then."

Warned by the off-key note in that small, obedient voice, their mother had turned to find Vivienne limping away, the arrow from a poacher's bow still lodged in her thigh. Cradled in their papa's strong arms, Vivienne had suffered in white-faced silence while the village physician drew out the arrow. It had been Portia's hysterical shrieks that had threatened to deafen them all.

With her own temper so quick to flare, Caroline had always envied Vivienne her serenity. And her gleaming golden curls. Caroline touched a hand to her own pale, wheaten hair. Compared to Vivienne's, it seemed almost colorless. Since the fine strands wouldn't hold so much as the ghost of a curl, she'd had no choice but to sleek it back in a tight knot at the crown of her head. For her, there would be no pretty fringe of ringlets to frame the angular bones of her rather plain face.

"I don't believe I've ever seen you wear your hair that way," she told Vivienne. "It's quite lovely."

Vivienne touched a hand to the shimmering cascade of curls. "Oddly enough, it was Lord Trevelyan who suggested the style. He said it would complement my fine eyes and the classical cut of my cheekbones."

Caroline frowned, thinking it odd that a gentleman would take such a keen interest in a lady's hair. Perhaps her sister's suitor was one of those fey dandies like Brummel, more interested in the quality of lace trimming a lady's collar than in more manly pursuits like politics or hunting.

"So just how exactly did you make Lord Trevelyan's acquaintance?" she asked. "You explained in your letter that the two of you met at Lady Norberry's ball, but you failed to provide any of the more delicious details."

Vivienne's smile softened. "The dancing had ended and we were all preparing to go into supper." She wrinkled her slender nose. "I believe the clock had just struck midnight."

Caroline grunted with pain as Portia drove an elbow into her ribs.

"I glanced over my shoulder to discover the most extraordinary man lounging against the door frame. Before I realized what was happening, he had elbowed aside my dinner companion and insisted on escorting me into the dining room." Vivienne ducked her head shyly. "There was no one to officially introduce us, so I suppose it was all rather improper."

Aunt Marietta tittered behind a gloved hand. "Improper indeed! He couldn't keep his eyes off the girl. I've never seen a fellow look so besotted! When he first spotted Vivienne, he went so white you'd have thought he'd seen a ghost. They've been nearly inseparable ever since. With me serving as chaperone, of course," she added with a prim sniff.

"So have the two of you ever enjoyed any daytime excursions?" Portia leaned forward in the seat, a cheery smile fixed on her lips. "Gone on a barouche ride in Hyde Park? Visited the elephant at the Tower of London? Taken tea in some sunny garden?"

Vivienne gave her sister a bemused look. "No, but he's accompanied us to the Royal Opera House, two musicales, and a midnight supper hosted by Lady Twickenham at her Park Lane mansion. I'm afraid Lord Trevelyan keeps gentleman's hours. Most days he doesn't even rise until after the sun has set."

This time Caroline was ready. Before Portia could elbow her, Caroline caught her forearm and gave it a sound pinch. "Ow!"

At Portia's involuntary yelp, Aunt Marietta lifted her quizzing glass to frown at the girl. "For heaven's sake, child, get control of yourself. I thought someone had stepped on a spaniel."

"Sorry," Portia mumbled, slinking lower in her seat and shooting Caroline a narrow glare. "One of my dress pins must have poked me."

Caroline turned to the window to watch the broad thoroughfares of Mayfair roll past, her serene smile mirroring Vivienne's. The carriage was just turning onto Berkeley Square to reveal a terrace of handsome brick town houses basking in the mellow glow of the streetlamps.

As the carriage rolled to a halt, Caroline craned her neck to peer up at their destination. There was little to distinguish the four-story Georgian-style house from its neighbors—no snarling gargoyles perched on the slate roof, no black-caped figures lurking about its wrought-iron balconies, no muffled screams coming from the coal cellar.

Rather than being veiled with heavy drapes, the Palladian windows were aglow with lamplight, spilling a cheery welcome over the paved walk and covered portico.

"Ah, here we are at last!" Aunt Marietta announced as she gathered up her reticule and fan. "We should make haste, Vivienne. I'm sure your Lord Trevelyan is frantic with impatience."

"He's hardly *my* Lord Trevelyan, Auntie," Vivienne pointed out. "After all, it's not as if he's declared for me or even hinted at his intentions."

Watching an enchanting flush of rose spread over her sister's fair cheeks, Caroline sighed. How could any man *not* fall madly in love with her?

She reached over to give Vivienne's gloved hand a fond squeeze. "Aunt Marietta's right, my dear. If you've captured this gentleman's heart, then it's only a matter of time before you'll win his name as well."

Vivienne squeezed back, giving her a grateful smile.

They descended from the carriage one by one, tucking their hands into the waiting footman's. When Portia's turn came, she hung back. The footman cleared his throat and extended his hand deeper into the carriage.

Caroline finally had to reach past him and yank her sister out of the carriage. As Portia tumbled into her arms, Caroline whispered through clenched teeth, "You heard Vivienne. It's hardly uncommon for a gentleman to host a midnight supper."

"Especially not if he's a—"

"*Don't* say it!" Caroline warned. "If I hear that word from your lips one more time tonight, I'll bite you myself."

Seeing that their aunt and sister had already disappeared into the house, Caroline urged a pouting Portia up the walk.

They were nearly to the front steps when a dark shape separated itself from the shadows with a brittle flap of wings.

Portia ducked and let out an earsplitting shriek. "Did you see that?" she gasped, her nails digging into Caroline's elbow-length gloves. "It was a bat!"

"Don't be ridiculous. I'm sure it was simply a nightjar or some other nocturnal bird." Even as Caroline sought to soothe her sister's nerves, she cast the eaves of the house a furtive look and drew the hood of her cloak up to cover her hair.

They soon found themselves standing in a brightly lit entrance hall with the tinkle of crystal, muted laughter, and the rich, sweet notes of a Haydn sonata drifting to their ears. The parquet floor had been waxed to such a high sheen that they could practically admire their reflections in it. Trying not to gawk, Caroline handed off her cloak to an apple-cheeked young maid.

The girl turned expectantly to Portia.

"No, thank you," Portia muttered. "I do believe I might be taking a chill." Clutching the collar of the cloak tighter around her throat, she manufactured a pitiable cough to lend credibility to her claim.

Offering the maid an apologetic smile, Caroline held out one hand. "Don't be foolish, *dear*. If you become overheated, your chill could very well prove fatal."

Recognizing the steely gleam of warning in Caroline's eyes, Portia reluctantly shrugged off the cloak. She'd bundled a woolen shawl beneath it, carefully draped to conceal the slender column of her throat. Caroline ended up in a tugging match as she sought to unwrap the shawl with Portia stubbornly clinging to the other end of it. She finally wrested it away, only to discover a silk scarf beneath it.

She was unknotting the scarf, fighting the urge to strangle her sister with it, when a pungent aroma drifted to her nose. She leaned forward, sniffing at Portia's skin. "What on earth is that stench? Is it garlic?"

Portia stiffened. "I should say not. It's simply my new

perfume." Sticking her nose in the air, she went sweeping past Caroline, trailing the earthy scent behind her. Caroline tossed the scarf to the gaping maid and followed her sister into the drawing room.

As she surveyed the elegant assemblage, Caroline almost wished she had refused to surrender her own cloak. Vivienne was a vision of loveliness in celestial blue poplin, and Portia managed to look charmingly girlish in her finest Sunday frock. Since hems had risen and it was all the rage for one's bosom to spill over the top of one's bodice, Caroline hoped no one would notice that Portia's gown was over two years old.

Caroline had been forced to scavenge her entire London wardrobe from one of their mother's old trunks. She could only be thankful that Louisa Cabot had been as tall, slender, and small-breasted as she was. The pale India muslin evening dress she wore was almost Grecian in its simplicity, with a square-cut bodice, high waist, and none of the frills and furbelows that had been steadily coming back into fashion for the past decade.

Painfully aware of the curious looks directed her way by the dozen or so occupants of the drawing room, she pasted an awkward smile on her lips. Judging from the smug expressions and the diamonds twinkling on both the hands of the women and the men, it appeared that Portia had been right. Adrian Kane's reputation didn't seem to have damaged his social standing. A few of the women were already shooting Vivienne resentful glances.

Vivienne and Aunt Marietta drifted through the room, exchanging murmured greetings and welcoming nods. Portia lurked behind them, her hand clamped over her throat.

The pianoforte in the corner fell silent. A dark figure rose from the instrument's bench, his appearance sending a ripple of anticipation through the gathered guests. It seemed that Caroline and her family had arrived just in time for some sort of recitation. Relieved to find herself no longer the center of attention, Caroline eased into an alcove along the back wall where she could watch the proceedings without being ogled. A nearby French window overlooked the courtyard garden, promising a hasty escape if needed.

Simply by striding over to pose before the marble mantel, the black-garbed stranger magically transformed the hearth into a stage and the drawing room's occupants into a rapt audience. His fashionable pallor only made his soulful dark eyes and the rakish black curls tumbling over his brow more striking. He was broad-shouldered, yet lean-hipped, with a strong, aquiline nose and full lips that betrayed a tantalizing hint of sensuality. From the fond smile curving Vivienne's lips, Caroline deduced that he must be their host.

A reverent hush fell over the drawing room as he propped one foot on the hearth. Caroline found herself holding her own breath as he began to speak in a baritone so melodic it could have made the angels weep with envy.

> *"But first, on earth as Vampire sent,*
> *Thy corpse shall fall from its tomb be rent:*
> *Then ghastly haunt thy native place,*
> *And suck the blood of all thy race:*
> *There from the daughter, sister, wife,*
> *At midnight drain the stream of life."*

Caroline's eyes widened as she recognized the words of Byron's legendary Turkish tale, words she had heard Portia recite with an equal amount of drama only a few days before. She glanced at her baby sister. Portia's hand had fallen from her throat to her heart as she gazed up at the young Adonis, an adoring light dawning in her eyes. *Oh, dear*, Caroline thought. It would hardly do for Portia to start nursing an unrequited infatuation for her sister's suitor.

With his sulky mouth and cleft chin, the young orator might have been mistaken for Byron himself. But everyone in London knew that the dashing poet was currently languishing in Italy in the arms of his new mistress, the Countess Guiccioli.

As he launched into another verse of the poem, displaying his classical profile for everyone in the room to admire, Caroline had to cup a hand over her mouth to contain a hiccup of laughter. So *this* was the notorious viscount! No wonder he was offering Vivienne suggestions on how to style her hair. And no wonder society believed him to be a vampire. It was obviously a reputation as carefully cultivated as the *en cascade* folds of his cravat and the dazzling sheen on his Wellingtons. Such an affected dandy might steal her sister's heart, but Vivienne's soul appeared to be in no immediate peril.

Giddy with both mirth and relief, Caroline was still trying to choke back her giggles when a clock somewhere in the house began to chime midnight.

"Allow me."

Caroline started violently as a handkerchief appeared just beneath her nose.

"I try to come prepared. It's hardly the first time his performance has moved a woman to tears. The more sentimental ladies have even been known to swoon on occasion."

That droll masculine voice, pitched barely above a growl, seemed to resonate all the way through to her bones. How could she have been so foolish as to fret about vampires when a voice that full of smoke and brimstone could belong only to the devil himself?

She gingerly took the handkerchief before stealing a glance at the man lounging against the wall next to her. He seemed to have appeared out of nowhere. He must have slipped through the French window when she'd been distracted, no small feat for such a large man.

Although she would have sworn she'd felt his gaze on her only a second before, he was staring fixedly at the hearth, where their host was launching into yet another stanza of Byron's masterpiece.

"Your chivalry is much appreciated, sir," she said softly,

dabbing at her overflowing eyes with the expensive linen. "But I can assure you that there's no danger of my being overcome with emotion and swooning into your arms."

"A pity that," he muttered, still gazing straight ahead.

Taken aback, Caroline murmured, "Pardon?"

"Pretty hat," he said, nodding toward the pearl-and-feather concoction perched atop a matron's silvery curls.

Narrowing her eyes, Caroline took advantage of his purported indifference to study him. His thick hair was a warm honey shade threaded with brighter strands of gold and worn just long enough to brush the impressive shoulders of his russet tailcoat. Had he straightened instead of lounging against the wall with both ankles and arms crossed, he would have towered over her by nearly a foot. Yet he seemed utterly at home with his size, finding no need to use its power to intimidate or cajole.

"What I meant to say, sir," she whispered, unsure why it was so important that this stranger not mistake her for some maudlin ninny, "was that I wasn't overcome by sentiment, but amusement."

He slanted her an unreadable look beneath his generous lashes. His long, crystalline eyes were neither blue nor green, but some bewitching shade in between. "I gather you're not a fan of Byron?"

"Oh, it's not the poet who amuses me, but his interpreter. Have you ever seen such shameless posturing?"

One of the women in front of them turned around to glare at Caroline. Touching a gloved finger to her lips, she hissed, "Shhhhh!"

While Caroline struggled to dredge up a suitably contrite expression, her companion murmured, "You seem to be the only woman in the room immune to his charms."

There was no arguing with that. Portia was still gazing at the hearth as if she'd fallen into a trance. Several of the ladies had drawn out their own handkerchiefs to dab at their eyes. Even the gentlemen were watching the performance with slack mouths and glazed expressions.

Caroline swallowed a smile. "Perhaps he's bewitched them with his supernatural powers. Isn't that one of the traits of his kind—the ability to hypnotize the weak-willed and make them do his bidding?"

This time her companion turned to look her full in the face. His countenance might have been called boyish were it not for the furrowed brow, once-broken nose, and the teasing hint of a cleft in his broad chin. He had an oddly tender, expressive mouth for such a rugged visage. "And just what *kind* would that be?"

It was hardly in character for her to indulge in a tasty morsel of gossip with a total stranger, but there was something about his direct gaze that invited confidences.

Cupping a hand around her mouth, she leaned closer to him and whispered, "Don't you know? Our host is rumored to be a vampire. Surely you must have heard the gossip about the mysterious and dangerous Adrian Kane. How he rises from his bed only after the sun has set. How he prowls the streets and alleys of the city by night searching for prey. How he lures innocent women into his lair and enslaves them with his dark powers of seduction."

She had succeeded in bringing a sparkle of amusement to his eyes. "Sounds like quite a dastardly fellow. So what prompted you to brave his lair on this dark night? Have you no care for your own innocence?"

Caroline lifted her shoulders in an airy shrug. "As you can see, he's no threat to me. I'm utterly impervious to brooding, Byron-spouting young gentlemen who spend an inordinate amount of time in front of the mirror practicing their poses and curling their forelocks."

His gaze narrowed on her face. "I must confess that you have me intrigued. Just what sort of gentleman might pose a threat to you? What dark powers must a man possess to seduce such a level-headed creature as yourself? If a comely face and a nimble tongue won't make you swoon into a man's arms, then what will?"

Caroline gazed up at him, a kaleidoscope of impossible

images whirling through her head. What if this was her Season instead of Vivienne's? What if she was a dewy-eyed nineteen instead of a sensible four-and-twenty? What if it wasn't too late to believe a man like this might lure her into a moonlit garden to steal a private moment—or perhaps even a kiss? Wracked by a shiver of yearning, Caroline dragged her gaze away from that tantalizing mouth of his. She was a woman grown. She could hardly afford to succumb to a girl's foolish fancies.

She inclined her head with a dimpled smile, deciding it wisest to treat his words as the jest they undoubtedly were. "You should be ashamed of yourself, sir. If I confided such a thing, then you would have me at your mercy, would you not?"

"Perhaps it is you," he leaned down to murmur, his voice as deep and smoky as a forbidden swallow of scotch whisky, "who would have me at *your* mercy."

Caroline jerked up her head, mesmerized by the unexpected flash of longing in his eyes. It seemed a breathless eternity before she realized that the recitation had ended and the other occupants of the drawing room had burst into enthusiastic applause.

Her companion pushed himself away from the wall, straightening to his full height. "If you'll excuse me, miss . . . I'm afraid duty is a harsh and unforgiving mistress."

He had already presented his broad back to her when she called after him, "Sir! You forgot your handkerchief!"

She didn't realize she was waving the scrap of linen like a flag of surrender until he turned and one corner of his mouth slanted upward into a lazy smile. "Keep it, won't you? Perhaps you'll find something else to amuse you before the night is done."

As she watched him weave his way through the guests, Caroline smoothed the handkerchief over her gloved fingers. She had an absurd desire to bring it to her cheek, to see if it bore the manly scents of sandalwood and bay rum that still hung in the air around her.

Her fingertips blindly traced the initials stitched into the fabric as his deep, commanding voice carried over the crowd. "Bravo! Bravo, Julian! That was quite a performance. Dare we hope for an encore after supper?"

The lean, elegant satyr still posing with negligent grace in front of the hearth grinned at him. "Only if my brother and host commands it."

Caroline's fingers froze.

She slowly lifted the handkerchief, but even before she saw the satyr clap a hearty hand on his shoulder, even before she watched the guests greet him as one of their own, even before she saw a beaming Vivienne take her place at his side as if she had always belonged there, Caroline knew what she would find stitched into the expensive linen.

An elaborate *A* linked with a swirling *K*.

"Caroline!" Vivienne called out. A radiant smile lit her face as she tucked one slender hand in the crook of her companion's arm. "What are you doing cowering over there in the corner? You must come and meet our host."

Caroline felt all the blood drain from her face as she lifted her eyes to meet the equally stunned gaze of Adrian Kane, Viscount Trevelyan.

Three

"Would you care for some port, Miss Cabot?"

Although the query was perfectly innocent, there was nothing innocent about the teasing sparkle in her host's eyes. Or the way he swirled the bloodred liquor around the bottom of his glass before tilting it to his lips.

The glass of port would have looked more at home dangling from his brother's pale, aristocratic fingers. Oddly enough, Adrian Kane had a workman's hands—broad, strong, and powerful. His teeth were straight and white, with nary a fang in sight. Since she had been seated in the place of honor at his right elbow at the long, damask-draped table, Caroline had ample opportunity to study them every time he flashed her one of his enigmatic smiles.

It was hard to imagine anyone being foolish enough to believe this man embraced darkness and death. If anything, he seemed to be possessed of an almost unnatural vigor. Although according to rumor he shunned daylight, she would have sworn the gold threads in his hair had been spun by the sun. She even had the ridiculous notion that if she leaned closer, she might hear the steady thrum of the blood coursing through his mighty heart.

Before Caroline could decline his offer, Portia, who was sitting directly opposite her at his left elbow, thrust out her glass and chirped, "Why, thank you, my lord! I'd love some port!"

Caroline looked at her sister askance. Portia seemed to have momentarily forgotten her fear that Kane might lean over and nip her on the neck. She was too busy craning that neck to ogle Kane's brother, who was sitting just down the table from her, on the other side of Vivienne. No matter what she thought of his posing and preening, even Caroline had to admit that it was a tragedy Julian Kane's profile had never been minted on a Roman coin.

Their host crooked a finger at the footman hovering near the walnut sideboard, but gave the man a warning shake of his head before he could pour more than a splash of the ruby port into Portia's glass.

Aunt Marietta had been exiled to the far end of the table, where she was regaling a squat baron with a shrill account of her latest triumph at the boodle table. Since he couldn't very well slice open his wrists with a two-pronged fork, the poor man appeared to be steadily drinking himself into a stupor. He'd been sliding lower and lower in his chair for the past half hour. By the time dessert was served, he'd probably be *under* the table. Not that Aunt Marietta would notice. She'd probably just turn to the simpering marchioness on the other side of her and continue her recitation without bothering to pause for breath.

Caroline wondered if her aunt had been banished deliberately. Perhaps Kane had as little tolerance for her incessant chattering as she did. Of course, after the nonsense she had spouted to him in the drawing room, he must think her twice as bird-witted as Aunt Marietta.

Every time she remembered her careless words, she wanted to lean down and bang her forehead on the table. She didn't know whether she should be more mortified for insulting the man's brother or for repeating those ridiculous rumors about his nocturnal activities. She might have been able to forgive herself for both of those indiscretions had she not also indulged in a shameless flirtation with her sister's suitor.

"Miss?"

Thankful for the distraction, Caroline turned her head to find a footman proffering a silver platter laden with slices of rare roast beef swimming in bloody juice. Feeling her already shaky stomach turn over, she swallowed hard and murmured, "No, thank you."

"Oh, I'll have that." Instead of waiting for the footman to bring the platter around, Julian reached across the table and stabbed a slice of meat with his own fork. He brought the beef directly to his mouth, chewing with sensual relish.

He suddenly stopped and sniffed at the air, his perfectly aligned nose wrinkling in distaste. "You simply must tell Gaston to tone down the garlic, Adrian. It's nearly overpowering tonight."

Caroline was the only one who saw Portia dip her napkin in her crystal finger bowl and use it to scrub surreptitiously at her throat.

At least she thought she was the only one, until she glanced at their host and caught him watching not Portia, but her, with undisguised amusement. "You'll have to pardon my cook," he said. "He's French, and you know how the French love their garlic."

Caroline could not let his smirk go unchallenged. "What about you, my lord? Are you fond of it as well?"

"Quite. I find it adds an exciting element of surprise to even the most mundane of dishes."

She gave him an arch look. "Ah, but some people are not as fond of surprises as you seem to be. There are those who might even consider them a trial to be avoided."

Kane leaned back in his chair, the speculative gleam in his eyes deepening. "That would depend upon the nature of the surprise, now wouldn't it?"

"Indeed," she replied, meeting his gaze squarely. "And whether the surprise had been initiated by a simple misunderstanding or deliberate subterfuge."

He took another sip of the port. "I must confess, Miss Cabot, that you yourself have been something of a revelation to me. Since Vivienne informed me that you had all but raised her and young Portia here, I was expecting someone far more . . ."

"Old?" she offered.

"Experienced," he countered tactfully.

"Then I regret disappointing you, my lord. Had I known you were expecting a doddering crone, I wouldn't have bothered to wear my wooden teeth."

"Caroline was only sixteen when we lost Mama and Papa," Vivienne explained, regarding her sister with open affection. "She's been both mother and father to us ever since then. If not for her, Cousin Cecil might have shipped us off to an orphanage."

Caroline felt her color rise as Kane tilted his head to study her. "It couldn't have been easy taking on the responsibility of two young girls when you were little more than a girl yourself."

Julian waved his fork in her direction. "I'd think it would be deadly dull to be tucked away in the country with two brats to raise. No offense, pet," he added, leaning past Vivienne to offer Portia a teasing wink. She choked on a morsel of quail and pinkened to the roots of her hair.

Caroline remembered countless days spent hunched over the household ledgers, her fingers cramped with cold and fatigue; sleepless nights haunted by visions of her sisters locked away in a workhouse or slaving away as governesses in some household with a lecherous master and cruel mistress. Visions that might still come to pass if she couldn't secure a suitable husband for one of them.

But she simply said, "Contrary to what most of society believes, there are many rewards to be found in a quiet country life devoted to the pleasures of hearth and family."

Although she half expected their host to scoff at her words, his voice softened on a note that might have been longing. "I should imagine there would be."

"So tell me, my dear Miss Cabot," Julian said, turning the full force of his charm on her, "is it true that in the country one is expected to both sleep and rise 'with the chickens,' as it were?"

"Were we at Edgeleaf, I would have been abed hours ago," she confessed.

"Indeed," Kane murmured.

Caroline suddenly found herself unable to meet his gaze. How was it that the mere mention of bed in front of this man could make her blush like a green girl?

His brother shuddered. "Then I fear I shan't survive there for more than a fortnight."

Kane chuckled. "More than a night, I should say. You'll have to forgive my little brother, Miss Cabot," he said, the husky caress of his voice making her feel as if they were the only two in the room. "Poor Julian here is already dreading our return to the country next week. If I hadn't promised a ball to keep him amused, I doubt I'd have been able to drag him away from his favorite gambling hell. I fear the pleasures of country living are not for him. He much prefers a choking cloud of cigar smoke or coal dust to a breath of fresh air. And he has long shunned the sun for fear it would ruin his fashionable pallor."

Julian leaned back in his chair, flashing a good-natured grin. "You know as well as I do, dear brother, that nothing interesting ever happened before midnight."

As if to prove his point, there was the sound of raised voices and a sudden scuffle just outside the dining room.

Although the viscount didn't so much as twitch a muscle, danger suddenly spiced the air around him, its unspoken threat strong enough to stir the invisible hairs on Caroline's forearms.

The dining room doors flew open and a man appeared in the doorway, shaking off a panting footman. The footman's powdered wig sat askew on his head, revealing a thatch of coppery red hair.

The startled guests gaped, forks and goblets poised halfway to their mouths.

Jerking his waistcoat straight, the young footman shot

the interloper a black look. "I'm sorry, my lord," he said, still breathing heavily. "I tried to tell the *gentleman* you wasn't receiving callers, but he didn't take kindly to the refusal."

Despite Kane's laconic posture and heavy-lidded gaze, Caroline sensed that the stranger's appearance was definitely a surprise. And not a welcome one, either.

"Good evening, Constable," he said, rising from his chair just long enough to sketch a mocking bow. "Had we known you were going to grace us with your presence this evening, we would have delayed supper. Your regards must have been lost in the post."

"Oh, come now, Trevelyan," the man said, making a great show of brushing off his sleeve where the footman's hand had rested. "I like to think that old acquaintances like us are above such silly social niceties. We never used to honor them when we were at Oxford together."

With his long, lanky frame, ill-fitting and rumpled frock coat, and untidy thatch of light brown hair, Caroline suspected the stranger would look windblown even on a breeze-less evening. What his face lacked in charm it more than made up for in character. He might be thin-lipped and hawk-nosed, but both humor and intelligence glittered in his toffee-brown eyes.

Those eyes scanned the table until they found what they were seeking.

"Miss Vivienne," he said, his tone gentling as he nodded toward Caroline's sister.

"Constable Larkin," she murmured, swirling her spoon around her bowl of lobster bisque without sparing him so much as a glance.

Caroline jumped as Portia kicked her under the table. Neither one of them had ever seen their sweet-natured sister give anyone the cut direct.

The exchange was not lost on their host, either. Amusement rippled through his voice as he swept out a hand. "I don't believe you've made the acquaintance of Miss Vivienne's sisters—Miss Cabot and Miss Portia. You should be familiar with the rest of my guests. I'm sure you've harassed or interrogated them all at one time or another."

The viscount's guests continued to eye the intruder, some curiously, others with thinly veiled hostility. A sneer twisted Julian Kane's sculpted lips, and for once even Aunt Marietta seemed at a loss for words.

Undaunted by their regard, or lack of it, Larkin settled himself into an empty seat halfway down the table and cast the young footman an expectant look over his shoulder.

The footman stared straight ahead, his freckled jaw set, until the viscount blew out a noisy sigh. "Do offer the constable some supper, Timothy. If we don't feed the man, I fear we may never be rid of him. The only thing he loves more than barging in uninvited is eating."

Beneath the footman's glowering scrutiny, the constable proved Kane's words by helping himself to generous portions of stewed quail and vegetable pudding. Caroline suspected it would take more than one such meal to fill out his gaunt cheeks and narrow shoulders. She couldn't help but wonder what might have driven an Oxford graduate to seek out a career in the constabulary instead of a more profitable post in the clergy or the military.

Larkin polished off the quail in half a dozen bites, following the last swallow with a greedy gulp of wine and a rapturous sigh. "Whatever else your failings, Trevelyan, I have to admit that you do set one of the finest tables in London. I suppose that shouldn't surprise me since you're rumored to be a man of such vast and varied . . . appetites."

The harmless word sent a curious shiver down Caroline's spine.

"Is that why you came here tonight?" Kane asked. "To insult me and heap praise upon my cook?"

The constable leaned back in his chair, swiping at his mouth with his napkin. "I came here because I thought you'd be interested in knowing that there had been another disappearance in Charing Cross."

Adrian Kane didn't even blink. If anything, his gaze became even more somnolent. "And why would that information concern me? Given the unfortunate squalor of the rookery, debtors seeking to avoid their creditors probably vanish every day. And night."

Larkin held out his glass so the footman could pour another grudging splash of port into it. "That may very well be true, but as you know, there have been over half a dozen mysterious disappearances just since you and your brother returned from your travels abroad." He gave Kane an unmistakably pointed look. "In most of those cases, there have conveniently been no witnesses. But just yesterday morning a young woman came to us with a most extraordinary story."

"Fueled by hysteria and cheap gin, no doubt," Julian offered, draping one long, elegant arm over the back of Vivienne's chair.

Larkin shrugged. "Perhaps. I'd be lying if I said the girl was of sound moral character. But I can assure you that both her story and her terror were quite convincing."

"Do go on," Kane commanded, suppressing a yawn. "My guests were hoping for another poetry recitation from Julian after we supped, but I'm certain your tale will prove to be just as entertaining, if not more so."

The constable ignored the jibe. "According to the girl, the incident occurred shortly after midnight when she and her companion were strolling through Charing Cross."

"Am I to assume the fellow was a longstanding acquaintance?" Kane asked gently.

"Actually," Larkin admitted, "she'd met him only minutes before outside one of the gambling hells in Pickpocket Alley. The two of them had paused beneath a lamppost to . . ." He hesitated, stealing a pained glance at Vivienne's porcelain profile. ". . . *converse* when they were attacked by a stranger in a long black cloak."

"Attacked?" Julian echoed. "How? Did he threaten them with a club? A knife? A pistol perhaps?"

"The girl saw no weapon. She claims their attacker was possessed of extreme physical prowess. He simply snatched the man away from her and shoved him up against the lamppost, lifting him off the ground with one hand."

Caroline picked at her quail with her fork to avoid looking at Kane's brawny shoulders.

"The girl was so stricken with fright that she fell to her knees and hid her face. When she finally dared to lift her head, her companion was gone."

"Gone?" Aunt Marietta echoed shrilly, touching a hand to her fleshy throat.

Larkin nodded. "Vanished. As if into thin air."

"Pardon me, Constable Larkin, but if you have no body to provide any evidence of foul play, then how do you know the man didn't simply run away?" Caroline couldn't have said what prompted her to speak up. She only knew that a crystalline silence had fallen over the table and everyone was staring at her.

Including their host.

The constable cleared his throat, his gaze narrowing on her face as if he was seeing her for the first time. "A valid question, Miss Cabot, but with this incident following so closely on the heels of the other disappearances in the area, we have no choice but to treat it with equal suspicion. Especially after what the attacker did next."

"What did he do?" she asked reluctantly, wondering if it was too late to leap across the table and cover Portia's ears.

The guests held their collective breaths as they awaited his reply. Even Vivienne stole a glance at him, her lips trembling.

Larkin bowed his head, his long face somber. "According to the young woman, he approached her and helped her to her feet. His face was in shadow, but she described him as having the manners and demeanor 'of a gent.' He tucked a gold sovereign into her hand and told her to scurry home to her mum because there were worse monsters than him roaming the night. Then he turned, and with a swirl of his cape, disappeared back into the shadows."

Kane surged to his feet, making it clear that both his patience and his hospitality had reached their limits. "Thank you, Constable. It was very kind of you to drop by and share your riveting tale with me and my guests. I can assure you that we'll heed your warning and take care to avoid Charing Cross after sunset."

Larkin rose, facing him down the table. "See that you do." As two burly footmen appeared in the doorway, a wry smile curved his lips. "I appreciate the courtesy, but I do believe I can find my own way out." He paused in the doorway as if he'd forgotten something as inconsequential as a glove or a handkerchief. "I nearly forgot to mention that I ran into an old friend of ours from Oxford just the other day in Covent Garden—Victor Duvalier."

Although Julian visibly blanched, Kane's face could have been carved from stone.

"Apparently, he just returned to London after an extensive tour of the Carpathians. He said to give you his regards and to tell you that he hoped your paths would cross very soon."

"As do I," Kane murmured, something in his expressionless face sending another shiver down Caroline's spine.

Before turning to go, Larkin sketched a surprisingly graceful bow in Vivienne's direction. "Miss Vivienne."

"Mr. Larkin," she returned, going back to stirring her congealing bisque as if the entire future of England depended upon it.

Flanked by the footmen, the constable departed, leaving an awkward silence in his wake.

"Instead of you ladies depriving us of your company so we can enjoy our port, why don't we all adjourn to the drawing room for dessert?" Kane suggested. He leaned toward Portia. "If you will unfurl your prettiest smile, my dear, you just might be able to coax Julian into reciting another stanza or two of Byron for you."

Portia scrambled eagerly out of her chair while the rest of the guests rose and began to drift toward the dining room, slowly resuming their chatter.

"May I have a word with you, Miss Cabot?" Kane asked as Caroline slipped out of her chair.

"Certainly, my lord." She turned, startled anew by his size. Given her willowy stature, she wasn't used to having to look up just to gaze into a man's face. She'd always been quite comfortable looking down her nose at Cousin Cecil.

She wasn't sure how it had happened, but suddenly the two of them were all alone in the dining room. Even the servants seemed to have vanished. As had all traces of amusement in the viscount's luminous eyes.

"I just wanted you to know that I'm perfectly capable of handling both Larkin and his suspicions. I don't need you to defend me."

Taken aback by the rebuke, she lifted her chin. "I wasn't defending anyone. I was simply asking a question that anyone with an inkling of common sense would ask."

He leaned closer, his smoky baritone pitched just above a growl. "If you have an inkling of common sense, Miss Cabot, you won't involve yourself in my affairs."

Her mouth fell open, but before she could form a retort, he had sketched a curt bow, turned on his heel, and strode out of the room.

Caroline snapped her mouth shut. Constable Larkin might have couched his admonitions in civility, but there could be no doubt about Kane's blunt words.

She had been warned.

Four

The moon was riding low in the starless sky when the Cabot sisters finally murmured their polite farewells and departed the viscount's town house. A fine mist clung to the trees and grass, blurring the edges of the waning night. Even the irrepressible Portia was starting to drag her slippered feet. Caroline suspected her little sister would be fast asleep on her shoulder before their carriage pulled away from the curb. She smothered a yawn into her glove as Aunt Marietta took the footman's hand and heaved herself into the waiting carriage.

"Miss Cabot?" All three of the sisters turned as a man detached himself from the low stone wall bordering the walk. But it was Caroline who bore the brunt of his steady brown gaze. "Forgive me for startling you, but I was wondering if I might have a moment of your time?"

Constable Larkin stood before her, hat in hand. He must have been sitting on that wall waiting for them to emerge for nearly three hours. Judging from the shadows beneath his eyes, this wasn't his first sleepless night, nor would it be his last.

To Caroline's surprise, it was Vivienne who spoke up. "I shouldn't speak to him if I were you, Caro. It's hardly proper for a man to accost a young lady on the street."

"He's a policeman, dear, not an ax murderer," Caroline

replied. "Why don't the two of you wait for me in the carriage with Aunt Marietta? I'll only be a moment."

Vivienne hesitated just long enough to throw the constable a scornful look before climbing into the carriage, her soft, pink mouth compressed to a disapproving line.

Caroline led Larkin a few paces away, making sure they were out of her sisters' earshot. Portia had always been able to overhear a juicy tidbit of gossip at one hundred paces. "I'd appreciate it if you could make this brief, Constable. I need to get my sisters back to my aunt's lodgings. We're not accustomed to keeping such extravagant hours."

Although he made a valiant attempt, Larkin could not quite hide the longing in his eyes as he stole a glance at the carriage. "I can see that you take your responsibility for their well-being very seriously. Which is precisely why I had to speak to you. I wanted to warn you to have a care where Miss Vivienne is concerned." Still avoiding Caroline's gaze, he turned his hat over in his hands, his raw-boned fingers caressing its brim. "Although I've only known your sister for a short time, I hold her in very high regard and I would never forgive myself should any harm come to her."

"Nor would I, Constable. Which is precisely why you must stop dropping these lurid hints and simply tell me if you have any evidence to prove that Lord Trevelyan is a danger to my sister or any other woman."

He jerked up his head, plainly thrown off balance by her frankness. "Perhaps you should ask him what happened to the last woman he courted. A woman who bore a rather startling resemblance to your sister."

When he first spotted Vivienne, he went so white you'd have thought he'd seen a ghost.

As Aunt Marietta's shrill voice echoed in her memory, Caroline felt a chill ripple through her. "Perhaps I should ask you."

"I don't have the answer. Eloisa Markham vanished without a trace over five years ago. The mystery surrounding her disappearance was never solved. Her family finally decided that she must have simply spurned Kane's affections and eloped to Gretna Green with some penniless ne'er do well."

It was difficult to imagine any woman spurning the affections of a man like Kane. "But you don't believe that?"

The constable's silence was answer enough.

Caroline sighed. "Do you have any proof whatsoever that Lord Trevelyan is connected to her disappearance or to any of the others?"

Larkin grew very still, his gaze narrowing on her face. "Instead of interrogating me, Miss Cabot, perhaps you should be asking yourself why you feel compelled to defend him."

Caroline drew herself up. This was the second time she'd been accused of such a grave offense in only a few short hours. "I'm not defending him. I just refuse to dash my sister's hopes for a happy and prosperous future when you haven't a single shred of evidence to convict him."

"How am I to collect evidence on a phantom?" Catching the concerned glance Caroline threw the carriage, Larkin lowered his voice to a fierce whisper. "How can I hunt a man who moves like a shadow through the night?"

Caroline laughed, telling herself that it was only fatigue that gave the sound a hysterical edge. "What are you trying to say, Constable? That you—a man who has apparently decided to dedicate both his life and his calling to the unassailable pursuit of logic and truth—also believe that the viscount just might be a vampire?"

Larkin gazed up at one of the darkened windows in the third story of the town house, his face set in grim lines. "I don't know exactly what he is. I only know that death follows wherever he goes."

In any other circumstances, his words might have provoked more laughter. But standing in front of a stranger's house in an unfamiliar city in the predawn chill, Caroline was forced to hug her cloak more tightly around her. "That would be a sentiment more worthy of Byron's fanciful pen, don't you think?"

"Perhaps Byron is simply willing to entertain the notion that not every mystery can be solved by logic. If you're truly concerned about your sister's welfare, I strongly suggest that you do the same."

As he donned his hat and turned to go, she said, "I can't help but wonder if there isn't a more personal motive behind your suspicions, Constable. You mentioned that you and Lord Trevelyan attended university together. Perhaps this is just your way of settling a grudge against an old enemy."

"Enemy?" Larkin echoed, turning back. Even as one corner of his mouth tilted in a rueful smile, an ineffable sadness clouded his eyes. "On the contrary, Miss Cabot. I loved Adrian like a brother. He was my dearest friend."

He tipped his hat to her before strolling away, leaving her standing all alone in the mist.

"Damn Larkin to hell and back!" Adrian swore, watching the constable saunter away as if he hadn't a care in the world.

Caroline Cabot stood in the middle of the street below, looking like a lost little girl. Mist swirled around her, lapping hungrily at the hem of her cloak.

As Adrian watched from the shadows of the roof, she turned and cast a troubled look at the town house. Her gray-eyed gaze was so clear, so incisive, that he nearly ducked behind a brick chimney before remembering that the cloak of darkness shielded him, as it always did.

She turned and climbed into the waiting carriage, her shoulders slumping with exhaustion. As the carriage rolled away, Adrian strode to the edge of the roof, watching until it disappeared around a distant corner.

It was just as he had feared. Larkin had lain in wait for her like a cunning spider, hoping to entangle her in his web. By speaking up in his defense, she had marked herself with the same ugly stain of suspicion that tainted everything he did. He'd long ago grown accustomed to the nervous whispers and sidelong glances that followed him everywhere he went. There was no reason she should have to do the same.

"There you are!" Julian exclaimed, popping out of an attic window like an inebriated jack-in-the-box. His weaving was explained by the half-empty decanter of scotch he gripped in one hand. "I thought you'd gone out."

"What would be the point?" Adrian eyed the horizon. In the past few years, he'd become an expert at detecting the faintest shift from black to gray. "The sun will be up in less than two hours."

Julian staggered over and sank down on a crumbling chimney pot without a trace of the effete grace that had so dazzled Adrian's guests. "And not a moment too soon, as far as I'm concerned," he said, yawning broadly. "I don't know what was more exhausting—being forced to spew out overwrought poetry for hours on end or having that little girl gaze at me all night as if I hung the moon."

A wry smile touched Adrian's lips. "Didn't you?"

"No," Julian retorted, lifting the decanter to the sky in a mocking toast. "Only the stars."

Above their heads, those stars were winking out one by one, mourning the passing of the night. The fading shadows only deepened Julian's pallor and accentuated the hollows beneath his eyes. The hand clutching the decanter betrayed a visible tremor.

Adrian nodded toward the decanter, feeling his heart twist with a concern that was becoming all too familiar. "Do you really think that's wise?"

"Beats the alternative," Julian quipped, taking another deep swig. "There's only so much rare roast beef a fellow can choke down in one night. Besides, I have every right to celebrate, as do you. Didn't you hear Larkin? After tracking Duvalier through every sordid hellhole on seven continents, we finally have the bastard in our sights. He's falling right into our little trap."

Adrian snorted. "Or setting a trap of his own."

Julian leaned back on his elbows, crossing his long legs at the ankles. "Do you think he's seen her yet? Or was it just the rumors of your impending romantic bliss that finally lured him back to London?"

"I'm sure the mere thought that I could find happiness in the arms of any woman must be driving him insane with rage. I've tried to arrange it so he wouldn't catch more than a glimpse of her until the ball. That's why we've been frequenting darkened theaters and private suppers. I want to whet his appetite first, to draw him so deep into our net that escape will be impossible."

"What makes you think he'll take the bait and follow us to Wiltshire?"

"Because half of London will be following us to Wiltshire. You know as well as I do that a masquerade ball thrown by the mysterious Viscount Trevelyan will be the most sought after invitation of the Season. And Duvalier never could resist an audience."

Julian reached down to wipe a speck of soot from his boot, plainly weighing his next words with care. "I'm fully confident in your ability to keep Vivienne out of Duvalier's clutches, but aren't you just a little bit worried about breaking the girl's heart?"

Adrian offered his brother a rueful smile. "I might be. If it was mine to break." Julian frowned in bewilderment, but before his brother could question him further, Adrian continued. "Speaking of Vivienne, I don't believe her eldest sister was quite as enamored of you as young Portia was."

Julian pulled a long face. "She was all starch and vinegar, that one."

"On the contrary," Adrian said, keeping his face carefully impassive. "I found the elder Miss Cabot to be quite intriguing."

Vivienne had spoken of her older sister with such dismissive affection that Adrian had been expecting a dried-up spinster, not a slender, gray-eyed beauty garbed like Aphrodite herself. If Vivienne was sunlight, then Caroline was moonlight—silvery blond, misty, ephemeral. If he had dared to touch her, Adrian feared she would have melted like moonbeams through his fingers.

Julian finished off the scotch, then wiped his mouth with the back of his hand. "She didn't seem to be particularly enamored of *you*, either. If it was her blessing you were seeking, I fear you're doomed to disappointment."

"I stopped looking for blessings a long time ago. All I needed was some assurance that she wouldn't meddle in her sister's affairs. But thanks to Larkin's wretched timing, I'm afraid that all I succeeded in doing tonight was piquing her curiosity."

Julian sat up, a worried frown creasing his brow. "Now that we know our plan is working, we can't afford to let Duvalier slip through our fingers again. You don't think she could pose a problem, do you?"

Adrian remembered those unguarded moments before Caroline had realized who he was. He'd been blinded by the naughty sparkle in her eyes, the nearly imperceptible sprinkling of freckles over her cheeks, the inviting fullness of her lips and the flash of her dimples, so at odds with the angular purity of her high cheekbones and sharp little nose. He had never intended for his teasing to bloom into a full-blown flirtation. But all of his noble intentions had flown out the terrace door when she looked up at him as if she *wanted* him to gobble her up.

He turned his gaze toward the brightening horizon, wishing he could welcome the sunrise instead of dreading it. "Not if I can bloody well help it."

Five

"Despite being a vampire, I found Lord Trevelyan to be the very soul of kindness last night," Portia remarked.

"I thought vampires didn't have souls," Caroline muttered, pacing her aunt's octagonal parlor as if it were a cage.

Aunt Marietta and Vivienne had accepted an invitation to a Lady Marlybone's card party, leaving Caroline and Portia to their own devices. The servants had retired early, relieved to be free of their mistress's tyrannical demands.

Caroline made an abrupt shift in direction, nearly stumbling over an overstuffed bolster. Her aunt's three-story lodgings occupied exactly half of a narrow town house. The parlor was as fussy and overblown as Aunt Marietta. Caroline could barely reach for a teacup without snagging her sleeve on the crook of some simpering china shepherdess. A dizzying array of floral chintzes and busy brocades draped the numerous sofas, chairs, and occasional tables.

Portia was curled up in one of those chairs, her bare feet tucked beneath the hem of her linen nightdress, a book of Byron's poems nestled in her lap. Her dark curls peeked out from beneath a ruffled cap. "Don't you think Julian would make a far more dashing vampire than his brother? He has such elegant hands and soulful eyes." She hugged the leather-bound volume to her chest, a dreamy smile curving her lips. "He's not too old for me, you know. He's only two-and-twenty, five years younger than the viscount. If Vivienne should marry Lord Trevelyan, do you think she could persuade Julian to offer for me?"

Caroline turned and gazed down her nose at her sister. "Am I to understand that now that you've met his oh-so-handsome and ever-so-eligible brother, you're willing to overlook the fact that you believe Lord Trevelyan to be a vampire?"

Portia blinked up at her. "Aren't you the one who's always urging me to be more practical?"

As Portia tucked her nose back in the book, Caroline shook her head and resumed her pacing. She supposed she had no right to scold Portia for her ridiculous suspicions when she was starting to feel as if Adrian Kane had cast some sort of hypnotic spell over *her*. She'd thought of nothing—and no one—else since the moment he had first offered her his handkerchief. She certainly couldn't admit to Portia that she had tucked that innocuous scrap of linen beneath her pillow upon returning from the viscount's town house. Or that she had drawn it out upon awakening just to see if a tantalizing whiff of bay rum and sandalwood still clung to its luxuriant folds.

Although Kane had been the perfect gentleman for most of the evening, Caroline was still haunted by that moment in the dining room when his mask of civility had slipped, revealing that he might be even more dangerous than Portia suspected. According to Constable Larkin, dangerous enough to make a young woman who bore an uncanny resemblance to their sister vanish from the face of the earth.

She tried to draw in a deep breath, but the suffocating sweetness of her aunt's lavender perfume seemed to cling to every corner of the cluttered town house.

What if this Eloisa Markham did resemble Vivienne? Was it so terrible to imagine that a man might be attracted to a woman who reminded him of his lost love? Especially if she had been lost to another man.

Caroline had spent the evening searching for any sign of

a grand passion between Vivienne and her viscount—long, lingering looks, a discreet brush of the hands when they thought no one was looking, sneaking off behind a potted palm to share a passionate kiss. But they were the very model of propriety. Kane had chuckled at her sister's jests, heaped effusive praise on her rather mediocre harp playing, and stopped just short of rumpling her hair when she said something particularly clever. He seemed to treat Vivienne with the same fond affection one might show a beloved cousin.

Or a cherished pet.

Caroline rubbed her furrowed brow. What if Vivienne's affections were more deeply engaged than Kane's? Unlike Portia, Vivienne had never been one to wear her heart on her sleeve. Caroline couldn't bear the thought of breaking that gentle heart when her only weapons were rumors and unproven accusations. She was also keenly aware that Vivienne's heart wasn't the only thing at stake. Not with Cousin Cecil all but threatening to toss them into the streets if she didn't promise to "look upon him more kindly" in the future.

She hugged back a shudder. She wasn't yet ready to condemn Kane. Not when she knew for sure that Cousin Cecil was a monster.

But she still couldn't help wondering what sin could be so dark as to turn Kane's best friend into his sworn enemy? And who was the mysterious Victor Duvalier? The constable had obviously used the man's name as a taunt. Kane's stony-faced reaction had only made him look more guilty, not less. Especially when his brother had gone as pale as a corpse at the mere mention of the name.

Caroline wandered over to the window. In just a few short days she and Portia would be banished back to their drafty old cottage at Edgeleaf. But how could she leave London, knowing that she might be abandoning her sister to a villain's mercy?

As she gazed into the shadows of the night, wondering

what dark secrets they held, Constable Larkin's warning echoed through her memory: *I don't know exactly what he is. I only know that death follows wherever he goes.*

"Death won't be the only thing following him tonight," she murmured. If Constable Larkin couldn't provide her with the proof she needed to condemn or exonerate Kane, she would just have to do a little sleuthing of her own.

"Did you say something?" Portia asked, glancing up from her book.

"I most certainly did," Caroline replied, turning briskly away from the window. "Get dressed and fetch your cloak. We're going out."

Sensing that some rare excitement was afoot, Portia slammed her book shut and scrambled out of the chair, her eyes sparkling with eagerness. "Where are we going?"

As Caroline's gaze fell on a pair of dusty papier-mâché half masks resting on her aunt's mantel, souvenirs of some long forgotten masquerade, a grim smile curved her lips. "Vampire hunting."

As she and Portia slipped from the hired hack, even Caroline had to admit that it was a fine evening for vampires and other creatures of the night to be afoot—windy and unseasonably warm, with just enough threat of rain in the air to rattle the branches of the trees and set the budding May leaves to trembling. A shy half-moon peeked through the tattered veil of clouds. At least they would be safe from werewolves, Caroline thought wryly.

She had spent nearly every last coin of their meager allowance to hire the conveyance. Now she would have to return to Edgeleaf and beg Cousin Cecil for a pittance to tide them over until the end of the month. He would swear they'd squandered their money on high living in London. Instead, they'd spent an hour huddled in a rented hack that reeked of cigar smoke and stale perfume, waiting for Lord Trevelyan to emerge from his town house.

Caroline had been ready to admit defeat when the viscount's crested carriage emerged from the alley that ran behind the row of houses. She'd poked awake a dozing Portia and signaled the driver, who had already been instructed to follow the carriage at a discreet distance. Once it reached the viscount's destination, she and Portia had paused just long enough to fasten their cloaks and adjust the gold-leaf masks that covered only the upper half of their faces before eagerly forsaking the musty interior of the carriage for the warm, windy night.

"Oh, my!" Portia breathed, gazing upward in awe.

Caroline was tempted to do the same. She'd expected Kane to lead them to some dank alley, but instead he had lured them to one of Portia's imaginary fairy kingdoms, brought to vibrant life by a sprinkle of pixie dust and the tap of a magic wand.

As she gazed up at the flickering lanterns strung through the branches of the elms, and heard the distant strains of violin and mandolin, Caroline realized they were standing before the gates of Vauxhall, the most celebrated—and notorious—pleasure gardens in all of London.

Her heart skipped a beat as Adrian Kane emerged from the row of vehicles parked ahead of them. Unlike one of Portia's fantastical realms, this place held both enchantment *and* danger.

The viscount was hatless and the warm honey of his hair gleamed beneath the kiss of the lantern light. The waist-length cape of his coat made his shoulders look even broader and more intimidating. He glanced in their direction, his penetrating gaze scanning the crowd. Caroline grabbed Portia's elbow and ducked behind a stout matron, seized by the ridiculous notion that he was going to march right back to them and jerk her up by the ear.

But when she peeped around the woman's shoulder, he had swung around and started toward the gates, walking stick in hand.

"Quick! There he goes." Snatching Portia by the hand,

Caroline lurched into an awkward trot to match his long strides.

Despite Constable Larkin's insinuations, there was nothing furtive about Kane's movements. He walked the night as if he owned it, towering head and shoulders over most of the patrons streaming toward the garden.

"I was rather hoping Julian would be with him," Portia confessed, already out of breath from their brisk pace.

"From what I understand, most predators like to hunt alone," Caroline muttered without thinking.

Portia stopped dead in her tracks, jerking Caroline to a halt. Caroline turned to find her sister gazing at her, her eyes round with disbelief.

"I thought we were just here on a lark," Portia said. "Do you mean to tell me that you weren't joking about the vampire hunting? Do you really believe the viscount might be a vampire?"

"I'm not sure what I believe anymore," Caroline replied grimly, tugging her sister back into motion. "But I intend to find out tonight."

They were almost through the garden gate when a balding man in homespun trousers and shirt reached out from his wooden booth to block their path. "Whoa there, ladies!"

Although he addressed them as 'ladies', there was no mistaking the skeptical gleam in his eye. Caroline could hardly blame him for thinking the worst of two young unchaperoned females out on the town at this unholy hour. She was painfully aware that she was risking both of their reputations. But how could she weigh their reputations against Vivienne's entire future? She could only pray the masks would keep them from being recognized by anyone in Aunt Marietta's social circle.

Barely glancing at the man, she bounced up and down on her tiptoes, desperate to keep Kane in view. "We're in a terrible hurry, sir. Could you please stand aside?"

"Not until ye fork over three shillings apiece."

When she turned to stare at him blankly, he sighed and rolled his eyes. "For admittance to the garden."

"Oh!" Caroline recoiled in dismay. This was an expense she had not anticipated, one that would leave them with little more than a handful of pennies in their rapidly dwindling coffers. But unless they wanted to return to Aunt Marietta's lodgings no wiser than when they'd left, she had little choice. Kane was already melting rapidly into the crush.

Drawing her silk reticule from the inner pocket of her cloak, Caroline counted out the money and tossed it at the man's outstretched hand.

She and Portia scrambled through the gate hand in hand. Revelers thronged the garden's Grand Walk. Lanterns twinkled like stars among the majestic branches of the elms that lined the graveled thoroughfare. Lovers strolled arm in arm through air perfumed with night-blooming jasmine and roasted chestnuts.

A buxom lady swept past them, trailed by a liveried page, his powdered wig as white as snow, his smooth skin as dark as polished ebony. A handful of children darted through the crowd like sprightly elves, their eyes bright with mischief and their pudgy little fingers gripping sugar biscuits or whatever treat they'd most recently coaxed their parents into purchasing. A dark-eyed man stood beside a marble fountain, the violin tucked beneath his chin weeping out a wistful melody.

As she peered at all of the engaging sights around them, Portia's steps slowed. Caroline could hardly blame her. She was in grave danger of falling beneath the garden's enchantment herself. But she was jostled out of its spell by a swaggering pack of bucks, who stared just a little too hard and a little too long at Portia's bosom. Just a few days ago she'd overheard Aunt Marietta and some of her cronies whispering about an unfortunate young miss who had been dragged from her mother's side into one of the shadowy glades that bounded the gardens by a drunken pair of young bloods intent upon the worst sort of mischief.

"Hurry, Portia," Caroline urged, gathering her sister even closer. "We mustn't let him get too far ahead of us!" She kept her gaze locked on Kane, his powerful shoulders suddenly seeming more of a comfort than a threat.

They'd traveled only a few feet when Portia tugged her to a halt again. "Oh, look, Caro! They have iced cream!"

Caroline turned to find her sister gazing longingly at an Italian vendor who was handing over a paper cone filled with lemon ice to an elegantly garbed young lady close to Portia's age.

"Please Portia! We have neither the time nor the money for such nonsense right now." Caroline dragged her sister back into motion, but as her eyes scanned the path ahead of them, she realized it was too late. Kane was gone.

"Oh, no," she breathed, letting go of Portia's hand.

Leaving her sister standing there, she pushed her way through the crowd, tugging down her mask to frantically search for the viscount. But it was no use. Kane had vanished, swallowed up by the steady stream of revelers.

Revelers or prey? she wondered, touched by a sudden chill.

That chill hardened to a deep freeze when she heard a familiar cackle of laughter. Without thinking, she whirled around. Aunt Marietta and Vivienne were sweeping down the path, heading straight toward her. They had strolled right past Portia, too engrossed in their chatter to notice the masked young woman standing paralyzed in the middle of the walk.

Exchanging a panicked look with Portia, Caroline fumbled for the ribbons of her mask. In a few more seconds the women would be upon her.

"Aunt Marietta!" Portia shouted, dragging off her mask.

The two women turned as one. Caroline didn't know whether to burst into tears of dread or relief.

"Portia? Is that you?" Vivienne called out, bewilderment ringing in her voice.

Portia's face crumpled. "Oh, Vivienne! Aunt Marietta! I was so frightened! I'm so glad you've come!" She launched herself at their aunt, throwing her arms around Aunt Marietta's ample waist and burying her face in her ruffled bosom.

Behind their aunt's back, she gave Caroline a frantic hand signal. Caroline took the cue, ducking behind the graceful column of a Gothic temple at the edge of the path.

"What on earth are you doing here, child?" Aunt Marietta trumpeted, grimacing with distaste as she struggled to pry Portia's hands from her gown. "You're supposed to be at home in bed."

Portia straightened, but not before using one of her aunt's ruffles to dab at her nose. "I'm afraid I've been very naughty," she confessed, still sniffing pitiably. "I was terribly angry at you for leaving me behind tonight when I knew it would only be a few days before I was shipped back to the country. I've always wanted to see Vauxhall so I waited until Caroline fell asleep, stole some coins from her purse, and snuck out of your lodgings. But as soon as I got here, I realized I'd made a terrible mistake. I got so scared, and now I just want to go ho-o-o-ome!" Portia's voice broke on a wail.

Caroline rolled her eyes, grateful for once that her baby sister had always been such a convincing liar. One would have to possess a heart of stone to doubt her brimming eyes and trembling lips.

"Why, you wicked girl! I ought to send you back to Edgeleaf first thing in the morning." As Aunt Marietta lifted one hammy fist as if to box Portia's ears, Caroline tensed, ready to spring out of her hiding place.

"What are the two of *you* doing here?" Portia demanded, her tone just accusing enough to startle Aunt Marietta into lowering her hand. "Why aren't you at your precious card party?"

"Lady Marlybone took ill and we hadn't a fourth for our table," Aunt Marietta explained.

"It was such a beautiful night that Auntie suggested we take a stroll through the gardens before retiring." A note of poorly suppressed merriment rippled through Vivienne's voice. "I can assure you that it had nothing to do with the fact that we spotted Lord Trevelyan's crest on a carriage parked just outside."

Aunt Marietta sighed. "There's no help for it now, is there? You might as well come along with us. I refuse to let a disobedient little chit spoil such a fine evening. I suppose it's not your fault that silly sister of mine never taught you any manners. It was my good fortune to inherit both the looks and the brains in the family."

Tilting her pug nose in the air, Aunt Marietta linked her arm through Vivienne's and went sailing away down the walk, giving Portia no choice but to drift along in their wake. Portia lingered behind just long enough to throw a wink over her shoulder at Caroline, giving Caroline her unspoken blessing to proceed with their mission.

Caroline slowly straightened, her heart swelling with gratitude. Her little sister's ruse had bought her both time and opportunity.

Setting her mask back in place and tightening its ribbons, she hastened down the walk where Kane had vanished, determined to find him before they did.

Caroline had never realized it was possible to feel so alone while surrounded by so many people. As she wandered the garden's crowded walks, she searched every gentleman's face and form in vain. Twice she would have sworn she caught a glimpse of honey-gold hair and the commanding swirl of a shoulder-cape just ahead of her, but she would battle her way through the crush only to find herself bobbing along in a sea of strangers.

As the night deepened and the crowds began to thin, a group of giggling beaus and belles ran past, their faces also masked. The dappled shadows gave their hollow eyes and leering lips a sinister cast. One of them thrust a branch of bells in her face, laughing wildly.

She recoiled, gritting her teeth. She was just beginning to wish that she'd been the one to run into Aunt Marietta's arms, weeping and begging for forgiveness, when she spotted a lone man through the trees, strolling on a path that ran parallel to hers.

Her pulse quickening, Caroline ducked beneath the feathery branch of a cedar and darted through the glade. She emerged on a deserted stretch of walk. There was no sign of the man she had seen.

The path was narrower here, the lanterns spaced farther apart, the trees closer. Their interlaced branches formed a murky canopy over her head, blocking out the last traces of the moonlight. With a sinking heart, Caroline realized that she must have stumbled upon the infamous Lover's Walk, the most legendary trysting place in all of London.

The Walk's notoriety had spread all the way to Edgeleaf. It was whispered that here, among these winding paths and leafy glades, ladies who had married for money came to find love. Here that gentlemen who had been banished from their wives' chilly beds came to seek warmer and more welcoming arms. Here that both libertines and respected members of the House of Lords came to indulge their appetites for pleasures so dark and delicious that no one dared even whisper of them.

Caroline started as a low moan came out of the darkness ahead of her. She took an involuntary step toward the sound, fearing that someone was in distress. And as it turned out, they were, but not the sort of distress she had anticipated.

Just a few feet off the path, a man had a woman pinned against the smooth trunk of an elder tree. Their casual dishabille was somehow more shocking than if they'd been naked. The man's coat and shirt hung half off of his sun-bronzed shoulders, while the woman's skirt had been gathered to just above her knees, revealing a glimpse of silk stocking and milky thigh. The man was lavishing caresses and kisses on the one plump breast that had escaped the top of the woman's bodice. His other hand had disappeared beneath her skirt.

Caroline couldn't even begin to imagine what he might be doing to her under there to make her writhe and moan in such a shameless manner.

Against her will, she felt her own breath quicken, her own flesh begin to heat. The woman's glazed eyes drifted open and met Caroline's over her companion's shoulder. Her kiss-swollen lips curved in a smug smile, as if she possessed an exquisite secret Caroline would never know.

Drawing up the hood of her cloak to shield her flaming cheeks, Caroline hastened past them. She longed to retrace her steps, but couldn't bear the thought of passing by the lovers again. Perhaps if she just kept going, she could find another way out of this bewildering maze of paths.

For several minutes she didn't pass a single soul. Her sense of unease grew with each step, as did the rhythmic rustling of the leaves behind her.

"It's just the wind," she murmured, quickening her pace yet again.

A branch cracked in the woods to her left. She whipped around, clapping a hand to her pounding heart. Although her straining eyes failed to detect even a ghost of movement, she could not shake the sensation that someone—or something—was watching her from the shadows, some malevolent presence that was content to bide its time until she relaxed her guard. That quickly, the hunter had become the prey.

She whirled around to run. She'd barely taken three long strides before she crashed headlong into a masculine chest. If the impact hadn't dazed her, the man's breath would have. He'd obviously drunk far more than his share of the stout Vauxhall punch so prized by the garden's regular patrons. The fumes roiling from his breath were strong enough to make her eyes water.

Blinking to clear her vision, she saw that he was lanky, fair-haired, and barely old enough to grow whiskers, with an innocuous scattering of freckles across the bridge of his nose. Judging from his beaver top hat and the fine cut of his broadcloth coat, he was also a gentleman.

"Excuse me, sir," she said, relief flooding her as she fought to catch her breath. "I seem to have lost my way. Perhaps you'd be kind enough to direct me back to the Grand Walk?"

"Well, what have we here?" he crooned, steadying her with one hand while plucking down her hood with the other. "Little Red Riding Hood on her way to Grandma's house?"

A second lad came swinging out from the trees behind him, landing on the balls of his feet with the grace of a young cat. His top hat sat askew on his dark curls. "Didn't anyone tell you that these woods were full of big bad wolves just waiting to gobble up little girls like you?"

As Caroline's startled gaze darted from one face to the other, she saw that these two required no masks. Their leers were genuine.

She gave her captor's chest a shove, breaking free from his possessive grip. "I'm not on my way to Grandma's house and I'm hardly a little girl!" Fighting to keep her voice more steady than her hands, she added, "I can see that the two of you are gentlemen. I was hoping you'd be willing to lend assistance to a lady."

Hitching his thumbs in the pockets of his waistcoat, the dark-haired young buck snorted. "No *lady* would come strolling down this walk all alone unless she was looking for a little sport."

"I was looking for a man," Caroline blurted out, desperate to make them understand.

The fair-haired lad's grin was all the more chilling for being so genial. "Then I'm sure two of them will be twice the sport."

As they advanced on her, their swaggering gaits none too steady, Caroline began to back away. Through a haze of fear, she remembered the unfortunate girl who had been dragged from her mother's side. According to Aunt Marietta, no one had heeded her screams until it was too late.

Knowing she had to try anyway, Caroline was opening her mouth to let loose a bloodcurdling shriek when she backed right into the arms of a third man.

One powerful arm encircled her shoulders from behind, settling just above the swell of her breasts. "Sorry to disappoint you lads," said a deep, smoky rumble of a voice, "but there's more than just wolves roaming these woods tonight."

Six

Caroline sagged with relief, cradled by the sandalwood-and-bay-rum-scented warmth of Adrian Kane's embrace. She'd promised him she wasn't the type to swoon into a man's arms, but his undeniable strength made such a notion oddly enticing. Especially coupled with his devastating self-assurance. She couldn't escape the notion that he was the sort of man who would know exactly what to do with any woman he happened to find in his arms.

"Who in the bloody hell are you?" her fair-haired attacker demanded, his genial grin replaced by a sullen scowl.

Kane's voice was matter-of-fact, almost jovial. "I'm the one who ate the Big Bad Wolf and left nothing behind but bones."

The lad exchanged an uncertain glance with his companion. The dark-haired boy stepped forward until the two of them stood shoulder-to-shoulder. "We're just out for a bit of sport on this fine spring night," he said earnestly, tugging off his top hat. "We've no quarrel with you, sir."

"If you want to keep it that way, I suggest that you and your friend here move along and forget you ever strayed down this path."

"That's not fair!" snarled the other boy, poking his chest

out with the foolish bravado of youth. "We were the ones who snared her. She's ours!"

Before Caroline could so much as sputter a retort, Kane said smoothly, "Not anymore. She's mine now."

That primal claim, coming from Kane's lips and delivered with such absolute conviction, sent an involuntary shiver dancing along Caroline's skin. His grip tightened, warning her that he had felt it.

"You can have her when we're done, if you like," offered the dark-haired young man, obviously planning a future career as a diplomat in the Home Office. "The two of us, we know how to treat a lady." He wet his top lip with his tongue, his suggestive gaze flickering over Caroline. "She may start out begging for mercy, but by the time we're through with her, she'll be begging for more."

Kane's entire body tensed, as if poised to spring. But he simply said, "No, thank you. I've always had a taste for fresh meat."

Appalled by his deliberate crudity, Caroline stiffened. She tried to twist around to see his expression, but his implacable grip held her steady.

"This is a lot of rubbish," declared the fair-haired lad. "There's two of us and only one of him. I say we take her back."

As the two exchanged a defiant glance, Kane murmured, "Excuse me, dear. I'll only be a moment," and set her away from him with firm but gentle hands.

He was right. One minute both of her attackers were rushing toward him, the next they were sprawled on the ground, groaning aloud. Blood streamed from the blond's freckled nose. The other boy hung his head and spit out a tooth, his split lip already swelling to twice its size.

Kane stood there in the middle of the path without so much as a bead of sweat on his brow, tapping the end of his walking stick across his palm.

He took an almost imperceptible step in their direction,

and they both went scrambling backward on elbows and heels like wounded crabs. "The next time you two cubs want to do a little hunting, I suggest you invest in a pack of hounds and join a fox club. Otherwise, you just might find your own pelts mounted on my wall."

Still glaring daggers at him, they staggered to their feet and stumbled away through the trees, groaning and cursing beneath their breaths.

Kane slowly turned toward Caroline. Although he didn't so much as twitch a muscle in her direction, his intentions were clear.

He had dealt with them. Now he would deal with her.

She straightened her mask, still hoping against hope that he had not recognized her. "Thank you, sir. Your gallantry is much appreciated."

"Is that so?"

Unnerved by his inscrutable gaze, she began to back away from him. "I don't know what I would have done if you hadn't come along at such an opportune moment."

"Opportune for the both of us, it would seem," he replied, matching her retreat step for step.

Was it her imagination or was his gaze lingering on the pale curve of her throat? On the pulse that fluttered beneath her soft white skin? She touched a hand there, but it seemed a feeble defense indeed.

I've always had a taste for fresh meat.

His words drifted back to haunt her. What if he'd been talking about satisfying a different sort of hunger altogether?

Fighting to ward off the ridiculous fancy, she backed right into a pool of moonlight. Its misty glow did not deter him. He just kept coming, his every step as measured as the tolling of the distant church bell heralding the arrival of midnight.

"I should be getting back to my party," she said, growing more breathless with each step. "We were separated and they're probably frantic with worry by now."

"As well they should be . . ."

She turned to flee, half expecting one of his powerful arms to encircle her again. One of his big, warm hands to splay over the delicate curve of her jaw, to tilt her head to the side and expose the vulnerable curve of her throat so he could lean down and sink his—

". . . Miss Cabot," he finished.

Caroline froze in her tracks, then whirled back around to face him, unaccountably angry that he'd seen through her ridiculous little masquerade. "How did you know?"

Propping his walking stick against a nearby tree, he closed the distance between them in a few long strides. "By your hair. I don't think any other woman in London has hair quite that hue." He reached to tug a strand from her tightly woven chignon, sifting the wispy stuff through his fingers as if it was the rarest of silks. "It's like liquid moonlight."

Caught off guard by the unexpected caress, Caroline slowly lifted her gaze to his. Despite the tenderness of his touch, his eyes still glittered with anger.

Jarred by the traitorous tingle both his touch and his words invoked, she rescued the errant strand, then drew up her hood to cover her hair.

Accepting the unspoken rebuke, he folded his arms over his chest. "Perhaps you'd care to explain why you were following me and just how you managed to lose your little sister and end up in such a predicament. I thought you were supposed to be the sensible one in the family."

"But I am the sensible one! Or at least I was. Until I met—" She stopped, biting her lower lip. "How long have you known I was following you?"

"Since the moment your hack pulled out behind my carriage in Berkeley Square. I strongly suggest you never seek a position in the War Office. You seem to lack the required skulking and creeping skills required for a career in espionage."

"How did you manage to disappear so quickly?" she

asked. "I just looked away for an instant and you were gone."

He shrugged his broad shoulders. "I never know when Larkin and his men will be trailing me. I learned a long time ago that losing yourself in a crowd is the best way to lose someone else." He cocked his head to the side. "Is that why you were following me? Has the constable offered you a position on his payroll?"

Caroline lowered her head to escape his penetrating gaze. It was one thing to stand in a crowded drawing room and laughingly admit that there were those in London who believed him to be a vampire, quite another to stand on a deserted path with his white teeth gleaming in the moonlight and confess that some fanciful corner of your imagination was starting to wonder if they might not be right.

"There were rumors," she murmured.

"There always are, aren't there?"

She swallowed hard, desperately wishing she was as accomplished a liar as Portia. "These rumors gave me reason to doubt your fidelity to my sister. I followed you tonight because I believed you might be engaging in an assignation with another woman."

"I *am* engaging in an assignation with another woman." He tilted her chin up with two fingers, no longer allowing her to avoid his gaze. "With you."

The frank challenge in his eyes made her wonder just what might have happened had they met on these dark and secret pathways under other circumstances, in another lifetime.

She met his gaze boldly, the lies and half-truths flowing more smoothly to her lips. "I realize now how foolish I was to listen to wagging tongues. I should have never doubted your devotion to my sister. And I certainly should have never risked my reputation to spy on you."

His expressive mouth hardened to a grim line. "If I hadn't doubled back to follow you, those black-hearted scoundrels would have seen to it that you lost far more than just your reputation."

She could feel the heat rising in her cheeks. "We don't know that for sure. Given more time, I'm quite certain I could have reasoned with them. After all, they weren't common thugs, but gentlemen."

"Perhaps it's time you learned, Miss Cabot, that beneath the silk waistcoat of every gentleman beats the heart of a beast."

With him looming over her in the moonlight, his voice a smoky growl, that claim wasn't difficult to believe.

"Even beneath yours, Lord Trevelyan?"

He leaned even closer, his brandy-scented breath grazing her lips. "*Especially* beneath mine."

He might have leaned closer yet if a trio of familiar feminine voices hadn't come drifting through the trees.

"Must we go on? These cursed slippers have rubbed blisters on both my heels."

"Poor Auntie! I just don't understand. I was quite certain I saw the viscount come this way."

"You can't be right about everything, you know. I tried to tell the both of you that I spotted him near the Hermit's Walk nearly a quarter of an hour ago."

"Why should we trust you? You once swore you saw a crocodile in the attic at Edgeleaf. And what about all of those years you went around insisting you were a changeling left beneath a cabbage leaf in Mama's garden?"

"Oh, no!" Caroline whispered in horror. "It's Aunt Marietta and my sisters!"

Kane scowled down at her. "Is there anyone else from your family stalking me tonight? A doddering great-uncle or a second cousin thrice removed perhaps?"

She clutched at his arm without realizing it. "Shhhh . . . if we're very quiet, maybe they'll turn around and go back the way they came."

The voices drifted closer, approaching the curve in the

path. It seemed there was to be no going back. For any of them.

"Are you quite sure this is the right walk?" Aunt Marietta's petulant whine warned them it would only be a matter of seconds before she came teetering around the corner on her satin heels, Caroline's bickering sisters in tow.

"Would you like to be the one to explain to your sister why we're enjoying a rendezvous on the Lover's Walk?" Kane murmured, his expression grim. "Or shall I?"

Suddenly Caroline remembered another rendezvous and a sloe-eyed gaze so ripe with pleasure and passion it had sent her scurrying on her way like a frightened rabbit. Just as her aunt's ruffled bosom appeared, she seized the front of Kane's coat and urged him backward into the veil of shadows cast by the trees.

Gazing up at him with pleading eyes, she urgently whispered, "Make love to me!"

Seven

 "Pardon me?" Kane muttered hoarsely, fighting Caroline's frantic grip.

She dug her fingernails into his coat. "If they think we're lovers, there's a chance they might rush past without recognizing us. You have to pretend to make love to me!"

He shook his head, his breath coming hard and fast. "Miss Cabot, I really don't think this is the wisest—"

Knowing that there was no more time for either of them to think, Caroline took a deep breath for courage, rose up on her tiptoes and pressed her lips against his. For several heartbeats he stood as rigid as stone, resisting her clumsy embrace. Then he muttered an oath and his arms went around her. The forbidding line of his mouth softened against hers, curving to embrace the plump swell of her lips. Suddenly, neither one of them was pretending.

Through a haze of delicious sensation, she heard Vivienne blurt out, "Oh, my!" and her aunt snap, "Portia, cover your eyes immediately! And stop peeking through your fingers!"

Portia's startled gasp was followed by the distinct *thwack* of a fan striking tender flesh.

"Ow!" Portia wailed. "Don't tug my hood over my eyes! I can't see to walk!"

Then Kane's tongue flicked gently over Caroline's lips, coaxing them open, and the rushing in her ears drowned out everything but the pulse of pleasure thrumming deep in her veins and the erratic drumbeat of her heart.

When Cousin Cecil had sought to penetrate the defenses of her tightly clamped lips, she had felt only revulsion. But Kane stormed the same gates with irresistible tenderness, seducing her into surrender. She might not know how to kiss, but he was a more than willing tutor. He brushed his lips back and forth across hers, creating a tingling spark of friction that threatened to ignite them both. His tongue delved deeper into the virgin sweetness of her mouth, swirling and stroking and entreating her own tongue to sample a taste of him.

When she obliged him, his arms tightened, gathering her against him until the aching softness of her breasts was crushed against his chest. He deepened his kiss, drinking of her lips as if he wouldn't be satisfied until he'd consumed the very essence of her. Caroline clung to him, growing light-headed with longing.

Everyone had leaned on her for so long that it felt absolutely wonderful to lean on him, to lean *into* him and simply melt into his heat and his strength. Without even realizing it, she sighed into his mouth—a sweet, helpless sound of abandon.

With a shuddering groan, he tore his mouth from hers. As he gazed down at her, his eyes gleaming with primitive hunger, she realized that her aunt and sisters were long gone, leaving the two of them all alone in this moonlit paradise.

For the first time in her life she understood why a man and woman might seek such a haven. Understood the desire to escape society's prying eyes, to hide in the shadows and explore the tantalizing lure of the forbidden. She had surrendered her will for a mere kiss. What would she be willing to sacrifice for other, even more provocative, pleasures? Her self-respect? Her sister's happiness? If she remained in this man's arms much longer, she was afraid she just might find out.

Lowering her eyes, she pushed at his chest. "I believe they're gone now. We can stop pretending."

At first he didn't budge, letting her know just how ineffective her struggles could be when matched against his strength. But then he slowly lowered his arms, freeing her from his embrace.

As he stepped away from her, a gust of rain-scented wind stirred his hair and lifted the shoulder-cape of his coat. His gaze was even more inscrutable than before. "That was a very convincing performance, Miss Cabot. Have you ever considered a career on the stage?"

"Since you've assured me I'm not fit for the rigors of espionage, perhaps I should." She straightened her mask, hoping the shadows would hide the nervous fluttering of her hands. "If I'm not tucked soundly in my bed by the time Aunt Marietta arrives home, I may very well end up selling Banbury cakes on some street corner."

"I hope that won't be—"

Kane's words were cut off by the sharp crack of a nearby branch. Caroline started, fearing that perhaps her aunt and sisters had returned. Moving with lightning quick speed and soundless grace, Kane retrieved his walking stick and tucked her behind him in a motion that warned he would brook no disobedience. Shielding her with his body, he scanned the moon-dappled shadows, his wariness seemingly out of proportion to the harmless sound.

Gripping the back of his coat with one hand, Caroline peered around his shoulder, remembering the overwhelming sense of menace she had experienced earlier. She had assumed that Kane was the one following her, but what if she had been wrong? What if there was something else out there in the darkness, watching and waiting? Something dangerous? Something hungry?

She shivered, wondering where such a wayward thought had come from. "What is it?" she whispered. "You don't think those ruffians have returned, do you?"

Instead of answering, Kane startled her by drawing her

back into the shadows of the trees and clamping a hand firmly over her mouth. Her eyes widened as a man came striding around a bend in the path. Her squirming and squeaking subsided as she recognized Constable Larkin's ill-fitting coat and loose-limbed stride. He was followed by a quartet of men in nondescript hats and coats. At Larkin's discreet signal, they melted into the woods in different directions, one of them passing within a few feet of Caroline and Kane.

When they were all safely out of earshot, Kane released his grip on her. It might have been her overwrought imagination, but his hand seemed to linger against the softness of her lips for a heartbeat longer than necessary.

"What are Larkin and his men doing here?" she whispered.

"Apparently, the same thing everyone else at Vauxhall is doing tonight," Kane murmured, shooting her a wry glance. "Looking for me."

Claiming her hand in a possessive grip, he urged her down the path in the opposite direction, glancing over his shoulder as they went. Caroline had to scramble to keep up with his long strides.

Still wondering if she'd simply leapt from frying pan to fire, she blurted out, "Where are you taking me?"

"Why, where else, Miss Cabot?" He stole a sidelong glance at her, allowing himself only the faintest hint of a smirk. "To bed."

"Are you awake? Caro, wake up! Pssssst!"

Ignoring the frantic hissing just as she'd ignored the creak of the door opening and the telltale groan of the floorboards, Caroline dragged her pillow over her head and burrowed deeper beneath the covers. It had always been useless to feign sleep around Portia. She would start out by poking you in the ribs, then pluck a feather from the nearest hat and begin tickling your toes. Once, in a frenzy to share her latest theories regarding the mermaid she'd spotted splashing around in the bottom of the garden well, she dumped the entire contents of the wash basin over Caroline's head. Caroline had come up swinging, boxing Portia's ears so hard she would whine about their ringing for a week.

But this time Portia chose a strategy that was far more diabolical.

She tugged away a corner of the blanket and put her mouth next to Caroline's ear. Lowering her voice to a mock baritone, she crooned, "Don't be so shy, Miss Cabot. Come on—give us a kiss."

Caroline sat up so fast they nearly bumped heads. "Why, you wretched little brat! You recognized us, didn't you?"

Portia scrambled backward, curling up against the narrow iron footboard like a smug little cat. Aunt Marietta had tucked the both of them into a room beneath the eaves that was little more than an attic. The chamber was furnished with two iron bedsteads and several nicked and scratched cast-offs deemed too unfashionable to be seen belowstairs. A tallow candle burned on the washstand, illuminating the impish twinkle in Portia's eyes.

She kicked off her slippers and wiggled her stocking-clad toes. "Believe me—it wasn't easy to recognize you with Aunt Marietta jerking my hood down over my eyes and smacking me with her fan every five seconds. I stumbled into a tree and nearly knocked myself insensible."

Caroline settled back against the pillows, glaring at her sister. "It's a pity you didn't. At least then I might have been able to get a decent night's rest."

Tugging off her gloves one finger at a time, Portia leaned forward and confided, "At first I thought the viscount was biting you. I couldn't understand why you weren't trying to fight him off. I was getting ready to scream my fool head off when suddenly I realized he was . . . *kissing you.*" She whispered the last as if it were some sort of ancient carnal rite, dark and forbidden and far more lascivious than any act a vampire might commit.

"He was only pretending to kiss me," Caroline insisted,

trying not to remember the intoxicating taste of his lips against her own, the tender sweep of his tongue through her mouth.

Portia's skeptical snort was less than ladylike. "Then he must have a very vivid imagination indeed because he was certainly going about it with a great deal of enthusiasm."

"He had no choice," Caroline retorted, only too aware that her own enthusiasm had been even more damning. "If Aunt Marietta had recognized the two of us, it would have spelled disaster for everyone—especially Vivienne."

Her conscience quailed before the thought of her sister. She almost wished she could believe Kane had cast some sort of spell over her. Then she would have an excuse for behaving like such a shameless wanton in his arms. For being willing to abandon everything she'd always held dear—including Vivienne's trust—for a pleasure as fleeting as a kiss.

"You needn't worry about Vivienne," Portia assured her. "She hadn't an inkling of suspicion. Aunt Marietta was too busy hurrying us along and denouncing your character. Well, not *your* character, but the character of the brazen doxy in the viscount's arms. Of course, she didn't know *you* were the brazen doxy in the viscount's arms. And she didn't know they were the viscount's arms. She thought—" Portia waved away her own hastily spun web of confusion. "Oh, never mind all that. How on earth did you get home? Was the hack still waiting for you?"

"Lord Trevelyan sent me home in his own chaise."

He had bundled her into the vehicle's luxurious interior with nothing more than a curt command to the driver, instructing the man to deliver her to her aunt's door. *Directly* to her aunt's door.

"He didn't accompany you?"

Caroline shook her head, grateful that they hadn't had to share the close confines of the carriage. "I doubt he wanted to spend another minute in my company after I made such a cake of myself."

Portia listened raptly while Caroline told her all about the two young bucks who had accosted her and the viscount's dashing rescue.

When she had finished, Portia leaned against the footboard with a puzzled sigh. "How very odd. I wonder why a vampire would spend his evenings wandering around Vauxhall Gardens rescuing maidens in distress?"

"If it weren't so impossible, I'd almost be tempted to believe he *was* a vampire. You should have seen how he dispatched those two ruffians. I've never seen a man exhibit such astonishing speed and power." Caroline shook her head, shivering at the memory. "There was something almost . . . supernatural about it."

Portia studied her face for a moment before softly asking, "What about his kiss? Was there something supernatural about it as well?"

Caroline inclined her head, cursing her fair complexion. "It's not as if I have anything to compare it with," she lied stiffly, feeling a flush creep into her cheeks. "I'm sure it was a perfectly ordinary kiss."

A perfectly ordinary kiss that had made her dizzy with longing. A perfectly ordinary kiss that had melted her every misgiving and sent every practical thought fleeing from her head—including the fact that the man kissing her belonged to her sister.

No longer able to bear Portia's knowing scrutiny, Caroline slid back down in the bed and rolled over, facing the wall. "Why don't you take yourself off to your own bed and leave me in peace so I can get back to my perfectly ordinary dreams?"

The bells were chiming midnight.

She stood with her feet rooted to the cobblestones as he came striding out of the mist, his hair glowing in the moonlight, his cape swirling around his ankles. She knew he was coming for her, yet she couldn't force a scream from her paralyzed throat, couldn't move so much as a muscle.

The moonlight vanished, leaving her lost in his shadow. He drew her into his arms, his gentleness as irresistible as his strength.

His teeth gleamed as they descended toward her. Too late, she realized that it was not her lips he sought, but her throat. Even so, she could not stop herself from tilting her head to the side and inviting him—no, begging him—to partake of her, to drink his fill of the current of life pulsing just beneath the smooth silk of her skin.

He was only offering her what she wanted, what she had always secretly craved.

Surrender.

As his teeth pierced that fragile veil, sending a rush of unholy ecstasy through her soul, the bells kept ringing, heralding the arrival of some eternal midnight where she would forever belong to him.

Caroline sat bolt upright in the iron bedstead, fighting the crushing pressure in her throat. It took her a panicked moment to realize it was her own hand wrapped around the slender column. Her pulse was racing madly beneath her fingertips. She slowly lowered her hand, gazing at her trembling fingers as if they belonged to someone else.

Even more disconcerting than her panic was the inexplicable flush that seemed to have seized the rest of her body. Her mouth was dry, her skin tingled with awareness, and there was a tender ache in her breasts and between her legs that was more pleasurable than painful.

She glanced around the room, struggling to shake off the dream's lingering daze. Portia's narrow bed was empty and the dormer room was shrouded in gloom, making it impossible to tell what time of day it was. Caroline's fitful sleep had been haunted by fragments of other dreams where she was pursued down shadowy paths by masked assailants, their mouths twisted into cruel and sensual leers.

She rubbed at her bleary eyes. What if the entire night had been nothing more than a dream—she and Portia's mad trek to Vauxhall Gardens; those delicious moments in the viscount's arms; the intoxicating taste of his kiss? What if they'd all been nothing more than a feverish fantasy, born of an excess of both conscience and imagination?

She was almost tempted to believe she was still dreaming because the midnight bells were still ringing.

She frowned, finally recognizing the harsh jangle of the front doorbell pull. Tossing back the blankets, she climbed down from the bed and hastened to the window. An elegant chaise drawn by a pair of handsome bay steeds was parked in the street. By craning her neck just so, she managed to catch a glimpse of a lone man standing on the stoop. Although the curled brim of his beaver hat hid his features, there was no mistaking the way the shoulder-cape of his coat hugged his imposing shoulders.

Adrian Kane had come calling. And in broad daylight no less.

Caroline sagged against the windowsill in relief, not realizing until that moment just how firmly Portia's fantasies had seized both her dreams and her imagination.

Shaking her head at her own folly, she cast a rueful glance heavenward. A steady rain was falling from clouds so low and leaden it looked as if the sun might never shine again.

Her eyes narrowed as she studied those ominous clouds. Was it daylight that was supposed to destroy vampires?

Or sunlight?

She rubbed her brow, suddenly wishing she had paid more heed to Portia's ramblings. The bell rang again. Aunt Marietta was no vampire, but she rarely rose before noon or received callers before two o'clock. Even so, Caroline could hear a frantic stirring, punctuated by barked orders, coming from the floor below, as if Aunt Marietta and Vivienne were both rushing about their spacious chambers, trying to make themselves presentable.

As she lowered her gaze to the stoop, Kane tipped back his head and looked straight up at the window where she was standing. Caroline ducked behind the curtains. There could be no denying the power of his gaze. Not even the dusty lace could shield her from its hypnotic pull.

The bell ceased its jangling. In the deafening silence that followed, a single stray tidbit of Portia's vampire lore rang out loud and clear in Caroline's mind.

A vampire could not enter his victim's home unless invited.

Caroline tried to shake away the ridiculous notion, but the dream was still too vivid in her memory. What if she was ignoring Portia's cry out of habit and there really was a wolf standing right out there on her aunt's stoop?

Since she couldn't very well rush downstairs in her night-dress, fling herself across the door, and pretend she'd come down with some dreadfully contagious disease like cholera or the bubonic plague, she stole another peek out the window.

The front door had swung open. But instead of her aunt's elderly footman, it was a beaming Portia who was ushering the viscount out of the rain and into the house.

Caroline's mouth fell open. *"Et tu, Brute?"* she whispered, shaking her head in disbelief.

Caroline went creeping down the stairs a short while later after donning a severe blue walking dress that did her slender form no favors. The starched ruff that served as a collar would have looked just as fitting on Queen Elizabeth two centuries ago. She'd ruthlessly smoothed every last wisp of her hair into a knot and plopped a matronly lace cap over the rigid structure. She was determined to vanquish all traces of the wanton creature who had clung to her sister's suitor with such shameless abandon.

She hesitated on the landing, her hand on the banister. The viscount's smoky baritone might melt away a woman's every inhibition, but its low pitch made it devilishly difficult to eavesdrop. She strained to hear, but all she could catch were tantalizing snatches of conversation. Portia's steady stream of chatter was punctuated by the amiable clinks of teacup on saucer, Vivienne's polite murmurs, and Aunt Marietta's shrill titters.

Suddenly, the parlor fell into a deferent silence. Even Portia ceased her babbling.

As the viscount began to speak, Caroline eased down another step. But all she could make out was, ". . . come here today . . . presume upon your affections . . . a very important question . . ."

Her hand tightened on the banister, her knuckles going white. Kane was going to propose. He was going to offer to make Vivienne his wife, and once he did, nothing would ever be the same again. She felt a curious pressure in the vicinity of her heart, as if some heretofore unrecognized vein had sprung a mortal leak.

Without giving herself time to examine the sensation, she went hastening down the last few steps. "Absolutely not!" she proclaimed as she swept into the parlor. "I forbid it!"

Eight

Everyone in the parlor turned to gawk at her as if she'd lost her wits. Although the damp was making Portia's ringlets curl merrily around her face, and a cloud of fresh face powder still enveloped Aunt Marietta, Vivienne looked as cool as a spring morning with her hair upswept in the viscount's preferred style. Her shapely form was garbed in a satin-sprigged gown of willow green crepe that would have perfectly complemented Caroline's gray eyes had she ever had the opportunity to wear it.

Resting his teacup on its saucer with deliberate care, Kane rose to face her. Towering over the cluttered chaos of her aunt's parlor, he appeared larger than life and twice as robust. If he *had* been a vampire, he could have probably drained them all dry of their lifeblood and still had room left over for tea and scones.

"I do hope you'll forgive my impudence, Miss Cabot," he said, amusement warring with wariness in his gaze. "I had no idea you would have such a passionate objection to my inviting your sister to visit my ancestral estate."

She blinked up at him. "Your estate?"

He blinked back at her. "Of course. Just what did you think I was proposing?" His innocent demeanor didn't fool her. He knew *exactly* what she had thought.

Her knees going weak with relief, she collapsed into a wing chair upholstered in a hideous floral brocade, nearly missing its edge. "I thought perhaps you were suggesting . . . an outing in this dreadful weather. Vivienne has always had a rather delicate constitution and I feared for her health."

Vivienne rolled her eyes. "You'll have to forgive my sister, Lord Trevelyan. You'd think she was a mother hen and Portia and I were her chicks."

Following Caroline's lead, Kane sat and reclaimed the teacup, his powerful hands dwarfing the fine bone china. "I can assure you, Miss Cabot, that I would never knowingly put your sister's health at risk." She might have imagined the mocking slant of his gaze. "As you may have heard, I'll be hosting a masquerade ball at Trevelyan Castle next week, and with all of the preparations to be made, I thought it would be best to retire to the country a few days early. I came here to invite your sister to join me." He nodded at Aunt Marietta, evoking a fresh simper. "With your aunt serving as chaperone, of course."

Naturally he would have a castle. A castle where Vivienne would someday be mistress. The pressure in Caroline's breast deepened to a dull ache.

"And just where is this castle, my lord?" she asked. "Romania?"

Portia choked on her tea, earning a hearty slap on the back from Aunt Marietta. Everyone knew that the eastern European country was rife with Gypsy stories of vampires, werewolves, and other dastardly creatures of the night. It even boasted its share of real monsters, including Vlad Dracula the Impaler, the infamous ruler whose reign of terror had become the stuff of both legend and nightmare.

Kane acknowledged her jibe with the flicker of a smile. "Somewhere far more pedestrian, I fear. Trevelyan Castle is located in Wiltshire, west of Salisbury."

Caroline wondered if his sudden desire to flee London had anything to do with what had transpired between them last night. Was he seeking to remove Vivienne from her influence? Or himself? Whatever his intentions, she could not afford to let him succeed. She needed more time to ensure that he was no threat to her sister.

She accepted a brimming teacup from the maid, amazed at the sudden steadiness of her hand. "It's very dear of you to include Aunt Marietta in your invitation, my lord, but it won't be necessary to inconvenience her any more than we already have. I'm quite capable of acting as my sister's chaperone."

It was Aunt Marietta's turn to choke on her tea. With a spark of glee in her eye, Portia whacked her between the shoulder blades with more force than was strictly necessary.

While she was still sputtering, the viscount's eyes narrowed ever so faintly. "Forgive me, Miss Cabot. I was under the impression that you and Portia would be returning to Edgeleaf in a few days."

Caroline took a genteel sip of her tea. "There's really no rush, is there? Cousin Cecil will hardly miss us, and I've heard that the air in Wiltshire can be quite invigorating at this time of year."

"I can't imagine what put such an outlandish notion in your head, child," Aunt Marietta snapped, dabbing droplets of tea off her bodice with her handkerchief. "Talk about the blind leading the blind!"

"I fear your aunt is right. I shouldn't have to remind you that you, too, are a young, unmarried woman." The teasing note in Kane's voice somehow mocked them both. "It would hardly do for you to throw yourself upon the suspect mercies of a jaded bachelor such as myself."

Waving away his objections, Caroline laughed. "I can assure you that you've nothing to fear on that account. I'm far past the age where I believe every man I meet is intent upon seducing or ravishing me."

"Caro!" Vivienne exclaimed, blushing to the roots of her fair hair.

"Yes, I was wondering how you were going to gum those biscuits now that you've entered your dotage," Kane said dryly as Caroline helped herself to a sugary treat from the tea tray.

She took a dainty nip of the cookie. "I refuse to wear the title of 'ape leader' without claiming any of its advantages. As a woman who will most likely never come under the protection of a husband, I should be able to move about society as I choose, just as Aunt Marietta does." She cast him a look from beneath her lashes, unable to resist a mocking flutter. "I'm also confident that I can rely upon your good character. According to Vivienne's letter, you're a veritable saint among men—a self-appointed champion of the downtrodden and lost kittens in every alley."

"And of foolish young women who insist upon wandering where they're not welcome."

As he met her challenging gaze with one of his own, the two of them might have been right back in that moonlit garden at Vauxhall, just a kiss away from falling into each other's arms. Although Kane's gracious smile never wavered, the frosty glint in his eye warned her that he wasn't accustomed to having his will thwarted. Nor did he care for it.

Aunt Marietta's protests were drowned out by the sound of Portia clapping her hands. "Oh, a masquerade ball! What a thrilling development! I can hardly wait to pack! Tell me, my lord, will your brother be joining us right away?"

"Once Julian learns that I'm to be accompanied by a bevy of lovely young Cabots, I'm sure I won't be able to beat him off with my walking stick." Taking up that implement, Kane stood. "Now if you'll excuse me, ladies, I do believe I've imposed upon your hospitality long enough. I must go and make arrangements for our journey."

While Aunt Marietta beckoned for the maid to fetch his damp coat and hat, Vivienne rose. "I'm so glad you called on us, my lord. It's been an unexpected pleasure."

"The pleasure was all mine," he murmured, bringing the back of Vivienne's hand to his lips.

The same lips that had so tenderly caressed hers. The

same lips that had stroked and glided and cajoled until she had opened to the possessive heat of his tongue. The same lips that had claimed her as if she had always belonged to him and always would.

"An unexpected pleasure indeed," Caroline said stiffly, her tone implying the opposite. "I was under the impression that you rarely venture out during daylight hours."

As Kane lowered Vivienne's hand and turned to her, even Caroline had to admire his aplomb. "I rarely do unless there's a very strong enticement, such as indulging in the company of four charming young ladies." The sweep of his hand included Aunt Marietta. She tittered like a schoolgirl, making Caroline cringe.

He was accepting his hat and coat from the maid when Caroline innocently said, "I hope that coat isn't too warm for you, my lord. While I was dressing, I would have sworn I saw the sun peeping out from behind a cloud."

For a long moment Kane stood stock-still, nothing moving but a muscle in his cheek. Then, without waiting for the maid, he strode to the door and threw it wide open. The rain was still falling in a silvery torrent from the bruised canopy of the sky.

He turned, his imposing figure silhouetted against the curtain of rain, and offered Caroline a tender smile. "I appreciate your concern, Miss Cabot, but it appears the rain is here to stay."

Adrian came storming into the town house, banging the door shut behind him. There was no footman to welcome him, no maid to rush forward and whisk away his dripping hat and coat. The servants weren't accustomed to anyone stirring during daylight hours. Most of them had probably taken to their own beds or slipped out for an afternoon in Town. Every drape and shutter in the house had been drawn tight in accordance with their master's instructions. Even the lowliest footman and scullery maid knew that a single infraction of that particular rule would lead to immediate dismissal.

For one treacherous moment Adrian allowed himself to wonder what it might be like to have a wife waiting for him. Some lovely creature who would come bustling out of the shadows to help him out of his dripping things and offer him a hot cup of tea and a tender kiss, all the while scolding him for venturing out on such a wretched day. But when that creature materialized as a slender, gray-eyed girl with a sleek waterfall of pale blond hair tumbling down her back, he ruthlessly vanquished her back to his imagination.

Accustomed to navigating the gloom, he shrugged off his wet coat and tossed it and his hat on the hall tree. He was running a hand through his damp hair when Julian came stumbling down the stairs, his dusky curls standing on end just as they had when the two of them were boys and Adrian would awaken to find a terrified Julian standing at the foot of his bed. Although he would grumble and scold, Adrian would always end up crawling out of his own warm bed so he could slay the imaginary monster lurking beneath Julian's.

"Good Lord, man!" Julian exclaimed, jerking a knot in the sash of his black velvet dressing gown. "Why all the ruckus? You're loud enough to wake the dead."

Adrian shot him a dark look before striding over to the marble-topped sideboard and pouring himself a healthy splash of brandy. He frowned at the nearly empty bottle as he replaced it on the blotter. He would have sworn the butler had refilled it only yesterday.

His brother sank down on one of the lower steps, yawning and rubbing his eyes. They widened as he noticed the rain puddling around the foot of the hall tree. He gave the window a disbelieving look. An unmistakable ribbon of daylight was peeping through the crack in the heavy drapes. "Have you been *out*?"

Adrian turned to lean against the sideboard. He rubbed

the back of his neck, trying not to think about how many hours it had been since he slept. "I have."

"And what would possess you to leave the house at this ungodly hour? Did you have a bad night? Was your hunt unsuccessful?"

"Oh, on the contrary, my hunt was quite successful." Adrian tossed back a swallow of the brandy, remembering the lush feel of Caroline in his arms. "I just caught something I hadn't expected."

Julian surveyed him wryly. "Knowing your devotion to duty, I'm sure it wasn't the French pox. Although popping into one of those brothels in the alleys you frequent for a few hours just might improve your temper."

For some reason the thought of a fleeting release at the hands of some overblown doxy held little charm for Adrian. Not with the irresistible sweetness of Caroline's mouth still so fresh in his memory.

He polished off the remainder of the brandy in a single swallow, but not even its heat could completely sear the taste of her from his lips. "The only thing that would improve my temper at the moment is the rapid return of one Miss Caroline Cabot to her home in Surrey."

"I gather from your dour countenance that Miss Cabot's departure for more pastoral climes is not imminent."

"On the contrary. It seems that she and her lovely sisters are going to be accompanying us to Wiltshire later this week."

Julian sat up straight, blinking his dark-lashed eyes. "This week? Are you sure it's not too soon? I thought we weren't going until next week. What about Duvalier? How can you be sure he'll follow us?"

"Oh, I'd say that we've managed to successfully pique his interest." Adrian met his brother's eyes squarely, refusing to shy away from the blow he was about to deliver. "He was there tonight. At Vauxhall."

Julian went so still his lips barely moved when he whispered, "Did you see him?"

Remembering the near panic he had felt stalking Duvalier through the night as Duvalier stalked an oblivious Caroline, Adrian shook his head. "I didn't have to. I could feel him. I could sense him. But the minute I got too close to the bastard, he melted back into the shadows."

Adrian hadn't realized until later that Duvalier's disappearance had been a blessing. If Duvalier had witnessed him kissing Caroline with such undeniable passion, it might have spoiled all of their plans.

"I'm afraid we haven't much choice but to leave London as soon as possible," Adrian said grimly. "Duvalier wasn't the only one at Vauxhall tonight. Larkin is growing more persistent. If I don't throw him off our scent, we're both going to end up in Newgate *before* the ball. And I don't have to tell you what a disaster *that* would be." He ran a weary hand over his jaw. "I have business to tend to in Wiltshire as well. I received word from Wilbury this morning. Someone—or something—has been terrorizing the villagers and slaughtering livestock in Nettlesham," he said, referring to a small village near their home.

"It wasn't me," Julian quipped. "I never have developed a taste for mutton." He averted his eyes, but not before Adrian could glimpse the shadow of doubt in them. "I know how difficult this must be for you. But you won't give up on me, will you?" he asked, keeping his voice light to hide the cost of the question.

Adrian crossed to the stairs. Although his first inclination was to rumple his brother's dark curls, he rested a hand on Julian's shoulder, squeezing gently until Julian was forced to meet his gaze. "I'll never give up, Jules. Not on you. And God help anyone who tries to stand in my way."

Julian lifted one eyebrow. "Including Miss Caroline Cabot?"

Ignoring a keen stab of regret, Adrian replied, "*Especially* Miss Caroline Cabot."

Nine

Rain lashed against the plate glass windows of the coach, obscuring everything but Caroline's pensive reflection. She strained her eyes, trying to catch a glimpse of the passing countryside of Wiltshire, but it was no use. What the rain didn't veil, the night did.

Lightning flashed, flooding the landscape with preternatural daylight and dazzling her unprepared eyes. For one startled blink she would have almost sworn she glimpsed a hulking shape galloping along beside the coach. Then the darkness descended once again, leaving her with only her startled reflection.

Unsettled, she drew the mahogany shutters over the window and settled back against the Morocco sleeping cushions. The viscount's handsome coach didn't smell of cheap perfume and stale cigars, but of leather and bay rum and some indefinable masculine presence. The gleaming brass trim and the frosted globes of the coach lamps perfectly complemented the restrained elegance of its interior.

Portia was curled up in the seat opposite her, with her head sprawled on Vivienne's shoulder, lulled to sleep by the cozy drumming of the rain on the coach's roof and the gentle swaying of the well-sprung vehicle.

At least she and her sisters were warm and dry. Caroline could only imagine how miserable the coachman and outriders must be. The rain had been falling steadily since the viscount's carriage had arrived at Aunt Marietta's doorstep to collect them early that afternoon. To Vivienne's disappointment and Caroline's keen relief, Kane had departed for Wiltshire a day earlier to prepare the servants for their arrival.

They'd stopped to change horses twice and had to wade through the ankle-deep muck of a coaching inn courtyard just to warm themselves before a smoky fire with a cup of tea. At this rate of travel, they probably wouldn't reach Trevelyan Castle before midnight.

Perhaps their host had planned it that way.

Caroline shook off the ridiculous notion. Adrian Kane might exude authority from his every pore, but surely his influence didn't extend to control of the weather.

She glanced over at Vivienne, who was patiently stitching a needlework sampler by the dim light of the coach lamps. This might be her only opportunity to find out just how strong a claim Kane had on her sister's heart. Portia's mouth had fallen open and her even breathing had deepened to snores.

"You must be looking forward to our visit and the viscount's ball," Caroline tentatively began.

"Oh, very much." Vivienne drew the needle through the fabric without even bothering to look up.

Caroline puffed out a sigh. Coaxing information from Vivienne could be as maddening as getting Portia to stop blurting out every thought that popped into her head. "Lord Trevelyan seems to be quite taken with you."

A demure smile curved her sister's lips. "Then I should consider myself fortunate, should I not? He's everything a girl should want in a suitor—courteous, intelligent, well-spoken, kind."

A marvelous kisser.

Caroline bit her lip, feeling a sharp pang of guilt as she remembered the persuasive heat of Kane's mouth on hers.

She stole another glance at Portia to make sure her little sister wasn't peeking through her eyelashes. "So tell me,

Vivienne—I can't help but be curious—in all the time you've spent together, has the viscount ever tried to take any . . . um . . . untoward liberties?"

Vivienne finally lifted her gaze from the sampler. A flush seeped into her cheeks, a startling contrast to the white rose tucked behind her ear. She leaned forward, earning a tiny snort of protest from Portia as her sister's head lolled back on the cushions.

Oh, no, here it comes, Caroline thought. She was about to learn that Kane spent all of his free time kissing inexperienced young women insensible.

"Once," Vivienne confided in a near whisper, her blue eyes enormous, "when we were disembarking from his carriage, I stumbled and Lord Trevelyan rested his hand on the small of my back to steady me. Given the circumstances, I felt I had no choice but to forgive him for the indiscretion."

Flooded with an emotion that felt dangerously like relief, Caroline snapped her gaping mouth shut. "That was very magnanimous of you." She chose her next words with even more care. "Has he ever spoken to you of any previous romantic entanglements?"

Vivienne looked taken aback. "I should say not! He's far too much of a gentleman."

Caroline was wracking her brain for a less inflammatory question when she noticed a glint of gold. She leaned forward and tugged at the chain encircling her sister's throat. A delicate cameo of a woman's profile framed in a lacework of gold emerged from Vivienne's bodice. Caroline studied it, puzzled. When he had evicted them from the main house, Cousin Cecil had laid claim to all of their genuine jewels—even the pearl earrings Caroline's papa had given her on her sixteenth birthday. Since then the girls had worn nothing but paste.

"This is a lovely piece," Caroline said, turning it toward one of the carriage lamps. "I've never seen you wear it before. Was it in the trunk from home?"

Vivienne lowered her eyes, looking as guilty as Caroline

had felt when she remembered the viscount's kiss. "If you must know, it was a gift from Lord Trevelyan. I was afraid to tell Aunt Marietta for fear she would make me return it." She lifted her beseeching eyes to Caroline's face. "Please don't scold! I know it's improper to accept such a personal trinket from a gentleman, but he seemed so pleased when I agreed to wear it. He's a very generous man."

"Indeed he is," Caroline murmured. She frowned at the cameo, her gaze drawn to the ivory gleam of the woman's long, elegant throat.

A sharp crack of thunder sounded, jolting Portia awake. The cameo slipped from Caroline's fingers. Vivienne quickly dropped it down the bodice of her gown, where it would be safe from other prying eyes.

"Whazzit?" Portia muttered. Rubbing her eyes, she peered around hopefully. "Was that gunfire? Have we been set upon by highwaymen? Are we going to be abducted and ravished?"

"I'm afraid not, pet," Caroline replied. "We'll have to save that adventure for another time."

Portia yawned and stretched, nearly poking Vivienne in the eye. "I'm starving. Did you save any of those little iced tea cakes from the last inn?" As she bent down to fumble for the brocaded valise sitting at Caroline's feet, Caroline swept it out of her reach.

Portia straightened, giving her a wounded look. "There's no need to be so selfish, Caro. I wasn't going to eat them all."

"I do believe we're stopping," Vivienne said as the coach's rocking slowed. "Do you think we've arrived?"

Grateful for the diversion, Caroline rested the valise carefully on the seat beside her. "I should hope so. If we travel much farther, we'll drive right into the River Avon."

Vivienne's question was answered when a liveried footman swept open the coach door and said, "Welcome to sunny Wiltshire!"

No one could question the man's sense of irony. Rain still

spilled from the sky in wind-driven gusts, its uneven patter accompanied by sullen growls of thunder.

Suddenly reluctant to abandon the cozy haven of the coach, the sisters spent an inordinate amount of time gathering up gloves and adjusting the hoods of their cloaks. When there was nothing left to collect, Caroline descended from the coach, clutching the valise beneath her arm.

A second footman hastened forward to take it from her. "No, thank you! I can manage!" she shouted over the howling of the wind. At least she hoped it was the wind.

As Portia and Vivienne descended behind her, Trevelyan Castle loomed up out of the darkness. The towering fortress of weathered stone might be modest by the standards of Wiltshire's more famous castles, but it hadn't been allowed to fall into ruins like nearby Old Wardour Castle. Numerous renovations throughout the centuries had cunningly blended the medieval, the Renaissance, and the Gothic. The castle boasted all of the gargoyles and flying buttresses the viscount's town house had lacked. It also looked quite capable of sporting a fully equipped dungeon, complete with manacles and iron maiden.

As Caroline lifted her gaze to the ramparts to watch a stream of rain pour between a snarling gargoyle's jagged teeth, foreboding seized her. What if she'd made a terrible miscalculation in bringing her sisters here? One that couldn't be corrected by re-adding the numbers in a ledger?

Before she could order them back into the coach and demand that the driver make a mad dash for London, the castle's iron-banded oak door swung open and they were ushered inside.

They stood dripping on the flagstones in a massive entrance hall. A centuries-old chill seemed to permeate the air, making Caroline shiver. A mounted stag's head glared down at them from the far wall, a feral gleam in its glassy eyes.

Portia tucked her small hand into Caroline's before whispering, "I've always heard a house should reflect its master's personality."

"That's what I'm afraid of," Caroline whispered back, eyeing the ancient tapestries with their vivid scenes of bloodletting and mayhem.

Some depicted ancient battles in all of their violent splendor while others glorified the savagery of the hunt. In the tapestry nearest to Caroline, a snarling hound was leaping up to tear out the throat of a graceful doe.

Even Vivienne looked a little doubtful when she peered around and said, "I'm sure it will be quite lovely by daylight."

They all jumped as a butler with a slightly hunched back and a startling shock of white hair emerged from the shadows, gripping a candlestick in his gnarled hand. He was so old Caroline could hear his bones creak and pop as he shuffled toward them.

"Good evening, ladies," he intoned, his voice nearly as rusty as the ancient suit of armor lurking in the alcove to Caroline's right. "I gather you would be the sisters Cabot. We've been expecting you. I trust you had a pleasant journey?"

"Simply divine," Portia lied, bobbing a sprightly curtsy.

"My name is Wilbury and I'll be at your service during your stay at the castle. I'm sure you're more than eager to be out of your damp things. If you'll follow me, I'll show you to your chambers."

The butler turned to shuffle toward the broad stone staircase that led upward into darkness, but Caroline stood her ground. "Pardon me, sir, but where is Lord Trevelyan? I had hoped he would be here to greet us when we arrived."

Wilbury turned to give her a withering look from beneath his snowy white brows. Long stray hairs poked out from their bushy depths like a cat's whiskers. "The master is out."

Caroline stole a glance at the enormous arched window

over the door just as a jagged fork of lightning split the sky and a fresh gust of wind rattled its panes.

"Out?" she echoed dubiously. "In *this*?"

"The master has a very vigorous constitution," he intoned, looking insulted that she would dare suggest otherwise. Without another word, he started up the stairs.

Vivienne made a move to follow, but Caroline touched a hand to her sister's arm, staying her. "What about Master Julian? Is he also *out*?"

Wilbury turned again, heaving such an exaggerated sigh that Caroline almost expected to see a puff of dust emerge from the creaking bellows of his lungs. "Young Master Julian won't be arriving until tomorrow night." Portia's face fell. "Unless you'd care to stand here in the entrance hall and wait for his arrival, I suggest you accompany me."

Caroline's gaze followed the shuffling path of the butler to the first landing. She supposed he was right. Unless they wanted to stand there all night, shivering in their wet cloaks and awaiting the onset of lung fever, they had no choice but to follow him into the shadows.

Wilbury left Portia and Vivienne nestled in adjoining chambers on the second floor. By the time Caroline had followed the wavering light of his candle up three more long flights of winding stairs, her legs had begun to ache and her spirits to sink. The stairs finally ended in a narrow door. Apparently, Kane planned to punish her for imposing upon his hospitality by banishing her to some airless attic even more devoid of charm than Aunt Marietta's.

As the butler swept open the door, she braced herself for the worst.

Her jaw dropped. "There must be some sort of mistake," she protested. "Perhaps this room was intended for my sister Vivienne."

"My master doesn't make mistakes. Nor do I. His instructions were quite explicit." Wilbury deepened his voice to a creditable impersonation of Adrian Kane. " 'Miss Caroline Cabot is to be housed in the north tower.' You are Miss Caroline Cabot, are you not?" He squinted down his blue-veined nose at her. "You don't seem to have the shifty air of an imposter."

"Of course I'm not an imposter," she retorted, taken aback. It was impossible to tell if the twinkle in the butler's eye stemmed from mischief or malice. "I just wasn't expect-ing . . . *this*." Caroline waved a hand at the chamber before them.

While her sisters' accommodations had been both cozy and charming, they bore little resemblance to this opulent nest situated at the very peak of the castle.

A fire crackled on a hearth framed by a mantelpiece of dove marble, its cheery glow reflected in the leaded glass of the mullioned windows. Slender wax tapers in iron sconces ringed the circular room. The stone walls had been white-washed and painted with a border of entwining ivy. A tow-ering four-poster dominated one wall, its graceful canopy draped in hangings of sapphire silk.

As Wilbury took his leave, promising to send a footman with her trunk and a maid to assist with her evening toi-lette, Caroline ventured into the chamber, still clutching her faded valise. Beneath one of the windows a ceramic wash basin and a pitcher of steaming water sat on a half-moon table inlaid with satinwood. An overstuffed wing chair had been drawn up before the hearth, where a tray of meat and cheese rested. An emerald dressing gown of cut velvet had been draped across the bed, inviting her to peel off her chill, wet garments and slip into its seductive warmth.

No comfort for the weary traveler had been spared. Every aspect of the chamber had been designed to make its occu-pant feel both welcomed and cherished—a sensation Caro-line hadn't enjoyed since her parents died.

Her gaze wandered to the pair of French doors on the op-posite side of the room. After tucking the valise safely be-neath the bed, she pried one of the candles from its sconce and moved to unbolt the doors. Just as she'd suspected, they opened onto a rain-drenched stone balcony. Although the river was nowhere in sight, the gusting wind carried a hint of its metallic tang.

Her gaze searched the cloud-tossed sky. Was Kane out there somewhere, all alone and drenched to the skin? And if so, what desperate errand would drive a man to brave such a wild and perilous night?

The candle flame fluttered, threatened by both the wind and her sigh. She cupped her hand around it and drew the doors closed, securing herself in the cozy nest her host had provided for her.

Battered by the storm, Adrian drove his horse through the night. His oilskin cloak did nothing to stop the wind from hurtling chill gusts of rain into his face or the damp from sinking its fangs deep into his bones.

He had ridden all the way to Nettlesham only to discover that the mysterious creature that had been terrorizing the villagers and ripping the throats out of their livestock was nothing but a mangy cur—half wolf and half dog—that had been driven completely mad by cruelty and starvation. Adrian had been left with no choice but to dispatch the poor beast. In the moment before he'd planted a pistol ball in its brain, he'd gazed into its savage and lonely eyes and felt a startling flare of kinship.

As he topped a steep scarp blanketed in gorse, Trevelyan Castle came into view. He wished his heart could have quickened at the sight as it once had, but ever since he and Julian had taken to wandering the world one step behind Duvalier, the castle had become little more than a cold hunk of stone, devoid of warmth or welcome.

He had nearly reached the courtyard wall when he realized the castle wasn't as bereft of warmth as he'd supposed. Blinking the rain from his lashes, he gazed up at the north tower. The window facing him was aglow with candlelight. That fragile glimmer seemed to beckon him home, promising him respite from the wild and lonely night.

Tugging the horse to a halt, he slid to his feet beneath the dripping branches of a gnarled old oak. The mare tossed her head, nearly jerking the reins from his hand. Despite her exhaustion, she still snorted and pranced with a restlessness Adrian recognized only too well.

As long as he walked like a gentleman, bound by the rigid strictures of London society, he could contain it. But here in this ancient keep with the wind whipping through his hair and the scent of the river in his nostrils, it threatened to consume him.

He tensed as Caroline Cabot appeared in the window of the tower, her piquant face illuminated by the flame of a single candle. Her hair was loose and flowing over her shoulders. She had donned the dressing gown he had left for her. The velvet hugged her slender curves, betraying the softness she fought so hard to hide beneath her prickly exterior.

Adrian sighed. It seemed there was to be no escaping her. Not among the throngs at Vauxhall and not here, in the only retreat left to him. Not even in his dreams, which she had haunted ever since he tasted her kiss.

Make love to me, she had whispered only last night as he thrashed restlessly in his tangled sheets. Her voice was no longer frantic with desperation, but languid with desire. She had gazed up at him, her gray eyes misty with longing. Her hands had tenderly stroked his face while the silky petals of her lips parted to invite him inside.

Adrian swore, cursing himself and his traitorous imagination. His life would be so much simpler if it was Vivienne who haunted his dreams. Vivienne who stood at that window and gazed wistfully into the night as if she was searching for something. For someone.

For him.

Cupping one hand around the candle's flame, Caroline turned away from the window, taking the light with her.

Adrian had always prided himself on his control, but there were some appetites that were simply too powerful to be denied. Wrapping the horse's reins around his fist, he strode toward the castle, rejecting the sheltering arms of the darkness.

Caroline opened her eyes, slipping from sleep to wakefulness with barely a shift in breathing. For a few disoriented seconds she believed she was back in Aunt Marietta's attic with Portia snoring in the other bed. But it wasn't so much a noise that had awakened her as the absence of it. The rain had stopped, its cessation magnifying the silence to deafening proportions.

She sat up, feeling dwarfed by the extravagant four-poster. The chamber had been so warm and cozy when she crawled into the bed that she hadn't bothered to draw the bed curtains. But now the fire was waning on the hearth and a faint chill clung to the air.

She reached for the bed curtains, but her hand froze in midair. One of the French doors on the opposite side of the tower was cracked open, inviting in a creeping tendril of moonlight and mist.

She drew back her hand, her fingers beginning to tremble. Her nervous gaze searched the chamber. All of the candles had guttered out, leaving the tower draped in shadows.

The ghost of a sound jerked her attention back to the balcony. Was it just the wind? she wondered. Or a furtive footfall? But how could it be a footfall when she was at least five stories above the ground?

She licked her parched lips, surprised she could hear anything at all over the frantic thudding of her heart. She wanted nothing more than to jerk the blankets over her head and cower beneath them until morning.

But she'd lost the luxury of cowering on the night her parents had died. Portia and Vivienne might be able to hide beneath the covers when trouble loomed, but she was the one who always had to creep out of her warm bed on stormy nights to fasten a loose shutter or add another log to the fire.

Mustering her courage, she tossed back the blankets, slid her feet to the floor, and crept across the flagstones toward the spreading pool of moonlight. She was halfway to the door when a shadow flickered across the balcony. She recoiled, a gasp of fright lodged in her throat.

"Stop being such a silly goose," she scolded herself aloud through chattering teeth. "It was probably just a cloud passing across the moon." She took another reluctant step toward the door. "You simply forgot to bolt the door and the wind blew it open."

Trying not to imagine one of the gargoyles from the ramparts unfurling its stone wings and diving straight for her throat, she took a deep breath and crossed the rest of the floor in three determined strides. She flung both doors open wide and marched right out onto the balcony, all but daring some unseen monster to spring out at her from the darkness.

The balcony was deserted.

A veil of mist rose from the damp stone, its gossamer threads burnished to silver by the glow of the moon. Caroline crossed to the parapet that sheltered the balcony, using its rough stone to steady her shaking hands. Torn between relief and chagrin at her own foolishness, she peered over the wall, gauging the impossible distance to the ground. If anyone wanted to accost her here, they would surely require wings to fly.

"Good evening, Miss Cabot."

As that mocking voice came out of the shadows behind her, borne on a cloud of brimstone, Caroline whirled around and let out a terrified shriek.

Ten

Caroline stumbled backward. As the rough stone of the parapet bit into her back, the sky took a careening dive and threatened to swap places with the ground. Suddenly Kane's arms were there, encircling her, roughly at first, then gentling as he gathered her quaking body against his chest.

One of his big hands smoothed her hair, pressing her cheek to the warm, broad haven of his chest. "Sweet Christ, woman," he said hoarsely. "What are you trying to do? Frighten me to death?"

As the world slowly righted itself and her trembling subsided, Caroline wanted nothing more than to sink into his strength and his warmth. To believe that no harm could befall her as long as she was in his arms. To forget, even for one unsteady heartbeat, that such a foolish notion was the most seductive danger of all.

She shoved against his chest, extracting herself from his embrace with a desperation that surprised even her. "Frighten *you*? You're the one who came pouncing at me out of the shadows! If I'd have tumbled to my death and poor Wilbury would have had to spend his morning scraping me off the cobblestones of your courtyard, it would have been no more than you deserved for sneaking up on me in such a distressing manner." Her suspicions mounting, she began to back away from him. "Just how did you get up here anyway?"

He tracked her progress without moving a muscle, his eyes glittering with unmistakable amusement. "I walked."

Caroline stopped, scowling in bewilderment. She followed the sweeping path of his hand, realizing for the first time that the structure she'd mistaken for a private balcony in the poor light was actually a walkway that ringed the entire tower. There was probably a bridge or staircase on the opposite side leading to another tower or a lower floor.

Kane folded his arms over his chest before gently asking, "Just how did you *think* I got up here, Miss Cabot?"

Caroline swallowed. "Well, I..." She wasn't sure what she had thought. After all, it wasn't as if he could have turned himself into a bat and flown up to her balcony just so he could slip into her bedchamber, cover her helpless form with his shadow, and...

As she envisioned him looming over her in the darkness of her bed, another image popped into her head, one even more disturbing—and far more provocative. She blinked frantically, trying to will it away. "Um, I—I... well, I assumed that perhaps... um..."

He took pity on her stammering ineloquence. "I didn't mean to startle you. I thought you'd be long abed. I'm afraid I haven't yet grown accustomed to your country hours. I couldn't sleep, so I came outside for a stroll and a smoke."

For the first time, Caroline noticed the slender cheroot still smoldering on the stones. He must have dropped it when he moved to snatch her back from the brink of disaster. Now she understood why she had smelled that whiff of brimstone just before he appeared.

As she became aware of the cheroot, she became aware of other things as well. Such as the rather scandalous absence of Kane's coat, waistcoat, and cravat. His thin lawn shirt was tucked into a pair of doeskin riding breeches that hugged his lean hips and accentuated every muscle of his sculpted thighs. The shirt hung open at the throat, revealing a gilded slice of muscle and a generous scattering of crisp, honey-colored hairs. Although he had gathered his hair into a careless queue at the nape of his neck, a few rain-dampened strands still hung around his face.

His appearance only served to remind her of her own disgraceful state. She hadn't even bothered to slip on the dressing gown he'd so generously provided. She stood before him in her faded nightdress and bare feet, with her hair streaming down her back like a schoolgirl's. The worn bodice of her nightdress clung to the swell of her breasts.

She awkwardly folded her arms over them, thankful for the first time in her life that she wasn't as well-endowed as Portia. "I hope my scream didn't wake the entire household."

"The servants probably slept right through it," Kane assured her, his heavy-lidded gaze flicking not to her chest, but to the graceful curve of her throat. "After all, they should be accustomed to such noises around here—blood-curdling screams, pleas for mercy, the tortured cries of the innocent."

He was doing it again. Mocking them both with nothing more than the devilish arch of one tawny eyebrow.

Caroline countered with a cool smile. "That doesn't surprise me. I had assumed such a fine estate must possess a working dungeon."

"Most certainly. That's where I keep all of those missing village virgins. Perhaps we can arrange a tour before your visit is over."

"That would be lovely."

He leaned against the parapet. "I'm afraid I've been sadly remiss as a host. I do hope you'll forgive me for not being here to greet you and your sisters when you arrived."

"Wilbury informed us that you were *out*." Her gaze strayed to his chest, where his damp shirt clung to the impressive expanse of muscle and sinew. The sight made her feel curiously light-headed. She touched a hand to her brow. Perhaps she was still dizzy from her near tumble off the balcony. "It must have been an urgent errand indeed to require your attention on such a frightful night."

"On the contrary, I found the storm to be far less frightful than being cooped up in some overcrowded ballroom or smoky theater. I'd much rather battle the elements than the wagging tongues of the society gossips. But I am sorry I wasn't here to greet you."

Perfectly aware that he had neatly dodged her unspoken question, she gestured toward the French doors, which still stood agape, offering them both a moonlit view of her rumpled sheets. "I can hardly accuse you of being remiss in your hospitality when you've provided me with such extravagant accommodations."

He snorted, his jaw tightening. "More extravagant than the ones your aunt provided, no doubt. I'm surprised she didn't house you in the coal cellar."

Caroline frowned. "How did you . . . ?" But then she remembered him standing on her aunt's stoop in the rain, lifting his gaze to that dusty dormer window. She must have ducked behind the curtains a second too late.

Inexplicably embarrassed that he knew exactly how little regard her aunt had for her, she lifted her chin. "As your guest of honor, Vivienne should have been given her own room. Portia and I are quite accustomed to sharing."

"I thought you would approve of the arrangement. After all, I can hardly be accused of trying to sneak into your sister's bedchamber and compromise her virtue with Portia standing guard, can I?"

But who will guard my virtue?

Caroline didn't dare ask him that question. Not when she had insisted she was past the age where she believed every man she met was plotting to seduce or ravish her. Even one who appeared outside the open door of her bedchamber in the dead of night, half dressed and smelling of wind and rain and an intoxicating blend of tobacco and bay rum.

"I fear that Portia's more of a terrier than a mastiff," she said.

He gave a mock shudder. "Then I consider her an even more formidable foe. I'd much rather be savaged by a mastiff than have a yapping terrier nipping at my boots."

Caroline smiled in spite of herself at his apt description of her little sister. "I usually find whacking her on the nose with the *Morning Post* to be quite effective."

"I'll keep that in mind." He cocked his head to the side, giving her one of those penetrating looks she was coming to both covet and dread. "So tell me, Miss Cabot, what do you think of my humble home? Is it to your liking?"

She hesitated. "Your guest chambers are lovely, my lord, but I have to admit that I did find the entrance hall to be a bit . . . intimidating. There were a few too many animal carcasses and gory battle scenes for my taste."

"I suppose it lacks the warmth that only a woman's touch can provide," he replied, his husky voice caressing the words.

"Ah, but that's a lack that can be easily rectified, is it not?"

For just an instant, as their gazes met and held, Caroline got the startling impression that neither one of them was talking about Vivienne.

The sensation was so disconcerting that she began to back toward her bedchamber. She almost expected him to follow, matching her step for step as he had on that moonlit path at Vauxhall. "If you'll excuse me, my lord, I really should be getting back to bed. Dawn will be here before we know it."

"Yes, it will, won't it?" Instead of following her, Kane turned to brace his hands on the parapet, his gaze straying to the far horizon, where the occasional flash of lightning still split the roiling underbellies of the clouds. "Miss Cabot?"

She paused, her hand already reaching for the door handle behind her. "Yes?"

He spoke without turning to look at her, his gaze still riveted by the night. "From now on, you might want to bolt those doors. You can't always depend on an element as capricious as the wind to exercise its best judgment."

Caroline swallowed before saying softly, "As you wish, my lord."

Backing into the chamber, she gently drew the doors shut after her. She hesitated for the briefest moment, then reached down and shot the iron bolt into its mooring. When she lifted her eyes, Kane was gone. The balcony was empty.

She was alone.

"Oh, my stars! Who died and made you Queen of England?"

Caroline couldn't have said what was more horrifying. Waking up the next morning to Portia's exuberant squeal or having her bed curtains ripped open to invite in a blaze of sunshine. As the searing rays struck her face, she threw a hand over her eyes, feeling as if she might actually burst into flames.

Long after Adrian Kane had vanished from her balcony, she had tossed and turned in the tangled bedsheets, wondering if it had been the wind—or some element even more primal and dangerous—that had eased open her door. Wondering why her every encounter with Kane had to either begin or end with her in his arms. And wondering what sort of wicked creature could find being in his arms so alarmingly agreeable when she had no right to be there.

As Portia bounced up on the feather mattress like some sort of high-spirited puppy, Caroline groaned and tugged the damask-covered quilt over her head. "Go away! I refuse to believe it could already be morning."

"Morning?" Portia echoed. "Why, it's nearly noon! Just because you've been housed in the queen's tower, it doesn't mean you get to languish in bed all day like royalty. If you're expecting me to play lady-in-waiting and ring for a maid to fetch you your chocolate in bed, you've got another think coming, Your Highness!"

"Noon?" Caroline sat up and threw back the quilt, accidentally tossing it over Portia's head. "How on earth can it be noon already? I would have sworn it was barely dawn."

Doubly horrified by this fresh evidence of her moral decay, Caroline scrambled out of the bed. She only had one week before the ball to determine if Kane was friend or foe and she'd already squandered half a day.

Batting aside the quilt, Portia flopped back into the warm hollow Caroline had vacated with a rapturous sigh. "I suppose I can't blame you for being such a lazyboots. If I had such a splendid room, I'd never want to leave my bed."

As Caroline unlatched her trunk and tossed open the lid, she tried not to think of other, even more compelling, reasons not to leave a bed.

Portia rolled to her feet and began to meander around the room, examining its many treasures. "Now, I know why Vivienne insists that the viscount is so generous. So tell me—just what did you do to deserve such bounty?"

"Nothing!" Caroline blurted out, burying her head in the trunk to hide a traitorous blush. "Nothing at all!"

She pawed through several well-worn chemises and petticoats before finally locating a plain morning gown of cambric muslin with long sleeves and a high collar.

To spare her from ringing for the maid, Portia came over to lace her into her corset. Lifting her hair out of harm's way, Caroline asked, "So where is Vivienne this morning?"

Portia rolled her eyes. "Probably curled up in some corner, stitching a Bible verse onto a sampler. You know it doesn't take much to amuse her."

"We should all be so blessed." Still determined to salvage the last few minutes of the morning, Caroline hurried to the wash basin to splash water on her face and scrub her teeth with a cloth and some mint-flavored powder.

"I don't know why you're in such a rush," Portia said.

"According to that dour butler, Julian won't be arriving until tonight. And you know Lord Trevelyan won't be able to make an appearance until well after sunset."

"Don't you think it's time to stop nursing that ridiculous fancy of yours?" Sinking down on the upholstered bench of the baize-covered vanity, Caroline lifted its hinged lid and began to search for the paper of hair pins the maid had unpacked the night before. Gathering the sleek fall of her hair at her nape, she said, "I don't believe Lord Trevelyan is a vampire any more than I believed you when you decided you were Prinny's illegitimate daughter and rightful heir to the throne of . . ." She trailed off, gazing fixedly into the interior of the vanity.

"What is it?" Portia asked, drifting closer. "You really don't look all that frightful. If you like, I can fetch my rabbit's foot and dab a little rice powder on those circles beneath your eyes."

When Caroline failed to reply, Portia peered around her shoulder. It took her a minute to recognize what Caroline was seeing. Or rather, *not* seeing.

The sisters slowly turned to look at each other, the truth reflected in each other's eyes. Although the burled oak of the vanity bore a distinct oval impression, there was no mirror.

There were no mirrors draped in crepe at Trevelyan Castle. There were no mirrors at all. No delicate ovals clutched in the chubby little fingers of gilded cherubs. No tall pier glasses situated between two windows. No handsome plates of mirror-glass hung above the mantel so that a guest might pretend to gaze into the fire while secretly admiring their reflection. No elegant cheval glasses standing at attention in the bedchamber corners, inviting a lady to pose and preen while she tilted the glass to show both her figure and her coiffure to their best advantage.

Caroline and Portia spent most of the afternoon ducking footmen and maidservants so they could slip in and out of the castle's deserted chambers. Their search failed to yield so much as a tarnished hand mirror tucked away in an armoire drawer.

"Perhaps you'll be more inclined to believe me the next time I tell you I'm the rightful heir to the throne of England," Portia said with a smug sniff as they hastened toward the south wing.

"I'm sure there's a perfectly reasonable explanation," Caroline insisted. "Perhaps the mirrors have been taken away so they can be polished before the ball. Or perhaps the Kane family simply isn't given to vanity."

Portia sighed wistfully. "If I was as beautiful as Julian, I'd sit in front of the mirror and admire myself all day long."

"You practically do that now," Caroline reminded her.

They both started guiltily when Vivienne's dulcet tones sounded behind them. "Where on earth have you two been all afternoon?"

They turned to find their sister standing beneath the vaulted beams at the far end of the broad flagstone corridor.

"I've finished two samplers, hemmed a dozen handkerchiefs, and taken tea all by myself," she informed them plaintively. "Mr. Wilbury isn't exactly the most scintillating conversationalist. I'm growing quite weary of my own company."

"We didn't mean to abandon you," Caroline called out. "We've just been doing a bit of exploring." Stealing a glance over her shoulder at the massive mahogany door that stood guard over the south wing, she gave Portia a gentle shove in Vivienne's direction. "Why don't you run along and keep Vivienne company, dear? I'll join the two of you shortly."

Portia reluctantly obeyed, shooting Caroline a wide-eyed look over her shoulder. "Do take care, won't you, *dear*? One never knows what sort of *creature* will pop up in these musty old rooms."

Caroline waved away Portia's warning. Not only had they failed to locate any mirrors. They had also failed to locate any trace of their host. Despite Portia's fears, Caroline refused to believe that he was napping in a coffin in the family crypt.

As she watched her sisters stroll away, arm in arm, she frowned. It wasn't like Vivienne to be so querulous. And hadn't her complexion looked a shade fairer than usual? Caroline shook away the notion. Perhaps it was just the lengthening shadows bleeding the color from her sister's cheeks. Through the leaded glass panes of the lancet window at the end of the corridor, she could see the lavender haze of twilight creeping toward the castle.

Her sense of urgency inexplicably growing, she turned back to the door and gingerly twisted the knob. The door swung open with an unnerving creak and Caroline found herself gazing down a windowless corridor draped in shadow. She fumbled in the pocket of her skirt, thankful that she had possessed the foresight to tuck a candle stub and tinder box in her pocket.

The candle wick hissed to life beneath her ministrations, casting a flickering glow around her. Slipping into the corridor, she held the candle aloft, only to find herself standing face-to-face with Adrian Kane.

She let out a sharp yelp and stumbled backward, so startled she nearly dropped the candle. It took her several thundering heartbeats to realize that it wasn't the viscount himself who stood before her, but a full-length portrait mounted in a gilded frame. Fighting to steady her breathing, she swept the candle in a shaky half circle. This was no ordinary corridor, but a portrait gallery, each of its residents frozen in time by a spell cast by an artist's brush.

She crept toward Kane's portrait, knowing she might never have such an unguarded opportunity to study him in the flesh. He stood silhouetted against a backdrop of stormy sky, one hand resting on his hip, the other curled around the silver head of a walking stick. A pair of bored spaniels reclined on the grass at his booted feet.

Caroline studied his face, dismayed to discover how very familiar it had become to her in so short a time. She knew exactly how the faint crinkles around his eyes would deepen when he laughed. How the furrow would appear between the tawny arches of his brows whenever she perplexed or challenged him. How his expressive mouth could tighten into a forbidding line, then soften whenever he fixed those luminous eyes on her.

She touched a fingertip to the plump swell of her own lips, remembering how that mouth had curved so tenderly over her own. Warned by the wistful pang in her heart, she tore her gaze away from his face. Only then did she realize that his clothing was all wrong.

Puzzled, she held the candle closer to the canvas. The man in the portrait wore a midnight blue satin coat with a flared skirt trimmed in gold braid. Elaborate falls of lace framed his muscular throat and powerful hands. He wore knee-breeches and gartered hose that tapered into a pair of black, buckled shoes—a style that had lost favor over a generation ago.

Perhaps he'd been painted by one of those eccentric artists who chose to costume his subjects in the garments of another era. Only a decade ago, everything Grecian had been the rage, resulting in an alarming number of family portraits depicting plump, toga-clad matrons fleeing bewigged centaurs who looked suspiciously like their gout-ridden husbands.

Stealing one last longing look at the canvas, Caroline drifted to the next portrait. Her mouth fell open in surprise. It was Kane again, this time garbed in a feathered hat and an Elizabethan ruff with a pleated cape swinging from his broad shoulders. His hair fell just past those shoulders, and a curling mustache and pointed goatee made him look even more devilish than usual. She might have doubted her eyes were it not for the wry twist of his mouth and the bold tilt of his head.

To her shock, the next frame also contained a likeness of Kane. In this one, he wore a mocking smirk, a short, fur-trimmed doublet and a clinging pair of dark green hose.

Caroline averted her eyes, trying not to notice how remarkably well he filled out the hose.

"Must be wearing a padded codpiece," she muttered.

Shaking her head in bemusement, she lifted the candle to the next portrait. The breath whooshed out of her lungs. A warrior towered over her in full armor, a gleaming broadsword gripped in one fist. There was no mistaking the rusty stains on his blade—all that was left of the last person who had been fool enough to stand between this man and what he wanted.

He swaggered without moving a muscle, his heavy-lidded gaze daring the world to accept his challenge. This was a Kane stripped of the veneer of civility forced on him by society. This was the man Caroline had glimpsed at Vauxhall Gardens. The man who had dispatched her attackers without so much as breaking a sweat. His raw masculinity was both terrifying and irresistible.

A fierce hunger glittered in his eyes—an appetite for life that refused to be denied. She recognized that hunger because she had felt it when he crushed her against him on the Lover's Walk, tasted it when his kiss had deepened and his tongue boldly claimed her mouth, demanding a surrender she had been only too willing to give. She reached up to brush her fingertips over his cheek, wondering if it was possible to tame such a wild creature with only a touch.

Despite the muted colors and crackled paint, he looked as if he was perfectly capable of stepping right out of that tarnished frame and sweeping her into his arms.

Which was why Caroline barely jumped when his voice came out of the darkness behind her. "A remarkable resemblance, is it not?"

Eleven

Caroline snatched her hand back from the painting as if it had scorched her fingertips, then slowly pivoted to find Kane leaning against the wall behind her, his arms folded over his chest. She could hardly accuse him of sneaking up on her this time. She had been so engrossed in his portrait, she doubted she would have heard an entire regiment of bleating bagpipers march into the gallery.

He was once again garbed in the guise of a proper gentleman. Although he wore no coat, his waistcoat of burgundy-and-gold-striped silk was fully buttoned. Its deep V revealed nothing more than the frilled front of his shirt. His starched wing collar and neatly tied cravat ensured that she wouldn't catch so much as a glimpse of the crisp hair that furred his chest. Ignoring a pang of disappointment, she wondered just how long he had been standing there, watching her. Wondered if he had seen her touch that fierce warrior in the portrait as she would never have the right to touch him.

"A remarkable *likeness*, don't you mean, my lord?" she replied, nodding toward the glowering knight. "I was just admiring the extraordinary brushstrokes. I can't imagine where you found such a skilled artist. The man rivals Reynolds or Gainsborough."

Kane straightened, his effortless grace reminding her that

no artist, no matter how skilled, could completely capture his raw vitality in the flesh. "I'm afraid that artist is long dead. As is his subject. This portrait is all that remains of either of them."

As he drew nearer to her, Caroline sought to escape his penetrating gaze by turning back to the portrait. "I don't understand. Isn't he you?" She gestured to the wall. "I thought they were *all* you."

"You thought that I'd commissioned multiple portraits of myself, garbed in various costumes from ages long past?" His smoky chuckle stirred the tiny hairs at her nape. "I can assure you, Miss Cabot, that while I'm a man of many vices, vanity is not among them."

She shrugged, wondering just what those other vices might include. "Some might call it vanity. Others simply a yearning for immortality."

Even though he was behind her, she could feel his sudden stillness to the depths of his soul. "Not every man is willing to pay the price for immortality. It can be a very costly boon indeed."

Reaching around to gently pluck the candle from her hand, he swept it toward the tarnished brass plate fastened at the bottom of the frame. Accepting his unspoken invitation, Caroline leaned closer, squinting to read the numbers carved there.

"Thirteen ninety-five," she whispered, slowly straightening to turn her disbelieving gaze on Kane.

He swept a hand toward the portrait. "Allow me to introduce you to Sir Robert Kane, Miss Cabot. He built this castle in thirteen ninety-three after lopping off a lot of French heads in the Hundred Years War. He conveniently neglected to apply for a crenellating license from King Richard II, but was granted a pardon soon afterward. I'm afraid we Kanes have always excelled at asking for forgiveness rather than a polite by-your-leave. That's why most of the men you see on this wall were considered both reprobates and scoundrels." *Just like myself*. Although the words were not spoken, they might as well have been.

Caroline stole another look at the warrior's steely eyes. "I would have sworn he was you. The similarities are extraordinary."

Surveying the rugged row of Kanes, her host sighed. "There is a rather inescapable family resemblance, isn't there? I suppose my sons will be cursed with it, too, the poor devils."

His sons. The sons he would give Vivienne. Tall, strapping boys with blue-green eyes and honey-colored hair who would call her Aunt Caro, put crickets in her bed, and secretly pity her for having no babes of her own. Although Caroline didn't even blink, she felt as if the warrior in the portrait had just rammed the point of his sword through her heart.

"How did Julian escape this terrible fate?" she asked, keeping her voice deliberately light.

"He had the good sense to take after our mother." Kane turned, the sweep of the candle revealing the portraits on the opposite wall for the first time. Caroline followed its glow to an oval portrait of a petite woman with hair the color of mink and laughing dark eyes.

Her merriment was so infectious Caroline could not help smiling, too. "She's quite lovely. Is she still living?"

Kane nodded. "She's been abroad since my father's heart gave out nearly six years ago. She suffered from a severe fever as a girl, and the climate of Italy is much kinder to her scarred lungs than the air in this damp and drafty old place. I was just finishing up at Oxford when she sent Julian to live with me."

"Ah, so you know what it's like to become a parent before your time?"

"Indeed. Although I'd say you were much more of a success at it than I was. When he first came to Oxford, Julian desperately wanted to tag along wherever I went, but I thought he was too young so I patted him on the head and tried to send him on his way. To spite me, I'm afraid he fell in with a rather unsavory pack of young bloods."

"He seems to have turned out all right," Caroline offered.

"As well as can be expected, I suppose."

Surprised by the unmistakable note of bitterness in his tone, she cast him a startled glance. A shutter had fallen over his face, closing the window to the past.

Noting a curious omission among the portraits, she asked, "Why are there no portraits of you and your brother?"

He shrugged. "My mother always claimed she couldn't get us to sit still long enough."

Caroline returned to the very first portrait. The man with the walking stick and the spaniels could only be Kane's father. The bold grace of his stance and the wicked sparkle in his eyes made it far too easy to understand why Kane's mother had fallen in love with him. She envied her the joy of loving such a man. But not the anguish of losing him.

Unable to resist the commanding pull of his gaze, she drifted back to the portrait of the medieval warrior. She stole a furtive glance at Kane, then leaned closer to the portrait, an impossible suspicion beginning to niggle at the back of her mind. "The resemblance is absolutely uncanny. One would almost swear it was you. Why, you even have the exact same mole right there above your left—" The candle went out, casting them into inky blackness.

"My lord?" Caroline whispered uncertainly.

Kane muttered a husky oath. "You'll have to forgive my clumsiness. I seem to have dropped the candle."

The door at the end of the corridor failed to beckon in so much as a sliver of light, warning Caroline that outside the castle, full night had fallen. The velvety cloak of darkness brought her other senses to aching awareness. She could hear the uneven rasp of Kane's breathing, smell the bay rum cologne perfuming the freshly shaven curve of his jaw, feel the heat radiating from his flesh.

Although she was so disoriented she doubted she could have located her own nose, his hand unerringly found hers in the darkness. He laced his big warm fingers through hers, gently tugging her toward him. Her first instinct was to resist, but some more primitive impulse compelled her to obey, to go willingly into his arms or anywhere else he cared to lead her.

"Follow me," he murmured. "I'll look after you."

At that moment, she feared she would have followed him into hell itself. But her feet betrayed her and she stumbled. His arms went around her to steady her, the whisper of his breath against her cheek warning her just how dangerously close his lips were to hers.

Her tongue darted out to wet those lips. They felt alien to her somehow—swollen, tender, aching for a kiss that must never come.

Light blazed. She caught just a glimpse of Kane's eyes, smoky with an emotion that might have been desire, before she realized they had an audience.

They turned as one to find Julian leaning against the door frame, an artfully tousled forelock tumbling over his brow and a branch of candles in one hand. "If you're going to show Miss Cabot the skeletons in our family closet, dear brother," he drawled, "you really should remember to bring a candle."

Adrian knew he ought to be blessing Julian for his timely intervention, but instead he wanted to strangle him. It was hardly the first time he'd wanted to choke the life from his little brother. Nor would it be the last, he suspected.

Caroline had stiffened in his arms. She was no longer soft and yielding, but prickly with suspicion, her lips set in a rigid line. It was hard to believe that only seconds before, those lips had been parted in invitation, glistening with nectar, begging without words for his kiss.

When she had come into his arms without hesitation, it had nearly been his undoing. Her trust, both unearned and undeserved, had unleashed a hunger deeper than mere want. *I'll look after you*, he had said. Uttering those careless words aloud had only made him realize just how impossible their promise would be to fulfill. He was still haunted by the ghost of the last woman who had been foolish enough to believe them.

Striding forward, he wrested the branch of candles from his brother's hand. "Your timing, as always, is impeccable. I'm afraid Miss Cabot was an innocent victim of my clumsiness. I dropped our only candle."

"How tragic for you both," Julian said, a smirk playing around his lips. "Had I not come along when I did, I shudder to think what might have happened."

"As do I," Constable Larkin said, emerging from the shadows behind Julian.

Adrian gaped at Larkin in disbelief, then turned his glare on his brother. "What in the devil is *he* doing here?"

Crossing his long legs at the ankle, Julian sighed. "If you must know, I invited him."

Keenly aware of Caroline still hovering behind him, Adrian struggled to keep his voice somewhere below a roar. "You *what*?"

"Don't be too hard on your brother." Larkin's smile was studiously pleasant. "I gave him a choice. I would come stay with him in Wiltshire. Or he could come stay with me . . . in Newgate."

"On what charges?" Adrian demanded.

Larkin shook his head sadly. "I'm afraid deep play and shallow pockets don't mix. Your brother has made quite the rounds of the gambling hells *and* the ladies since your return to London. He had every intention of leaving behind a fat sheath of unpaid gambling vowels, a bevy of broken hearts, and several irate gentlemen willing to charge him with losing his money, but winning the hearts of their fiancées."

Adrian rounded on Julian. "Haven't I warned you about that? You know you haven't a head for cards or women when you've been drinking." He shook his head, fighting the urge to tug at his hair—or Julian's—in frustration. "I gave you two hundred pounds only last week. What in the devil did you do with it?"

Ducking his head sheepishly, Julian devoted all of his attention to flicking the imaginary wrinkles from his French cuffs. "I paid my tailor bill."

Adrian knew he would want to strangle his brother again. He just hadn't realized it would be so soon. Or that he'd want to do it with Julian's outrageously expensive silk cravat. "Why didn't you come to me when you realized you were in over your head? I couldn't have mended the broken hearts but I would have given you the blunt you needed to buy back those vowels."

As Julian lifted his head, there was no mistaking the bitterness in his soulful dark eyes. "I already owe you more than I could ever repay."

Feeling Larkin's sharp gaze like a dagger pressed to his throat, Adrian raked a hand through his hair, swallowing both his retort and his pride.

Sensing a chink in his armor, Larkin pressed his advantage. "When I heard you'd invited the charming Cabot sisters to visit Trevelyan Castle and attend your masquerade ball, I didn't see any harm in joining your little house party. After all, I used to spend every holiday here when we were at Oxford. Weren't you the one who once implored me to think of this place as my second home?"

Before Adrian could stop them, the years melted away and Larkin was once again standing in the castle's entrance hall, all flyaway hair and gangly limbs, so shy he could barely stammer out his name to a glowering Wilbury.

Don't worry, mate, a laughing Victor had said, reaching around Adrian to give Larkin a gentle shove. *Wilbury only eats Cambridge boys.*

That wayward memory only served to remind him of how inseparable he, Larkin, and Duvalier had once been. Until Eloisa had come between them.

He was still trying to shake the memory's echo when Caroline slipped past him to take Larkin's arm. The wariness she had exhibited toward the man in London seemed to have miraculously vanished.

As she offered him a dimpled smile, even the unflappable Larkin looked dazzled. "I, for one, am delighted that you could join us, Constable. And I'm sure my sisters will be just as pleased as I am."

"I'm rather starved for some civilized company myself, Miss Cabot," he told her. "Young Julian here was a bit of a bore during the journey. He insisted on sleeping the afternoon away and went into a fit of the sulks every time I tried to open the carriage shutters."

"Perhaps while you're here, you could tell me all about your days at the university with Lord Trevelyan." Drawing the constable away down the corridor, she cast an unreadable glance over her shoulder at Adrian. "So tell me—has the viscount changed much in the past few years? Or has he always been so . . . imposing?"

Larkin's voice drifted back to them. "Actually, he must take excellent care of himself. I would almost swear he hasn't aged a day since our years at Oxford."

"A well-matched pair, aren't they?" Julian observed, watching Adrian watch the two of them stroll away down the corridor, arm in arm. "I've often thought a pretty young wife would be just the thing to occupy that inquisitive brain of his."

Adrian turned his glare on his brother. "Don't you have some boots to polish or a cravat to starch?"

Julian might be foolish, but he wasn't stupid. Plucking the branch of candles from Adrian's hand, he sauntered away down the corridor, whistling a tuneless song and leaving his brother in darkness.

The cellar of Trevelyan Castle might very well host a medieval dungeon, but its great hall had been converted into a cozy drawing room. Turkish rugs in warm shades of crimson and gold had been scattered across the salon, blunting the chill of its flagstone floor. Despite the high vaulted ceiling, open beams, and the wooden balcony that ringed the hall, several groupings of sofas, chaises, and overstuffed chairs gave the room an inviting feel. Argand lamps with frosted glass globes burned on nearly every table, casting a picturesque glow. The velvet drapes were tightly drawn, keeping the night at bay. Caroline couldn't help but notice that those heavily veiled windows also made it impossible to catch a glimpse of anyone's reflection.

They had retired to the drawing room after a relatively painless supper. Both Lord Trevelyan and Constable Larkin seemed to have entered into an unspoken truce, temporarily laying down their weapons to keep from wounding any innocent bystanders. Since Kane was attending to Vivienne, and Portia was turning the pages of Julian's music as he coaxed one of Haydn's more sprightly melodies from the grand pianoforte, Caroline ended up sharing a Grecian chaise with the constable, an arrangement that suited her purposes just fine.

She stabbed her needle through a circle of linen, struggling to put the finishing touches on a sampler she'd started over six months before. Give her a ledger, a column of figures, and a fresh pot of ink and she could balance the budget of Britain and still end up with a tuppence to spare. Give her an embroidery frame, a spool of thread, and a needle, and all she could produce was a hopeless tangle. But the task occupied her hands and kept her eyes averted from the harp in the corner, where Vivienne was receiving instruction from the viscount. Just as Caroline slanted them a glance from beneath her lashes, a laughing Kane leaned over her sister's shoulder, sniffing the white rose in her sister's hair before gently repositioning Vivienne's slender fingers on the strings.

It was only too easy to imagine the two of them behaving just so thirty years from now—their hair frosted with silver, their grandchildren playing around their knees, the affection in their eyes undimmed by time. Stung by both jealousy and shame, Caroline jerked her gaze back to the sampler, giving the needle a fierce tug that nearly snapped the thread in two.

With no needlework to occupy him, Constable Larkin was not so fortunate. Although he made a valiant pretense of sipping his tea and gazing into the fire, it was Vivienne's lovely profile that kindled the wistful glow in his eyes.

"If you keep ogling my sister that way, sir," Caroline murmured, "Lord Trevelyan is going to be forced to challenge you to a duel."

Larkin jumped guiltily and jerked his gaze back to Caroline's face. "I don't know what you're talking about. I was just admiring the Venetian stonework around the hearth."

"How long have you been in love with her?"

Larkin gave her a startled glance, then sighed, realizing there was no point in resisting her frankness. As he rested his teacup on its Sèvres saucer, his despairing gaze drifted back to Vivienne. "I can't really say, although I'd swear that every moment she scorns me is a lifetime. Did you see her at supper? She wouldn't even look at me. And she barely touched her food. One would have thought my very presence robbed her of her appetite."

Caroline frowned in bemusement. "My sister has always been exceptionally even-tempered. I've never seen her take such an open dislike to anyone."

He brushed an untidy lock of brown hair out of his eyes. "Am I supposed to be flattered? Should I strive to inspire loathing in every gentle creature that I encounter?"

Caroline laughed aloud, earning an unreadable look from the viscount. She would have sworn she'd seen Kane's glance stray in their direction more than once. It was hardly fair of him to begrudge her a pleasant exchange with the constable when he was so studiously courting her sister.

Deliberately turning to give her full attention to Larkin, she said, "Perhaps Vivienne is insulted by the notion that you've come here to protect her from her own foolhardiness."

Larkin snorted. "How could even the most practical of women be expected to keep her wits about her when Kane is wielding that notorious charm of his?"

Suddenly finding it difficult to swallow, Caroline cleared her throat and devoted all of her attention to tying a clumsy knot in the thread. "I wish I could offer you some encouragement, Constable, but both my sister's affections and her hopes for the future are otherwise engaged. I would advise you not to waste your time chasing a dream that can never come true." She stole a furtive glance at Kane beneath her eyelashes, thinking she would do well to heed her own counsel. "Speaking of our host, you promised to tell me how the two of you met."

Larkin dragged his gaze away from Vivienne, his eyes losing their moon-eyed glaze. "I met Adrian my first year at Oxford. He found me in Christ Church Meadow with a bunch of rowdy bucks gathered around me, shouting and shoving. I was an orphan and a charity student, you see, and they found much to mock in my speech, my shabby clothing, my secondhand books." A reluctant smile curved his thin lips. "While their interests consisted solely of gaming, wenching, imbibing too much brandy, and taunting those less fortunate, Adrian had devoted his free time to the study of boxing at Jackson's. He laid them out flat, every one of them. From that day forward, he appointed himself my champion and no one ever dared trouble me again."

"That's a role he seems to embrace with more than the usual enthusiasm," Caroline murmured, remembering his timely rescue of her at Vauxhall. "What about Victor Duvalier? Was he another one of Kane's strays?"

The constable's eyes sparked with something that might have been amusement in a less guarded man. "You're very attentive, aren't you, Miss Cabot? Are you considering a career in the constabulary?"

"Only if you'll allow me to continue my interrogation," she replied, unable to resist a smug smile.

He sighed. "If you must know, Victor's father was a wealthy count and both of his parents were sent to the guillotine during the Revolution. An aunt smuggled him to England a few years later. Unfortunately, he could never quite rid himself of his accent, which provided endless amusement to our fellow students, especially since we were at war with France at the time. Until Kane took him under his wing, they made his life a living hell."

Her curious gaze searched Larkin's face. "From what you told me in London, Kane wasn't just your champion. He was your friend."

Larkin's smile faded. "That was a long time ago."

"Before Eloisa Markham disappeared?" she ventured, lowering her voice to ensure that their conversation remained private.

"After Eloisa disappeared, Adrian never confided in me again," Larkin admitted, unable to hide the note of bitterness in his voice. "It was as if our friendship had never been."

"What about Victor? Did Kane continue to confide in him?"

"Victor returned to France shortly after Eloisa's disappearance."

A tingle of excitement made Caroline sit up straight. "How do you know she didn't secretly accompany him?"

"Because it was a broken heart that drove him back to France. You see, Miss Cabot, the three of us were very dear friends, and of the three of us, Victor loved Eloisa the most. I don't think he ever forgave Adrian for being the one she chose to love in return."

"What about you?" Caroline dared to ask. "Did you ever forgive him? Or Eloisa?" she added pointedly.

Larkin rested his tea cup on his saucer. "If I had anything to do with her disappearance, do you honestly think I would have abandoned my dream of joining the clergy and devoted my life to hunting down those who commit such crimes?"

Caroline knew that guilt had driven men to do stranger things. But there was something about Larkin's clear-eyed gaze that invited trust. "It was a great loss for the clergy, sir," she said, absolving him with her smile. "You would have made a capital vicar."

As he took a sip of his tea, the rebellious lock of hair flipped back into his face. Caroline managed to resist correcting it, but she'd spent too much time tweaking Portia's various bows and ribbons to ignore the clumsy loop of his half-untied cravat.

Laying her needlework in her lap, she reached over and retied the cravat in a neat bow, surprised to find her exasperation mixed with genuine fondness. "I must say, Constable Larkin, that you are in dire need of either a valet or a wife."

"Which position are you applying for, Miss Cabot?"

At that resonant growl, Caroline glanced over her shoulder to find Adrian Kane looming over the chaise. He was glowering down at them with little evidence of his "notorious charm." Vivienne had begun to pluck out a melody on the harp, leaving him free to prowl the room. Caroline couldn't help but wonder just how long he had been standing there and just how much of their conversation he might have absorbed.

His impertinent query brought a fierce blush to her cheeks. Before she could whip up a suitably scathing denial, Larkin smiled ruefully and said, "I'm afraid I couldn't afford either a valet or a wife on my meager commissions."

The constable's gaze drifted back to Vivienne. Her slender fingers played over the harp strings, coaxing a delicate glissando of notes from the instrument. The flickering lamplight seemed to milk the color from her fair cheeks, leaving her looking particularly ethereal, like a golden-haired angel who might be summoned back to heaven at any moment.

Linking his hands at the small of his back, Kane leaned over the back of the chaise and tilted his head to study Caroline's sampler. " 'Bless Our Elves,' " he read. "Now those are certainly words to live by."

"It's supposed to read 'Bless Our Lives,' " Caroline retorted, squinting at the lumpy letters of the homily. As Kane sauntered over to sink down on the sofa opposite them, his mocking gaze inspired her to attack her needlework with fresh vigor. "I wasn't aware you were following our conversation, my lord," she said, wielding the needle as if it were a tiny wooden stake and the sampler the viscount's heart. "Had I known, I would have spoken more clearly to make it easier for you to eavesdrop."

Kane simply smiled. "That's hardly necessary. I have extremely good hearing."

"So they say," she replied more loudly than she intended, her simmering indignation making her careless. "Along with exceptional night vision and a passionate fondness for blood pudding."

"They only say that because everyone thinks he's a vampire," Vivienne said matter-of-factly, her fingers poised over the harp strings.

Twelve

Larkin's teacup clattered into its saucer. Portia's mouth fell open. Julian's fingers struck a jarring off-key note on the pianoforte. Caroline jabbed the needle into the tender pad of her thumb. They all gaped at Vivienne, but not one of them could bring themselves to look at Kane.

"You *know* about that?" Caroline whispered into the awkward silence that had fallen over the drawing room.

"Of course I do," Vivienne replied, rolling her eyes. "You'd have to be both blind and deaf not to see the sidelong glances or hear the whispers every time he walks into a room."

"And it doesn't bother you?" Caroline asked cautiously.

Vivienne shrugged and ran a graceful finger down one of the harp's strings. "Why would I pay any heed to such nonsense? Weren't you the one who always taught me to scorn idle gossip?"

"Yes." Caroline sank back into the cushions of the chaise, shamed by her sister's words. "I suppose I was, wasn't I?"

Until that moment, she hadn't realized how close she was to being swept along on that unsavory tide of gossip and innuendo. She didn't even have Portia's youth or rioting imagination to blame for her willingness to condemn an innocent man who had shown her and her family nothing but kindness.

As Portia flipped a page of the music so Julian could resume his song, Caroline glanced down and realized she had spattered blood all over the pristine linen of the sampler. She absently brought her thumb to her mouth, then glanced at Kane, having finally worked up enough courage to gauge his reaction to Vivienne's words.

He wasn't watching Vivienne. He was watching her. His hungry gaze was riveted on her lips as she sucked away the welling drops of blood. The polite mask he so often wore had vanished, revealing a naked need that stole her breath away.

She could almost feel *his* lips curving around her tender flesh. *His* mouth gently suckling away all of her hurts until there was no pain, only pleasure. Her heart seemed to slow, growing fuller and heavier with every beat until she could feel its primitive rhythm echoing deep in her womb.

Kane slowly lifted his gaze from her lips to her eyes. Instead of breaking the spell, the motion only intensified it.

Come to me.

She heard the words as clearly as if he had spoken them aloud. Both command and entreaty, they made it nearly impossible to resist the hypnotic pull of his will. For one terrifying yet exhilarating moment, Caroline thought she was going to rise, to cross the room in front of them all and go into his arms. She could almost see herself settling into his lap, twining her hands through the glossy silk of his hair, offering him her mouth and anything else he wanted, including her immortal soul.

She stood abruptly, dumping her embroidery to the floor. Setting aside his teacup and saucer, Larkin politely scrambled to retrieve it. As he handed it to her, his troubled gaze riveted on her face, she clutched at the ruined scrap of fabric, hoping to hide the violent trembling of her hands.

"Why, th-thank you, Constable Larkin. If you'll excuse me, I believe I shall retire for the night." Studiously avoiding Kane's eyes, she began to back toward the door, nearly upending a pier table in the process. "Please don't think me rude. I'm a country girl at heart and I still haven't adjusted to staying up until the wee hours of the morning."

"Sleep well, Miss Cabot," Larkin called after her as she turned to flee.

Although she flashed him a reassuring smile, Caroline wasn't sure she would ever sleep again.

Caroline paced the moonlit tower, her circular path perfectly matching the whirling of her thoughts. The beautifully appointed chamber no longer felt like a refuge, but a cage. If she didn't escape its gilded bars soon, she was afraid she never would. Even if she packed her things and fled tonight, taking her sisters with her, she was afraid her heart would remain here, held prisoner by a man who, for all of his power, was helpless to hide his desire for her.

But what exactly could a man like Kane want from her? Was it the sight of her blood that had kindled the hunger in his eyes? Or something even more unthinkable?

She had seen that look before. On the face of the medieval warrior in the portrait gallery. The warrior Kane had claimed was only a distant ancestor, though they were nearly identical, even sharing the same diabolically kissable little mole above their left eyebrows.

If that man had wanted her, he would have taken her, and no power on earth or in heaven would have stopped him.

Caroline hugged herself through her thin nightdress, fighting back a shiver of mingled fear and longing. She felt as if her flesh was being consumed by a terrible fever— one minute burning, the next chilled to the bone. Her usual calm logic seemed to have betrayed her. What if Kane was lying about the portraits? What if Portia had been right all along and he really *was* some sort of immortal creature who had existed since the dawn of time?

She didn't want to believe that monsters walked the earth. But how could a mere man exert such a ruthless grip on both her heart and her imagination? If he were only a man, how could he tempt her to betray her sister's trust with nothing more than a longing look?

From the corner of her eye she caught a flicker of movement, as if some sort of winged shadow had darted across the moon. Her startled gaze shot to the French doors.

From now on, you might want to lock those doors. You can't always depend on an element as capricious as the wind to exercise its best judgment.

As Kane's words echoed through her mind, Caroline remembered how unutterably lonely he had looked in that moment with his hands braced on the parapet and his face turned to the night.

She strode over to the doors, determined to heed his warning. But when she reached them, she hesitated, her fingers poised over the bolt.

He was out there.

She knew it with a certainty beyond mere female intuition. She could sense him, feel him, like an inescapable shadow cast over her soul. What if she wasn't afraid Kane would break down those doors? What if she was afraid she would throw them open herself? Perhaps it wasn't *his* will that she feared, but her own. After all, she was the one who'd spent six long, lonely years trapped in a prison of duty and obligation—stifling her needs, her wants, her desires. Growing old before her time and thinking only of what would be best for Portia and Vivienne. Was it any wonder she yearned to cast those doors wide open and invite the night into her waiting arms?

Pressing her brow to the cool glass, she closed her eyes against a helpless wave of yearning. Whether Kane was a vampire or simply a man, she was afraid that if she looked into his eyes at that moment, she would be lost forever.

Caroline slowly lifted her head and opened her eyes.

The balcony was empty, adrift in a silver wash of moonlight.

She slammed the bolt home with trembling fingers, then strode to her bedchamber door and made certain it was locked as well. Climbing into the bed, she jerked the bed curtains closed around her, shutting out the night and all of its dark temptations.

Adrian slowly backed into the shadows of the balcony. He no longer craved the light of the moon. He had once trusted her to keep his secrets, but now her unforgiving rays only illuminated the darkness in his soul.

It was the moon that had witnessed him standing there with only a fragile pane of glass separating him from the alabaster arc of Caroline's cheek, the plump swell of her lips, the enticing curve of her long, slender throat. The moon that had seen him lift his fingertips to the glass, stroking the cool pane as he ached to stroke the softness of her skin.

He knew that if she opened her eyes in that moment, the moon would no longer be his only mistress. So he had melted into the shadows and waited for the sound of the bolt being rammed into its moorings.

If she hadn't heeded his warning and bolted the door, would he have been content to slip into the room and watch her sleep as he had done the night before? Or would some darker force have driven him to lean over that bed and taste her, to cover her with his mouth and drink deeply until the burning hunger of his body was sated?

Adrian sagged against the wall and closed his eyes, growing dizzy with longing. He knew a taste of her would never satisfy him. It would only make him thirst for more. He had denied himself for too long. If he allowed himself even a single sip of her sweetness, he would never be satisfied, not until his hunger had consumed them both.

"Caroline! Caro, you have to open the door! I need you!"

As Portia's cry penetrated her groggy brain, Caroline rolled over and pried open her eyes, her limbs weighted by exhaustion. It had been nearly dawn before she'd finally drifted into a dreamless sleep, and the cozy patter of the rain against the tower windows only made her want to sleep the rest of the day away. After last night, she wasn't sure she could bear to face either Kane or Vivienne.

Ducking beneath her pillow, she snuggled deeper into the feather mattress.

"Caroline!" Her sister pounded on the door with both fists. "Open the door and let me in!"

Caroline sighed. It wasn't as if Portia in a state of near hysteria was cause for alarm. "Go away!" she shouted, pressing the pillow over her ears. "Unless we're being invaded by the French or the castle is afire, I wish to be left alone!"

"Please, Caro! I need you right now!" That plaintive plea was accompanied by a bout of renewed pounding.

"That does it," Caroline muttered.

Flinging away both pillow and blankets, she jumped out of the bed and stormed across the tower. Unlocking the door, she whipped it open to find her little sister standing there, her small fist poised just above Caroline's nose.

"What is it this time, Portia?" Caroline demanded through clenched teeth. "Mermaids in the moat? Leprechauns doing a merry jig on the castle lawn? Zombies stumbling out of the Kane family crypt? A white lady floating down the corridor with Wilbury's head tucked beneath her arm?" She leaned down until her nose was nearly touching Portia's. "If you must know, I don't really care if you've spotted an entire flock of vampires winging their way up to the tower to sink their fangs into our throats and make us their eternal brides. As a matter of fact, if you don't leave me in peace, *I'm* going to start biting people out of sheer spite. Beginning with you!"

She was preparing to slam the door in her sister's face when Portia said in a near whisper, "It's Vivienne."

Caroline blinked, taking in Portia's tumbled curls, ashen complexion, and trembling lips for the first time. "What is it?" she asked, her heart already beginning to tighten with dread.

"She won't wake up."

Thirteen

"When did you first realize there was something wrong?" Caroline demanded as she hurried down the stairs, jerking a clumsy knot in the sash of the velvet dressing gown the viscount had so thoughtfully provided. She glanced at the long-case clock on the landing as she passed to discover the morning was half gone.

"At first I thought she was just sleepy," Portia confessed, following Caroline down a long corridor paneled in mahogany wainscoting, forced to take two steps for every one of her sister's purposeful strides. "After all, Julian had kept us both up until nearly three playing faro for hairpins. But when I tried to wake her up for breakfast, she wouldn't budge. I coughed in her ear, tickled her toes with a feather, even dribbled cold water on her forehead. I rang for the maids, but they couldn't rouse her, either. That's when I got scared and came for you."

Caroline tossed a comforting smile over her shoulder, struggling to hide her own fear. "You did well, pet. She's probably just being a lazyboots. I'm sure we'll have her back on her dainty little feet in no time at all."

As she marched through the cozy sitting room that connected her sisters' bedchambers, Caroline could only pray that she was right. She entered Vivienne's chamber to find three maids huddled near the door, whispering and wringing their hands.

As Caroline approached the elegant tent bed, her dread mounted. With all the roses washed from her cheeks and her golden curls spread across the pillow, Vivienne looked as if she was auditioning for the role of Sleeping Beauty in one of the amateur theatricals the girls used to put on for their parents.

Sinking down on the edge of the bed, Caroline touched the back of her hand to Vivienne's brow. Her sister's skin wasn't flushed with fever, but as cool as death. Chilled by the thought, Caroline stole a glance at Vivienne's chest. The even rise and fall of her nightdress's ruffled bodice betrayed no distress. She simply looked as if she had succumbed to some dark enchantment.

Capturing her sister by the shoulders, Caroline dragged her to a sitting position and gave her a gentle shake. "Wake up, Miss Lazybones! The morning's half over. No more lollygagging in bed for you!"

Vivienne's lashes didn't even flutter. She hung limp in Caroline's arms, her head lolling to one side.

Caroline tossed the maids a pleading look over her shoulder. "Have you any hartshorn on hand?"

After a brief consultation, two of the women hurried from the room. One of them returned a few minutes later with a small glass bottle.

Supporting her sister's weight with one arm, Caroline drew the stopper from the vial and waved the bottle beneath Vivienne's nose. Although the pungent aroma of the ammonia made Caroline recoil, Vivienne's nostrils didn't even twitch.

Trading a despairing look with Portia, Caroline gently laid Vivienne back against the pillows. She squeezed her sister's icy hand, wishing desperately that she'd paid more heed to Vivienne's fading color outside of the portrait gallery yesterday, the poor appetite Larkin had commented upon at supper. She should have known Vivienne would never complain about a physical ailment. But she'd been too busy mooning over Kane to give her sister the attention she needed. Now it might be too late.

Struck by a wayward thought, she felt the chill in Vivienne's fingers spread to her own heart. Reluctantly surrendering her sister's hand, she rose and strode over to the casement window tucked into the north wall. Just as she had feared, the window was unlocked and unlatched. A simple push sent it swinging outward. She leaned out the window, blinking against the rain. There was no balcony here, only a narrow ledge.

"Did you hear anything last night after you went to bed?" she turned to ask Portia. "Someone stirring in Vivienne's room? A frightened cry perhaps?"

Portia shook her head helplessly. "I heard nothing."

Caroline had no reason to doubt her little sister's words. Portia had always slept like the proverbial log.

She returned to the bed. Keenly aware of the maids' scrutiny, she sank back down beside Vivienne. She was gingerly reaching for the ribbon at the throat of her sister's high-necked gown when she heard the staccato click of booted heels behind her.

She turned to find Kane standing in the doorway in shirtsleeves and trousers, his leonine mane tousled. Larkin, Julian, and a white-faced young maid hovered behind him. She might have been surprised to see him up so soon after sunrise were it not for the steady patter of the rain against the windowpanes.

"What is it, Caroline?" he asked urgently, using her Christian name for the first time. "The maid told me something was wrong with Vivienne." His face a study in concern, he started for the bed.

Fighting a treacherous urge to run into his arms, Caroline rose to place herself between him and her sister. "Your presence is not required here, my lord," she said stiffly. "What is required is a physician."

Kane froze, as did everyone else in the room, including the slack-jawed maids. Although he towered over her, Caroline stood her ground, her hands clenched into fists. Kane met her gaze without flinching, but his jaw tightened as if she had struck him an unexpected blow. She had never dreamed she would have the power to wound a man like him. Or that the price for wielding that power would be so high.

"Mattie?" he finally said, still looking at Caroline.

The young maid darted forward, lifting her starched apron to bob a nervous curtsy. "Aye, m'lord?"

"Send one of the footmen to Salisbury to summon Kidwell. Have him tell the doctor that one of my guests has fallen ill and he needs to come right away."

"As ye wish, m'lord." The maid bobbed another curtsy and went scurrying from the room.

Larkin brushed past Kane and stood facing Caroline. Unable to resist the unspoken plea in his eyes, Caroline stepped aside and let him pass. As he went to his knees beside the bed, tenderly gathering Vivienne's limp hand in his own, Caroline had to avert her eyes for fear the tears swimming in them would spill over.

Portia instinctively moved closer to Julian, who remained slumped against the wall by the door, his expression dazed.

Turning on his heel, Kane stalked over to his brother and grimly said, "A word, sir, if you please."

Pushing himself away from the wall, Julian followed his brother from the room with all the enthusiasm of a man marching to the gallows.

Adrian strode into the library, still haunted by the image of Caroline gazing up at him, her clear gray eyes shadowed by suspicion.

Although he could have easily swiped her aside with one hand, she had defied him with the ferocious courage of a mother lioness protecting her cubs, her chin held high and her shoulders thrown back. He had never felt more like a monster.

He went to the towering walnut secretaire in the corner

and brushed aside books and papers until he located a dusty decanter of brandy. Eschewing a glass, he poured a swallow straight down his throat, welcoming its raw burn. Only after the liquor hit his belly and began to sear the edges off his temper did he turn to face his brother.

Julian had slumped into a leather wing chair in front of the cold hearth. His appearance was nearly as alarming as Vivienne's. There was no sign of the elegant dandy who had entertained them at supper with a witty anecdote about his latest visit to a Bond Street haberdashery. His mane of mahogany hair was uncombed, his white shirt rumpled and stained with drops of red wine. His cravat hung limp around his throat. The deep hollows beneath his eyes stretched the skin taut over his sculpted cheekbones and made him look a decade older than he was.

Adrian didn't say a word. He simply gazed at his brother without blinking.

"Why are you looking at me like that?" Julian finally snapped, his dark eyes burning with defiance. "I know what you're thinking, but I had absolutely *nothing* to do with this."

"I suppose it's pure coincidence that Vivienne collapsed after spending the evening with you."

"Spending the evening *playing faro* with me," Julian corrected. "I swear to you that I took only a few worthless hairpins from the girl. When the clock struck three, she went upstairs with her sister and I didn't see either one of them again until I heard that maidservant crying and followed you into their room."

"If you stopped playing cards at three, that still leaves the three hours before dawn unaccounted for. Where were you during those hours?"

Julian dropped his head into his hands, his defiance crumbling into defeat. "If you must know, I don't remember."

Adrian shook his head, too angry to try and hide the disgust in his voice. "You were drinking again, weren't you?"

His brother's silence was answer enough.

"Has it ever occurred to you that drinking yourself into such a state that you can't remember where you were or what you were doing just might be a wee bit dangerous?"

Julian surged to his feet. "And has it ever occurred to you that I might be even more dangerous if I didn't drink?"

The two brothers stood toe-to-toe for a tense moment, but it was Julian who looked away first, his eyes bleak. "Why would I trouble Vivienne? It's the little one who keeps following me around like some sort of lovesick puppy just begging for a morsel of my attention. She's the one who gazes up at me with those lovely blue eyes of hers as if I were the answer to her every prayer. If I were going to slip, don't you think it would be with her?"

Adrian's control snapped. Grabbing Julian by the front of his shirt, he snarled, "If you lay so much as one finger on that child . . ."

He didn't finish the threat. He didn't have to.

He released his trembling brother, only to discover his own hands were none too steady. Julian fought to reclaim his dignity by smoothing back his hair and jerking a flawless knot in his cravat. Refusing to meet Adrian's eyes, he went stalking toward the door.

"Where are you going?" Adrian called after him.

"To hell, most likely," Julian replied curtly without turning around.

"If the rain stops and the sun comes out before you can get back here, you're going to wish you were in hell."

Julian stopped in the doorway and slowly turned. "It would be easier for you and your precious Miss Cabot if I didn't come back at all, wouldn't it?"

Bewildered by his brother's words, Adrian shook his head. "If you had nothing to do with Vivienne's collapse, then why would you say such a thing?"

Julian's smile was a bittersweet ghost of the grin Adrian had always loved so well. "I wasn't talking about Vivienne."

Adrian opened his mouth to deny the words, but before he could, Julian was gone.

* * *

"Julian! Julian! Where are you going?"

That winsome cry echoed off the stone walls of the ancient bailey that had once hosted tournaments for kings, knights, and their fair ladies.

Ignoring it, Julian blinked the rain from his lashes and continued to stalk toward the stables. He didn't know where he was going. Even with the sky a sullen mass of clouds and rain pouring from the heavens, it wasn't as if there was anywhere he could flee to escape what he had become. Despite the careless boast he had hurled at his brother, he doubted that even hell would welcome the likes of him.

"Julian! Why won't you answer me? I won't be ignored, you know, so you needn't try."

He bit back a groan. There was no question about it. Portia Cabot was even more persistent than his brother. And infinitely more alluring.

He whirled around so quickly that she nearly stumbled into him. He wanted to reach out a hand to steady her, but was afraid of the consequences, so he simply stood gazing down his nose at her as she awkwardly regained her footing on the slick grass.

She was gripping a parasol in her gloved hand—a ridiculous confection of silk and lace that was in danger of crumpling beneath the weight of the rain. With her dark blue eyes aglow and her damp curls threatening to tumble out of their hairpins, she looked like a bedraggled sprite.

"Shouldn't you be at your sister's bedside?" he demanded.

She wrinkled her pert nose at him, plainly taken aback by his brusqueness. "I'm sure she'll be just fine now that she has Caro to look after her. I was concerned about *you*. You looked so pale back there in Vivienne's room that I was afraid you might be taking ill yourself."

He snorted. "I'm afraid there's no cure for what ails me. At least none a doctor can provide."

"Is that why you and your brother quarreled?"

"How do you know that?" He narrowed his eyes, lowering his gaze to study the faint circle of dust that marred the snowy muslin of her skirt. "Were you kneeling at the library keyhole, by any chance?"

A guilty flush tinted her delicate cheekbones as she brushed at her skirt. "I was getting ready to knock when I accidentally dropped my handkerchief. It was only by pure happenstance that I heard your raised voices."

Julian quickly deduced that was all she had heard. If she had heard him denounce her as a "lovesick puppy," he doubted she would still be dogging his heels.

"My brother was simply delivering his standard lecture. He thinks I drink too much," Julian confessed, surprised to find himself inching so close to the truth. He'd grown very accomplished at lying in the past few years, especially to himself.

"Do you?" she asked, looking genuinely curious.

He raked a hand through his hair, finding it suddenly difficult to meet her eyes. "On occasion, I suppose."

"Why?"

He shrugged. "Why does any man drink? To dull the thirst for something else he wants desperately, but can never have."

Portia moved almost imperceptibly closer to him, boldly capturing his gaze. "I've always felt that if you want something badly enough, then you should be willing to move heaven and earth to get it."

Julian gazed down at her dusky brows and lush lips, thinking it ironic that such an angelic face could bring him such hellish torment. With a restraint he didn't know he still possessed, he reached down and gently tweaked her nose. "You should be thankful, bright eyes, that I don't ascribe to the same philosophy."

Turning on his heel, he continued on toward the stables, leaving her standing all alone with her parasol drooping in the rain.

* * *

Leaning forward in the chair she'd drawn next to the bed, Caroline gently stroked her sister's golden curls from her brow. Vivienne's condition had neither improved nor worsened throughout the long day and night. She simply looked as if she might continue in her unnatural slumber forever.

The footman had returned to the castle just as night was falling and the rain was tapering off with word that the doctor was attending a difficult birth and might not arrive until morning. Portia was napping in her bed, while Constable Larkin had insisted upon keeping his own vigil in the sitting room that connected the two chambers. The last time Caroline peeked in on him, he had been nodding off over a cold cup of tea, his stocking feet propped on an ottoman, a well-worn volume of *Tyburn Gallows: An Illustrated History* sprawled in his lap.

Vivienne sighed in her sleep and Caroline wondered if she was dreaming. Did she dream of Kane's blue-green eyes dancing in the sunlight and wedding bells? Or did she dream of darkness and surrender and bells that eternally tolled the midnight hour? Just as she had a dozen times before, Caroline drew back the collar of her sister's nightdress to study the creamy expanse of her throat.

"I gather you didn't find what you were looking for."

At that somber drawl, Caroline glanced over her shoulder to find Kane's dark figure silhouetted against the moonlight. Why should it even surprise her that he was standing not by the door, but the open window?

"I don't know what you're talking about," Caroline lied, deftly knotting the ribbon at the throat of Vivienne's gown. She had searched every inch of her sister's pale flesh, but found no mark at all, no evidence of foul play.

He started forward. Caroline rose, once again placing herself between him and the bed.

This time he didn't stop until he was near enough to touch her. "Why won't you let me get closer, Miss Cabot? Are you afraid for your sister? Or for yourself?"

"Do I have reason to be, my lord?"

His searching gaze caressed her face. "If you believe me such a despicable villain, then why don't you scream for Constable Larkin? I'm sure he'd like nothing more than to rush in here and rescue you from my dastardly clutches." Almost as if he couldn't resist the urge, he lifted his hand to her face, the back of his knuckles brushing ever so lightly over the curve of her cheekbone.

At first Caroline thought the anguished moan had come from her own lips. Then she realized it was Vivienne. Turning away from Kane, she rushed back to her sister's bedside.

Vivienne was muttering and thrashing restlessly beneath the blankets, her cheeks no longer pale, but mottled and flushed. Caroline touched a hand to her sister's brow, then cast Kane a helpless glance. "She's burning up with fever!"

"We have to get her cooled down." Brushing Caroline aside, he ruthlessly stripped the heavy blankets from Vivienne's limbs, then gathered her limp form and carried her to the window.

Caroline's protest died on her lips as she saw that he was simply exposing her sister's overheated flesh to the cool night air. He braced one hip against the windowsill, his strong arms cradling Vivienne with such unmistakable tenderness that Caroline had to look away.

She found Larkin standing in the doorway, his penetrating gaze traveling between the three of them. The shadow of reproach in his eyes might have only been a figment of her stinging conscience.

"A messenger just arrived," he informed them curtly. "The doctor is on his way."

As they huddled in the sitting room outside of Vivienne's bedchamber, waiting for the doctor to finish his examination, the hazy glow of dawn began to soften the edges of the sky outside the window. Portia was curled up in the corner of a damask-draped sofa, her expression unusually pensive. Larkin restlessly paced the cozy room, his long legs carrying him from the hearth to the closed door of Vivienne's chamber and back again. Caroline sat stiffly in a ladder-backed chair, her hands folded in her lap while Kane leaned against the wall by the window, lost in his own thoughts.

Everyone but Kane jumped when the door swung open and the doctor emerged, trailed by the freckled young maid Kane had addressed as Mattie.

Although the physician's questioning gaze immediately went to the viscount, Caroline rose and stepped forward, with Larkin hovering just behind her shoulder. "I'm Caroline Cabot, sir—Vivienne's eldest sister."

Dr. Kidwell had both the stature and demeanor of a small, ill-tempered frog. He glowered at her over the top of the steel spectacles riding low on his pug nose. "Has your sister been exposed to the elements recently? Suffered a period of protracted dampness perhaps?"

Hampered by exhaustion, Caroline searched her memory. "Well, it was raining three nights ago when we arrived at the castle. I suppose Vivienne might have—"

"Ah-ha!" he crowed, cutting her off. "Just as I suspected! I believe I may have found the culprit."

It took the last ounce of Caroline's flagging willpower, but she managed not to look at Kane.

Dr. Kidwell snapped his fingers at the cowering maid. She crept forward and he whisked an object out of her hands, holding it aloft. Caroline blinked, recognizing it as one of her sister's leather half-boots. Flushed with triumph, the doctor slipped his finger between the sole and the scuffed toe of the boot, exposing an enormous gap.

Both Caroline and Portia gasped. When Aunt Marietta had invited Vivienne to come to London, Vivienne had inherited all of the lovely gowns and kid slippers intended for Caroline's debut. But there had been no money left over from their sparse allowance to buy new boots.

"There's another one just like it tucked beneath the bed,"

the doctor informed them, "along with a wadded-up pair of stockings that are *still* a little damp."

Caroline remembered wading through the muck of the coaching inn courtyards, their shoulders beaten down by the pouring rain. She shook her head in dismay. "It would be just like Vivienne to ride for hours without complaining once about the holes in her boots or her soaked stockings."

Larkin rested a hand on her shoulder, giving it a comforting squeeze. "Miss Vivienne seemed perfectly fine at supper the night I arrived. She was a bit pale, but other than that, she showed no signs of distress."

The doctor's bulging eyes were not unkind. "Sometimes these things lurk in the lungs for a time, sapping the strength and the appetite before they make themselves fully known."

Caroline took a deep breath before asking the most difficult question of all. "Will she recover?"

"Of course she will! She's young and strong. I suspect she'll be back on her feet in no time. I'm going to leave ingredients and instructions for a medicinal mustard poultice."

Caroline nodded, a belated swell of relief making her knees go weak. Larkin's arm went around her waist, bracing her.

Portia scrambled eagerly to her feet. "What about the ball, sir? The viscount's masquerade is less than a week away. Will my sister be well enough to attend?"

"I would think so," the doctor said. "Just apply the poultice twice a day and bundle her up well before she goes outdoors." He wagged a chiding finger under Caroline's nose. "And make sure the child gets some new boots!"

"I will," Caroline vowed. She would see to it that both of her sisters had new boots, even if that meant she had to go crawling to Cousin Cecil on hands and knees.

"Oh, please, sir, is she awake? May we see her?" Portia asked.

The doctor turned his stern gaze on her. "As long as you promise not to giggle and bounce on the bed, young lady."

"Oh, I shan't, sir! I'll be as quiet and still as a church mouse," Portia assured him, nearly bowling him over as she galloped gracelessly toward the door.

Larkin took an involuntary step forward, then glanced down at Caroline, his uncertainty reflected in his eyes. She nodded toward the door, giving him her blessing. As he followed Portia into the bedchamber, Mattie ushered the doctor into the corridor, leaving Caroline and Kane alone in the sitting room.

Caroline glanced over to find him surveying her, his blue-green eyes more inscrutable than ever before. She bit her lip, battling an emotion that felt dangerously like guilt. She had proved herself only too willing to believe the worst of him. But what else was she to do when he refused to defend himself against even the most outlandish of accusations? How could he condemn her for betraying his trust when he had never offered it to her in the first place?

Determined to dredge up an apology, however inadequate, she cleared her throat and said, "It appears that I misjudged you, my lord. I believe I owe you an—"

"That's where you're wrong, Miss Cabot. You don't owe me anything." Turning on his heel, Kane went striding from the room just as the first rays of the morning sun came spilling over the horizon.

Fourteen

Sunlight streamed over the stone wall surrounding the castle garden, transforming the motes of pollen into sparkling fairy dust. Beneath the leafy green branches of a linden tree, a pair of robins hopped about, chirping and fussing over which twigs and bits of moss would best put the finishing touches on their spring nest. A gentle breeze wafted in from the east, bearing on its wings the heady fragrance of blooming honeysuckle.

As Caroline strolled the garden's winding cobblestone path, she longed to turn her face to the sun. But her gaze kept being drawn back to the third-story window overlooking the garden. Only a mullioned pane of glass separated them, yet the sun-drenched garden with its verdant greenery and flitting butterflies might have been a world away from the castle's shadows. Somewhere behind those towering stone walls, its master slumbered, his dreams and secrets known only to him.

Kane hadn't betrayed so much as a hint of reproach toward her in the days since Vivienne's collapse. He seemed to have neatly and ruthlessly severed the invisible cord that had bound them. If he still felt its irresistible tug whenever she walked into a room, he hid it behind a mask of polite indifference. There were no more witty rejoinders, no teasing spark in his eye when he looked at her. He was behaving with perfect propriety, almost as if he was already her brother-in-law. One would have thought that they had never shared a midnight rendezvous on the Lover's Walk or a soul-shattering kiss.

Although she continued to bolt her balcony door each night before retiring, Caroline suspected that there was no longer any need to do so. She slept the entire night through and woke up feeling bereft—as if someone dear to her heart had died.

"Please, sir, would you ring for some more tea?"

As Vivienne's voice drifted to her ears, Caroline paused beneath the shade of the linden tree, her hand on its smooth trunk.

Her sister was reclining on a chaise at the bottom of the hill, a woolen lap rug tucked around her slender legs. Constable Larkin had just risen from a stone bench and was hastening toward the house. Judging from the open book he'd left on the bench, he had apparently been reading aloud to Vivienne. Caroline smiled in spite of herself, wondering if he was reading *Tyburn Gallows: An Illustrated History* or perhaps *The Halifax Gibbet: Dance of the Damned*.

Since her collapse, Vivienne was no longer content to suffer in silence. She actually seemed to enjoy ordering the constable about when the viscount wasn't in attendance, asking him to "fetch my shawl" or "ring for another heated brick wrapped in flannel, would you please, sir?" whenever he showed signs of relaxing his vigilance.

"There you are, Caro!" Vivienne called out, spotting her. "Won't you come keep me company while Constable Larkin fetches some fresh tea?" She waved her over with the regal grace of a young queen, leaving Caroline no choice but to obey.

"You seem to have made a most miraculous recovery," Caroline remarked, taking the seat Larkin had vacated.

Vivienne nestled deeper into the freshly plumped pillows and covered her mouth to muffle a rather unconvincing cough. "I can manage well enough as long as I stay out of the drafts."

At the moment, with the afternoon sun picking out the golden glints in her hair and the breeze teasing the roses back into her cheeks, she appeared to be positively glowing with good health. Had it been Portia, Caroline might have accused her of malingering.

"Lord Trevelyan's ball is tomorrow night," Caroline reminded her. "Are you sure you're going to be well enough to attend?"

Lowering her lashes to veil her eyes, Vivienne toyed with the chain around her neck. The cameo was still tucked safely into her bodice. "I'm certain I will. After all, I couldn't bear to disappoint the viscount after his many kindnesses to us."

As if on cue, Portia came hurrying down the walk from the house, struggling beneath the weight of a wooden box that was nearly as large as she was. Her face was wreathed in a delighted smile. "You won't believe what one of the maidservants just delivered to our chamber, Vivi! I couldn't bear to wait until you returned. I knew you'd want to see it now."

Her own curiosity piqued, Caroline rose so Portia could rest her burden on the bench.

"It's simply the loveliest thing I've ever seen!" Portia proclaimed, whisking the lid off the box with a flourish.

Caroline and Vivienne gasped in unison as yard upon yard of tulle in the most ethereal shade of maiden's blush came spilling out of the box. The tulle was draped over an underskirt of glossy white satin.

Portia held the gown's low-cut satin bodice up to her chin, taking care not to drag the deep blond flounce of its scalloped hem on the grass. "Isn't it beautiful?"

"Exquisite," Caroline murmured, unable to resist running her own fingertips over the row of gleaming pearls that adorned the gown's rose-colored satin sash.

"It's like something a princess would wear," Vivienne said, her own lips curving in a besotted smile.

Still gripping the gown as if loath to surrender it, Portia reached back into the box to retrieve a card of ivory vellum.

She handed the card to Vivienne. "I may have opened the box, but I wasn't so impertinent as to read the card."

"It's nice to know you haven't lost your scruples," Caroline said dryly. Portia poked her tongue out at her.

Vivienne studied the card. "It's a gift from the viscount," she said, her smile fading. "He means for me to wear it to the ball tomorrow night."

Caroline snatched her hand back as if the gown had burst into flames, caught off guard to find herself suddenly seething with outrage. "*How dare he*? Who does the man think he is, flaunting convention this way? Gifting you with something as personal as a necklace was ill-mannered enough, but this rises to a whole new level of impropriety. If it had been a fan or a pair of gloves, I might have been able to overlook his insolence, but this . . . this . . ." She waved an arm at the offending garment, sputtering into incoherence.

Portia clutched the dress even tighter, as if fearing Caroline might rip it from her arms. "Oh, please, don't forbid Vivienne to accept it, Caro! She'll be so very lovely in it!"

"I'm certain she would, but I simply can't allow it. If anyone should find out where the gown came from, Vivienne's reputation would be damaged beyond repair. Why, it's the sort of gift a husband might give his . . ."

Caroline's voice faded as Vivienne slowly lifted her eyes to meet hers. Lowering her voice to a near whisper, her sister said, "I may be speaking out of turn, but Lord Trevelyan has been behaving rather oddly in the past week. I think he might be planning on using the occasion of the ball to ask me to be his wife."

At first Caroline thought the crash of breaking pottery was the sound of her own impossible dreams shattering into a thousand pieces. Then she looked up to find Constable Larkin standing on the path. His hands were empty, but the jagged shards of a Sèvres tea set littered the cobblestones around him. Although his face could have been carved from marble, his eyes were a stricken mirror of her own.

Ducking his head, he dropped down to kneel in a puddle of tea, mopping ineffectually at the mess with his handkerchief. "That was frightfully clumsy of me, ladies. All thumbs, I fear. At least that's what my mum used to say when I was a lad. I'm so dreadfully sorry. I'll find a maid to clean up the mess right away."

Without meeting any of their gazes, he stuffed the sodden handkerchief back into his coat pocket and went striding back toward the house.

Caroline turned to find Vivienne scowling after him. "Odious man," she muttered, plucking fitfully at the lap rug. "Once my betrothal to the viscount is announced, I suppose he'll have no further excuse to plague me." Despite Vivienne's truculent expression, Caroline would have almost sworn she glimpsed a telltale sparkle in her sister's eyes.

"What is it, Vivienne? You're not crying, are you?" Caroline asked, as bewildered by her sister's mercurial moods as she was by her own.

Blinking away the moisture, Vivienne lifted her chin and smiled brightly. "I should say not. My eyes are still just a little sensitive to the sun. If I *was* crying, I can assure you that I'd be weeping tears of pure joy. Lord Trevelyan will make a splendid husband, don't you think? Why, I'll be the envy of every woman in the *ton*!"

Tenderly stroking the bodice of the gown, Portia gave Caroline a pleading look. "Especially when they see her wearing this at the masquerade tomorrow night."

Surveying her sisters' hopeful faces, Caroline sighed. Her outrage had been swept away by some darker and even more dangerous emotion. "I can't fight the both of you. As long as no one finds out the gown was a gift from the viscount, I suppose there won't be any harm in it."

Suddenly as eager to escape Vivienne's company as Larkin had been, she began to back toward the house. "I believe I'll just run up to the house and make sure the constable remembered to ring for a fresh tea tray."

Keenly aware of Portia's troubled gaze, she started for the refuge of the house, the soles of her slippers crunching over the broken china.

Caroline wasted no time once she reached her chamber. She strode over to the bed, knelt beside it, and drew out the brocaded valise she had tucked away her first night at the castle. Resting the bag on the bed, she extracted a small glass bottle from its silk-lined interior and held it up to the sunlight.

"And what's this? Have you been hoarding liquor?"

Caroline whirled around to find Portia standing in the doorway.

"Don't you ever knock?" Caroline demanded.

"Not when the door is already open," Portia pointed out, crossing the room. "I was worried about you," she confessed. "You were behaving so oddly down there. I had no idea you were coming up here for a little shot of something to steady your nerves."

Before Caroline could protest, her sister had plucked the bottle from her hand and tugged out its cork. She gave its contents a tentative sniff before bringing the bottle to her lips.

"Don't!" Caroline shouted, snatching for the bottle.

Portia froze, her lips already moistened with the clear liquid. Giving Caroline a wounded look, she licked away a drop of the stuff. "There's no need to startle me half to death. It's only water."

Despite Portia's shameless snooping, it was Caroline who could feel a guilty flush creeping up her throat.

Her sister's eyes slowly narrowed. "Or is it?"

Carefully re-corking the bottle and setting it aside, Portia reached into the valise and withdrew a silver chain. A gaudy silver crucifix dangled from the end of it, glinting in the sunshine.

"How interesting," Portia remarked, giving Caroline a bright-eyed look. "Before we left Edgeleaf, did you by any chance inform the village vicar that you were thinking of becoming a Papist?"

"I fancied the chain," Caroline replied weakly.

"And what have we here?" Reaching back into the valise, Portia drew out a long, round, smooth piece of wood carved to a lethal point on one end. "Were you planning on catching up on your needlework?"

Caroline winced in anticipation as the most damning item of all emerged from the interior of the bag—a dog-eared copy of the April 1819 issue of the *New Monthly Magazine*, the very issue that contained Dr. Polidori's controversial story, "The Vampyre."

"Why, you wretched little sneak!" Portia glared at her as she thumbed through the magazine's well-worn pages. "I've been looking for this all week! You filched it out from under my mattress at Aunt Marietta's, didn't you?"

Caroline sighed and nodded, knowing the time for denials and excuses had passed.

Portia tossed the magazine on the bed with the rest of her ill-gotten booty, then rested her hands on her hips. " 'Don't be ridiculous, Portia! There are no such things as vampires,' " she mimicked, perfectly capturing Caroline at her most imperious. " 'Or werewolves. Or ghosts. Or mermaids in the garden well. Or handsome princes who will rescue you from every peril before sweeping you away to their castles to live happily ever after.' " She shook a finger at Caroline. "Why, you're nothing but a fraud, Caroline Marie Cabot! You should be ashamed of yourself!"

"You don't know the half of it," Caroline muttered, side-stepping her sister to shove the holy water, crucifix, and magazine back into the bag.

"I thought you were supposed to be the practical one."

"Isn't being prepared for every eventuality part of being practical?" Caroline retorted. After a moment's hesitation, she tucked the stake into the pocket of her skirt.

Portia followed the motion, her eyes widening. "Just what do you intend to do?"

Caroline briefly toyed with the idea of lying, but her sister had already proved herself an excellent ally when it came to matters of subterfuge. Facing Portia, she said, "I'm going to search every chamber in this castle until I find the viscount. If I can find him before the sun sets today, then perhaps I can lay all of our fears to rest."

"A rather unfortunate choice of words, don't you think?"

"If Kane truly intends to propose to Vivienne tomorrow night during the ball, this might be my last chance to prove that he's simply a man—a mere mortal just like the rest of us." Ignoring the suffocating tightness in her throat, Caroline added, "If I can do that, then I'll be free to give him and Vivienne my blessing."

"Are you entirely sure that's what you want to do?" Portia asked, plainly choosing her words with care.

"What ever do you mean?"

Portia chewed on her bottom lip for a moment before replying. "I saw your face in the garden when Vivienne mentioned becoming Lord Trevelyan's wife. I was afraid you were starting to have feelings for him."

"Of course I have feelings for him," Caroline said briskly. "The sort of feelings one is expected to have toward a man who may very well end up saving her family from ruin."

Recognizing the determined glint in Caroline's eye, Portia sighed in defeat. "What do you want me to do? Shall I follow along behind you, waving the crucifix and sprinkling holy water?"

"Just keep Vivienne occupied and out of my way."

"You should have given that task to Constable Larkin. I doubt that a pack of howling werewolves could tear him from her side. I suppose I should be grateful that at least Julian's not in love with her, too." Portia's casual shrug couldn't quite hide the hurt that shadowed her eyes. "Of course, he's made it perfectly clear that he's not in love with me, either."

Caroline shook her head helplessly, wishing she had the power to untangle the chains that bound all of their hearts. "I don't believe you'll find the constable keeping company with Vivienne this afternoon. Which is why I need you to keep one eye on her until I return."

As Caroline brushed past her, Portia seized her arm. "Have a care, won't you, Caro? Even if the viscount doesn't turn out to be a vampire, he might still be dangerous."

For a place with so many secrets, Trevelyan Castle contained remarkably few locked doors. Caroline wandered its winding stairwells and flagstone corridors for what seemed like an eternity, feeling a bit like a princess in one of Portia's beloved fairy tales. But it remained to be seen whether this castle was enchanted or cursed. Or whether her invisible captor was prince or beast.

The castle was already bustling with servants seeking to prepare its myriad rooms for the influx of guests who would begin arriving on the morrow. Some of the viscount's guests would be staying at nearby inns, but many of them would be spending the night at the castle itself. Passing easily among the distracted servants, Caroline searched each floor with methodical precision, finding several chambers she and Portia had missed when they were looking for mirrors. After a futile search of the upper floors, she found herself standing outside the door of the portrait gallery.

She touched her fingertips to the knob, longing to slip inside and see if she still possessed the courage to stand toe-to-toe with that ruthless warrior who bore Kane's face.

She stole a glance over her shoulder at the lancet window at the far end of the corridor. Her time was running out. The daylight was waning; the moon would be rising soon. Turning her back on the portrait gallery, she lifted her skirts and hurried toward the stairs, her steps quickening along with her sense of urgency.

It wasn't that difficult to slip past the servants in the basement kitchen. They were already shouting orders and clanging pans as they peeled vegetables and baked bread for the extravagant supper that was to be served after the dancing tomorrow night. She flitted past an arched doorway, grimacing as she caught a glimpse of a fat copper kettle that had been situated beneath an iron hook to catch the draining blood from some unidentified haunch of meat.

She doubted she would find anything of significance off the labyrinth of rooms that comprised the kitchen, but she was running out of places to search. Stealing one last glance behind her to make sure she hadn't been spotted, she slipped down a narrow corridor, leaving the cheerful chaos behind.

The corridor had a sloping dirt floor and low oak ceiling beams. As she ducked beneath one of them, a cobweb tickled the back of her neck, making her shudder. If not for the rusty iron sconces spaced at uneven intervals along the pitted, water-stained walls, she might have sworn no one had traveled this particular path for centuries. The squat tallow candles cast more shadows than light. Caroline didn't even realize the corridor had taken a turn until she glanced behind her to discover its mouth had disappeared. There was only darkness behind and flickering shadows ahead.

Something went scuttling across the floor behind her, its sharp claws scrabbling at the dirt. Letting out an undignified yelp, Caroline sprang forward, running smack dab into a door. Frantic to escape what she feared was probably a large, hungry rat, she rattled the doorknob, only to discover that she had finally found what she had been looking for—a locked door.

Forgetting all about the rat, she twisted the knob again, testing it for any hint of vulnerability. What if she had inadvertently stumbled upon the door to the family crypt? Or to that fully equipped dungeon Kane had boasted about so glibly?

She was kneeling to press her eye to the keyhole when a voice as dry as grave dust came out of the darkness behind her. "May I assist you, miss?"

Caroline sprang to her feet and whirled around. Wilbury was standing just behind her, looking as if he'd just staggered out of the family crypt himself. His face was as drawn and pale as a death mask in the sallow light.

He wore a ring of iron keys at his waist, most of them rusty from disuse.

"Why, good afternoon, Wilbury," she said, dredging up a pleasant smile. "What fortuitous timing you have! I was just wishing someone would come along and unlock this door for me."

"Indeed."

His withering reply left her with no choice but to persist with her bluff. "Your—Your master sent me down here to fetch something for my sister."

"Did he now? And just why didn't he ring for it himself?"

"Because he knew I was coming this way and he didn't wish to trouble you." The butler's only reaction was to arch one snowy eyebrow. Caroline leaned closer and whispered, "It would behoove you to help your master please my sister, you know. She may someday be mistress of this castle."

Muttering something beneath his breath that sounded suspiciously like "Balderdash," Wilbury began to fumble his way through the keys. He finally located the one he sought and slipped it into the keyhole. Caroline pried one of the candles from its sconce, anticipation quickening her breath.

Wilbury swept open the door, his bones seemingly creaking nearly as loudly as the ancient hinges. Keenly aware of him lurking behind her, Caroline crept forward, holding the candle aloft. Instead of manacles and chains holding the rotting remains of naive young virgins, the modest chamber sported mundane wooden shelves that housed row upon row of jars, bottles, and canvas bags. Their carefully inscribed labels didn't read Wolfsbane or Eye of Newt, but Nutmeg, Ginger, and Thyme.

It seemed she had stumbled upon nothing more damning than a spice cellar.

"We respect the old ways here," Wilbury informed her. "In medieval times, it was customary for the castle's steward to keep the precious and costly spices under lock and key."

That had only been three or four hundred years ago. Wilbury had probably been a boy then, Caroline thought uncharitably.

"Ah, there it is!" Struggling to hide her disappointment, she swept the nearest bottle off the handiest shelf without bothering to read its label and tucked it into the pocket of her skirt. "I'm sure this will be just what my sister's tea requires."

As Caroline brushed past him, Wilbury said, "You might want to take her some extra sugar as well, miss."

Caroline turned, blinking brightly at him. "And why is that?"

He nodded toward her pocket. "It will mask the bitter taste of the laudanum."

Caroline sat on her bed, hugging her knees and watching the sun sink on the western horizon. Their last full day before the ball would soon be over and her search of Trevelyan Castle had left her with more questions than answers. Despite her bold intentions, she was no closer to learning the truth about Adrian Kane than she had been the first night she laid eyes on him.

"Adrian," she whispered, wondering what it would be like to have the right to address him by his Christian name. "Would you care for some more blood pudding, Adrian? Shall we plan a midnight supper for your birthday this year, Adrian? What would you like to name our first son, Adrian?"

Beset by an aching stab of loneliness, Caroline rested her cheek on her knee and watched the shadows of twilight creep toward her balcony doors. Perhaps she would tempt fate tonight and leave them unbolted.

Caroline stiffened. She lifted her head, her gaze sharpening on the balcony doors. She was remembering a furtive footfall, a shadow flitting across the night sky, a tendril of mist creeping out of the moonlight. Slipping off the bed, she went gliding toward the doors, her steps as measured as if she'd fallen into some sort of hypnotic trance.

When he appeared outside the doors her first night at the castle, Kane had claimed that he couldn't sleep. That he had forsaken his bed and come outside for a smoke and a stroll. Then he vanished as abruptly as he had appeared.

Throwing open the doors, Caroline stepped out onto the balcony. The cool evening air caressed her bare arms beneath the short, puffed sleeves of her cambric gown, raising a thin layer of gooseflesh. In all of her fruitless wanderings that afternoon, why had it never occurred to her to simply retrace his steps?

She glanced at the horizon. She had little time to lose. The sun had already dimmed to a hazy glow, edging the bottom of the gathering clouds in gilt.

Caroline slipped along the battlements of the castle, hugging the curve of the tower wall so she wouldn't be spotted by anyone who might be lurking on the grounds below. She could only pray that Portia was still keeping Vivienne occupied.

On the side of the tower already cast in twilight, she finally found what she was looking for—a winding set of stone stairs. She followed them down one flight, where they connected to a narrow footbridge that spanned the gap between the north and south towers. As she hastened across the bridge, the rising wind lashed at her thin skirt, making her regret leaving her cloak behind.

On the night she arrived, Wilbury had informed her that his master had been very explicit in his instructions: *Miss Caroline Cabot is to be housed in the north tower*. As Caroline reached the other side of the bridge and began to climb the steps to the south tower, she tried not to think about the dark implications of the butler's words. Tried not to think about how easy it would be for the occupants of the two towers to conduct a torrid liaison with no one else in the castle the wiser. Kane's request had probably been utterly innocent. After all, she had witnessed the frantic exertions of the servants today. Perhaps at the time of their arrival, the north tower had been one of only a few chambers fit for habitation.

She soon found herself standing outside a pair of French doors nearly identical to her own. She cupped her hands around her face and tried to peer inside, but heavy drapes veiled the glass. She glanced over her shoulder. Although the sun hadn't completely finished its descent, the stars were already beginning to twinkle against the indigo palette of the eastern sky.

She couldn't afford to linger much longer. As she closed her icy fingers around the brass handle of the door, she wondered if Kane had heeded his own counsel and bolted his doors against the wind. If he had, she would have no choice but to go creeping back to her own bedchamber where she would spend one more night in an agony of uncertainty.

Mustering her foundering courage, she turned the handle and gave the door a gentle shove. It swung open without so much as a creak of protest, inviting her into the viscount's shadowy lair.

Fifteen

Caroline slipped into the tower's inner sanctum, easing the door shut behind her. Her heart felt as if it was pounding loud enough to wake the dead. She winced, wishing the unfortunate thought away.

She hesitated, waiting for her eyes to adjust to the gloom. Although plush velvet drapes had been drawn over every window, the chamber hadn't been abandoned to complete darkness. A single wax taper was burning low in an iron sconce fixed to the wall on the far side of the tower.

As the shadows slowly retreated, she found her gaze riveted by the piece of furniture that dominated the room. To her keen relief, it wasn't a closed coffin on a marble dais, but a towering mahogany four-poster, similar to her own but festooned with hangings of ruby silk. Those hangings were drawn, shrouding the bed in mystery.

She inched forward, nearly stumbling over the clawed foot of another piece of furniture situated near the foot of the bed. Its tall, slender form was also draped in silk. She was lifting a corner of the stuff, determined to peek beneath, when she heard the distinct rustle of something stirring behind the bed hangings.

She whirled around, her last secret hope that the bed might be empty dashed. Reaching into the pocket of her skirt, she curled her trembling fingers around the stake. Feeling as if her feet were mired in quicksand, she crept to the side of the bed closest to the candle. Her fingers gliding over the silk, she eased back the bed's curtain to expose its occupant.

Instead of lying neatly on his back with his arms folded over his chest in corpselike repose, Adrian Kane was sprawled on his stomach among the red silk sheets. The sleek silk had ridden dangerously low on his lean hips, exposing the sculpted planes of his back and shoulders and making it impossible to tell what he wore beneath the sheet—if anything.

Caroline jerked her wandering gaze back to his face, swallowing to combat the sudden dryness of her mouth.

He slept with his face turned toward the gentle glow of the candle, the generous sweep of his lashes brushing his cheeks. Since they were edged in gilt, Caroline had never before realized just how long and luxuriant they were. Sleep had erased the strain that so often furrowed his brow and eased the weight of responsibility he always seemed to carry on his broad shoulders. With his thick hair tousled and his lips slightly parted, she could almost catch a glimpse of the boy he had been.

As a decidedly mortal snore escaped those lips, Caroline shook her head, overcome by a swell of tenderness. She had come here to prove once and for all that he was simply a man. Yet all she had done was prove what a fool she was. There was nothing simple about him. Or her feelings for him.

He hadn't been deceiving her; she had been deceiving herself. She had insisted upon believing that he posed a threat to her sister when the only danger had been to her own heart. As long as she could cling to the ridiculous notion that he might be a vampire, she didn't have to let him go.

Caroline closed her eyes for a moment, struggling to compose herself. When she opened them, they were still stinging, but dry.

She knew she should go, but she couldn't move. She

might never again have the chance to draw near to him in the dark, to watch him sleep and to wonder, for one selfish moment, if he was dreaming of her.

One touch.

That was all she would allow herself. Then she would creep away as silently as she'd come and leave him to his dreams. She would return to her chamber and gather all of her strength so that when he came knocking at her door to ask for Vivienne's hand, she would be able to welcome him as the brother he would soon become.

Caroline stretched out her hand, keenly aware that this was no portrait, but flesh and blood, seething with heat and strength and life.

One second her fingertips were grazing the warm golden satin of his back, the next she was flat on *her* back on the feather tick, both of her wrists manacled above her head in one of his hands, his other hand wrapped around the slender column of her throat.

She blinked up at him, mesmerized by the feral glitter of his eyes. Every breath was a struggle, but she couldn't tell if that was from being imprisoned beneath his weight or from inhaling the intoxicating aroma of his sleep-warmed flesh. Added to the usual mix of sandalwood and bay rum was a new and even more potent spice—danger.

Recognition slowly dawned in his eyes, leaving them wary and heavy-lidded. His grip on her wrists and her throat softened, yet still he made no move to free her.

She wasn't sure she could have fled if he had. A paralyzing languor seemed to have claimed her limbs, slowing time to a waltz measured by each throbbing beat of her heart. She was keenly aware of the weight of him, the heat of him, the well-muscled length of him pinning her to the mattress. Even in her innocence, Caroline recognized that the hand at her throat was by no means the greatest threat to her.

"Don't," she whispered as she watched his gaze drift to her lips. She couldn't speak, couldn't think, couldn't draw in a single shuddering breath that wasn't filled with the musky heat of his desire. "Please don't . . ."

Even as she choked out the words, she knew it was too late. Knew it had been too late from the first moment their eyes had met, their lips had touched.

His hand slid from her throat to her cheek. He seized her gaze with his own, holding it captive as surely as the rest of her. The callused pad of his thumb played over the softness of her lips, exploring their yielding contours with a tenderness that threatened to undo her.

Then his head was there, blocking out the last of the candlelight as he brought his mouth down on hers. His lips moved over hers, gently but firmly dragging them apart, rendering her utterly vulnerable to the smoky heat of his tongue sweeping through her mouth, claiming both it and her heart for his own. He used that tongue to woo, to cajole, to make wordless promises he could never hope to keep.

Caroline couldn't have said how her hands got free. She only knew that suddenly they were tangling in his hair, curling around his nape, drawing him even deeper into the kiss, into her.

Too late, she realized his hand was free as well. Free to sift through the silk of her hair until it slipped from its pins to glide over his fingers. Free to skate down her satiny skin to the delicate hollow at the base of her throat. Free to graze the gentle swell of her breast through the thin cambric of her bodice. She wasn't prepared for the erotic shock of his warm fingers delving beneath the fabric of both bodice and corset, bringing them skin-to-skin. His hand curled around her breast, his thumb flicking back and forth over her quickening nipple with exquisite care, sending tiny shockwaves of pleasure deep into her womb. Although she was the one dying from delight, he groaned as if in mortal agony.

For six years she had denied herself every pleasure. Now she felt as if she was drowning in it, sinking deeper into its velvety embrace with each sigh, each kiss, each deft stroke of his fingertips against her flesh. When his hand skated lower, skimming over the curve of her belly, tracing the elegant arch of her hipbone, she simply tipped her head back, drinking even more deeply of the forbidden nectar he was offering her.

He tasted like warm sugar biscuits on a snowy Christmas morning; chilled strawberries and cream on a sultry summer afternoon; steaming apple cider on a crisp autumn evening. For the first time since she'd lost her parents, it was as if all of the empty places inside of her were being filled and she would never have to go to bed hungry again.

As if determined to fill her everywhere, he parted her limp thighs with his knee, bringing it to bear against the warm hollow between her legs with just enough pressure to make her gasp into his mouth and arch off the bed. She didn't know what he was doing to her. She only knew that she wanted more of it.

More of him.

When he dragged his mouth from hers, she was the one to moan in protest. But her moans melted to sighs as he pressed feather-soft kisses against the corner of her mouth, the delicate curve of her jaw, the downy skin beneath her ear.

She arched her neck, unable to resist the softness of his lips searching for the pulse in her throat. A pulse thundering out of control, fluttering as if it were a baby bird cupped in the palm of his hand.

Lost in a daze of delight, she felt the scrape of his teeth an instant before he gave the tender flesh a sharp nip.

"Ow!" Her eyes flew open. Clapping a hand to her stinging throat, she glared up at him in wide-eyed indignation. "You bit me!"

He glared right back at her, his eyes glittering like exotic gemstones in the candlelight. "And why not? That's what you expected me to do, isn't it?" He held up the stake he had pilfered from the pocket of her skirt while she had been drifting mindlessly on a sea of pleasure. "If not, you wouldn't have brought *this* to my bed."

Caroline swallowed hard, her guilty gaze darting from the stake to his face. "I don't suppose you'd believe that I was going to catch up on some needlework?"

"What were you going to do? Embroider 'Bless Our Elves' over my heart?" Snorting in derision, he tossed the stake on her chest and rolled off of her. Jerking open the silk hangings, he slipped out of the bed.

Caroline sat up, her jaw dropping as she realized what he'd been wearing beneath the sheet.

Not a stitch.

From behind, he resembled Michelangelo's *David* brought to glorious life, every sinew and muscle sculpted with loving hands by a master artist. He padded across the room with such un-self-conscious masculine grace that she forgot to look away until after he'd stepped behind a gilded dressing screen.

Flushing to the tips of her toes, she ducked her head. "You can hardly blame me for believing the worst of you. It's not as if you've ever tried to deny those ugly things the gossips say about you behind your back."

His clipped voice came from behind the screen. "I thought you were the one who didn't believe in heeding idle gossip."

"I have no choice but to heed it as long as you're courting my sister!"

He reappeared, having hastily dragged on a pair of charcoal-colored breeches. Her gaze was drawn to his hands as he struggled to secure the buttons of the front flap. Despite their deftness, he seemed to be having an undue amount of difficulty. "Until tonight, had I ever given you any reason to believe that my intentions toward your sister were anything less than honorable?"

Yes! Caroline wanted to cry. *When you kissed me in Vauxhall Gardens as if I was the only woman you would ever love.* But she held her tongue. Because he hadn't kissed her. She had kissed him. "Your intentions toward my sister might be above reproach, but your intentions toward me just now were hardly innocent."

He jerked on a rumpled shirt and began to fasten its cloth-covered buttons. "You would have received the same treatment from any man had you gone tumbling into his bed with such reckless abandon when he was half asleep and fully aroused."

Caroline's flush deepened, but Kane didn't see it. For the first time since they'd met, his direct gaze had faltered. He couldn't seem to bring himself to look at her.

Beginning to suspect that he was lying not only to her, but to himself as well, she retorted, "I didn't tumble into your bed. I was tossed."

"And just what was I supposed to do? It's not every night that a woman sneaks into my bedchamber fully prepared to murder me in my sleep." Shaking his head, he raked a hand through his already disheveled hair. "What in God's name were you thinking? If one of the servants had seen you slip in here, your reputation would have been destroyed."

"I made sure that no one saw me," she told him.

"Then you're even more foolish than I thought." His voice lowered to a dangerous note as he moved toward the bed with the inexorable grace of some large jungle cat.

Caroline scrambled to her feet to face him, her hair slipping half out of its pins, but her chin held high. Following the mocking direction of his gaze, she slipped the stake back into the pocket of her skirt. "I didn't come here tonight to murder you. I came here to find out the truth once and for all. And I'm not going anywhere until I get it." She took a deep breath, determined not to squeak when she finally said the words out loud. "Are you or are you not a vampire?"

She startled him into stopping a scant foot away from her. He cocked his head to the side to study her. "You never cease to surprise me. At our first meeting, I would have sworn you were far too practical to believe in such creatures."

She shrugged. "Nobody denies the existence of Vlad the Impaler or Elizabeth Bathory, the notorious Countess of Transylvania who used to hang the village virgins upside down and slit their throats so she could drink their blood to maintain her eternal youth."

The silky note in his voice deepened. "I can assure you, Miss Cabot, that I have far more enjoyable uses for virgins."

Although her fair coloring betrayed her with another blush, she chose to ignore the deliberate taunt. "You can't deny that you have the instincts of a born killer. You had me flat on my back with your hand at my throat before I could so much as draw breath to scream."

Arching one eyebrow, he said, "As I recall, you weren't struggling very hard." He reached to tuck a wayward strand of hair behind her ear. "One would have almost sworn that escape was the last thing on your mind."

The barest brush of his fingertips against the sensitive skin behind her ear made her shiver with longing.

He drew his hand back as if he, too, was shaken by the contact. "So is that what you believe I am? A 'born killer'?"

"I don't know what you are," she confessed, her voice beginning to tremble with emotion. "I only know that from the first moment I laid eyes on you, I could think of nothing—and no one—else. I know that every time you walk into a room, I feel like my corset stays are too tight and I can't breathe. I know that I couldn't possibly be having such shameful thoughts and dreams about a man who is practically my sister's betrothed if he hadn't cast some sort of wicked spell on me!"

"The first time we met, you told me that only the 'weak-willed' were in danger of succumbing to my bidding."

A despairing laugh escaped her. "Then my will must be far weaker than I realized."

"If that's true, then what would happen at this very moment if I commanded you to come into my arms?" He moved close enough for her to feel the raw heat radiating from his body, smell the clean masculine musk of his skin, yet still he did not touch her. "Would you be able to resist if I ordered you to put your hands on me? To kiss me?" His voice softened on a husky note. "To love me?"

Caroline tried to turn away from him, but Kane caught her by the shoulders, forcing her to meet his smoldering gaze. "What if you're right, Caroline? What if I *have* cast a spell on you? What if it's the most inescapable enchantment of all? What if you're falling in love with me?"

She shook her head in mute denial, horrified that he had guessed her dark secret. No amount of holy water could wash away such a stain. There was no cure, no remedy, no spell to break. She might as well drive a stake through her own treacherous heart. "You insult me, my lord. I would never do such a thing to Vivienne. I'm not that sort of woman."

His grip on her shoulders softened to something dangerously near a caress. "Don't you think I know what sort of woman you are? You're the sort of woman who would give up every one of your own dreams just to make one of your sisters' dreams come true. But perhaps your heart isn't as scrupulous and self-sacrificing as the rest of you. It might selfishly insist upon having its own way even if you don't."

She gazed up at him, fighting back tears. "Then I suppose it deserves to be broken, doesn't it?"

"Not by a man like me," Kane muttered.

His expression grim, he retrieved a voluminous cloak from the back of a nearby chair and wrapped it around her shoulders.

"Where are you taking me?" she demanded as he gripped her upper arm through the cloak and urged her toward the French doors.

"I'm taking you back to your bedchamber. Unless, of

course, you'd rather I ring for one of the servants to escort you?"

Without waiting for her reply, he yanked open the French doors and swept her into the night. The wind had risen another notch, sending ghostly wisps of clouds skating across the silvery arc of the rising moon.

"I'll have you know that I won't be dismissed this easily," Caroline insisted even as he hastened her down the steps and onto the bridge. Keenly aware of the dizzying height they were crossing, she stumbled along beside him, already growing breathless from the effort of keeping pace with his long strides. "If you're not a vampire, I want to know why you sleep all day and refuse to show yourself in the sunlight. I want to know why your ancestors all look *exactly* like you. I want to know why you're willing to let society— and me—believe the worst of you instead of defending yourself against their accusations. And I want to know why there isn't a single mirror in this entire blasted castle!"

Biting off a blistering oath, Kane swung her around to face him. He loomed over her, his broad shoulders framed by the swirling clouds, his teeth bared. The moonlight gilded the planes of his face, making him look leaner and even more dangerous.

Before she could protest, his hand had plunged into her pocket and emerged with the stake. Wrapping his other arm around her waist to prevent her escape, he thrust the stake into her hand and forced her fingers closed around its smooth length. Although she struggled against him, it took very little effort for him to turn the primitive weapon and bring the point of it to bear against his chest.

"If you honestly believe I'm some sort of monster," he rasped, his gaze as fierce as she had ever seen it, "then go ahead and drive it home. My heart hasn't been my own from the first moment I laid eyes on you, so you might as well finish the job."

Caroline blinked up at him, utterly dumbfounded by his

confession. In that moment, she didn't care if he was man or monster. She only wanted him to be hers. No longer able to hide the helpless yearning in her eyes, she reached up and gently stroked the rigid curve of his jaw. His fingers slowly uncurled, as did hers, sending the stake clattering to the stone.

Groaning his surrender, he dragged her against him, taking her mouth in a kiss as dark and sweet as death itself. Despite the hair whipping at her face and the wild flapping of the cloak in the wind, it was as if the two of them were somehow frozen in time. For Caroline, there was no past or future. No Vivienne and no regrets. There was only this moment, this man, this kiss.

A breathless eternity later, he tore his mouth from hers and gazed deep into her eyes. He shook his head, looking even more powerless than she felt. "Whatever am I going to do with you, my darling Miss Cabot?"

"Whatever you like, my lord," she murmured dreamily, feeling the fervent touch of his lips in her hair as she rested her cheek against his chest.

"Adrian," he whispered, wrapping his arms around her.

"Adrian," she sighed.

She was so dazed with delight that it took her a moment to realize that the rhythmic shudder beneath her cheek was the pounding of his heart. Shooting him a startled glance, she tugged open his shirt and pressed her palm against the lightly furred warmth of his chest. His heart's cadence nearly doubled beneath that chaste touch. Like the rest of him, his heart was warm, coursing with life, and all too mortal.

"I always knew you weren't as heartless as you wanted me to believe you were," she murmured, slanting him a knowing glance.

"I suppose my secret is out, then. I'm not a vampire."

"Of course you're not." She laughed up at him, going almost dizzy with relief. "Because there are no such things! I can't believe I let myself be swayed by Portia's ridiculous fancies. You must think me a complete and utter cake-wit. I should have never—"

Adrian's arms tightened around her, halting her in mid-prattle. He gazed down at her, his eyes curiously somber. "I'm not a vampire, sweetheart. I'm a vampire hunter."

Sixteen

Caroline blinked up at Adrian, reminding him of a small befuddled owl. "You're not a vampire," she slowly repeated.

"That's right."

"You're a vampire hunter."

Adrian nodded.

"Someone who hunts vampires."

He nodded again.

"And kills them."

"Not precisely. Because they're already the living dead," he gently explained. "What I do is destroy them and send the soulless husks of their bodies to hell so that they can't do any more harm."

Even as she carefully extracted herself from his arms and began to back toward the middle of the bridge, Caroline nodded, as if what he was saying made perfect sense to her. "So that's why you sleep during the day. So you can go out hunting vampires at night."

"I'm afraid they're not very fond of the sun."

He could almost see the elaborate cogs and wheels of her brain turning. "I don't suppose you happen to share any of their other characteristics. Like, oh say—immortality, for instance?"

He arched one eyebrow. "Is this about the portrait gallery again?"

She nodded.

He folded his arms over his chest, hard-pressed to remember the last time they'd felt so empty. "I wasn't lying to you about the strong family resemblance. My great-great-great-uncle once sired a child on his wife's maid. He was able to deny that the babe was his until the day it was born with that telltale mole above its left eye."

"What happened then?" she asked, slowing, but still backing away.

"My great-great-great-aunt shot him. Fortunately for me and the rest of his descendants, she had poor aim and only managed to shoot him in the shin. He went on to sire fifteen more children, seven of those on my aunt. She was forced to shoot him twice more before he finally died in his bed at the ripe old age of ninety-two."

Caroline cocked her head to the side. "What about the mirrors? If you're a vampire hunter instead of a vampire, then why are you so averse to catching a glimpse of your reflection?"

Adrian blew out a stalling breath and ran a hand over his jaw. This was the question he had been dreading the most.

"If you must know, he got rid of the mirrors on my account," Julian drawled as he came sauntering out of the shadows behind her.

While Adrian bit off an oath, Caroline clapped a hand over her heart and whirled around to face his brother. "Because you're averse to catching a glimpse of *your* reflection?"

"No," Julian replied, taking another step toward her. "Because I no longer have one."

Caroline was silent for a long moment before quietly asking, "And I suppose you no longer have a soul either?"

Julian patted the pockets of his crisply tailored waistcoat, then shook his head ruefully. "Not on me, I'm afraid."

Caroline slowly turned back to Adrian, the warmth in her eyes chilling to frost. "Just how long did it take you and your brother to come up with this cruel little hoax? Did you think it would be great fun to dupe the gullible country girl? Did you plan the whole thing over a nice bottle of port and some fine cigars?" She lifted her chin, but couldn't quite hide its trembling. "It seems I was wrong about you after all, my lord. You're every bit as heartless as you wanted me to believe you were."

Adrian took a helpless step toward her. "If you'll just listen to me, Caroline—"

"Oh, no," she said, shaking her head. "I believe I've heard quite enough for one night. Now if the two of you are done making sport at my expense, I believe I'll return to my chamber."

Her slender shoulders rigid beneath Adrian's cloak, Caroline started toward the end of the bridge blocked by Julian.

Too late, Adrian realized what his brother was going to do.

As Caroline approached him, an inhuman growl rose from Julian's throat. He bared his teeth, the pools of darkness in his eyes swelling to engulf the whites.

Caroline gasped and went stumbling backward. Julian stalked her step for step, moonlight gleaming off the lethal curves of his fangs. He didn't relent until she had backed right into Adrian's arms.

Adrian gathered her trembling body against his and glared at his brother over her head. "Damn it all, Julian! That wasn't very sporting of you."

Julian shrugged, his angelic countenance restored to the contrite expression that had always allowed him to wiggle out of even the worst mischief. "Not sporting perhaps, but quite efficient."

Adrian had to admit it was no great sacrifice to have Caroline back in his arms. Still glaring daggers at Julian, he stroked the softness of her hair. "It's all right, sweetheart. I won't let the nasty boy hurt you."

As Caroline continued to gawk at him in open-mouthed astonishment, Julian gave her the sort of smile one might give a little girl after chucking her under the chin and assuring her that the monster beneath the bed has been safely vanquished. "There's no need for you to cower in terror, Miss Cabot. You may be a delectable morsel, but unlike my dear brother here, I'm able to control my appetites."

As he watched his brother's indolent gaze take in every damning detail of their embrace, including Caroline's tumbled hair and kiss-ripened lips, Adrian said, "I know what you're thinking, but this isn't what I wanted."

"Oh, for pity's sake, don't!" Julian snapped. "You can lie to her. You can even lie to yourself if you want. But don't lie to me. She is *exactly* what you wanted."

"Do it again," Caroline suddenly commanded. "That thing you did. With the eyes. And the . . ." Feeling a fresh shudder ripple through her, Adrian gently rubbed the small of her back. ". . . the teeth."

"I don't usually do encores, but for you . . ." Julian looked to his brother for approval.

Although he knew he would probably have cause to regret it later, Adrian sighed and nodded.

This time there could be no blaming Julian's transformation on a hoax or a trick of the moonlight. As the darkness swept through his eyes, turning him into something both less and more than human, it was all Adrian could do not to recoil. Then, just as quickly, the darkness subsided and his little brother was standing there before them.

"Oh, dear Lord, it's true, isn't it? He really is a vampire," Caroline breathed. Although she had once assured Adrian she wasn't the sort of female to swoon in his arms, she appeared to be in danger of doing just that.

"I'm afraid so," he murmured, holding her steady until she stopped swaying on her feet.

She couldn't seem to tear her gaze away from Julian. "Did . . . Did you . . . ?" Robbed of coherence, she made little flapping motions with her hands. ". . . turn yourself into a bat and fly up here?"

Julian recoiled. "Good Lord, woman, have you been listening to Portia's drivel again? You really should monitor that child's reading habits more carefully. If she keeps stuffing her head with Dr. Polidori's nonsense, she'll be seeing vampires behind every drape and potted palm. I may very well sleep in a coffin, but I can assure you that I've never—"

"You actually sleep in a coffin?" Caroline blurted out, curiosity beginning to overcome her shock.

Adrian rolled his eyes. "You'll have to forgive my brother. He always did have a flair for the dramatic, even *before* he became a vampire."

"I don't understand," Caroline whispered, turning to gaze up into Adrian's face. "If Julian is the vampire, then why do you let everyone believe it's you?"

"It's easier that way," Adrian explained. "They may suspect me, but they can never prove anything."

Julian spread his arms in an eloquent shrug. "And as long as I scorn the sun, dress all in black, and spout abominable poetry about blood and death at every musicale and midnight supper, how can anyone possibly take me seriously?"

Her wary gaze returned to him. "What about the mysterious disappearances in Charing Cross? Were you responsible for those?"

"No," Adrian said. "I was." As Caroline's startled gaze whipped back to him, he added, "They were vampires, darling. Every last one of them."

"So you destroyed them," she said, echoing his earlier words. "And sent the soulless husks of their bodies to hell."

"Whoa there!" Julian exclaimed. "There's no need to be so cavalier about the fate of the soulless."

"Julian isn't like the others," Adrian assured her. "Never once has he drunk from another human being."

"Only because my big brother here has spent a small fortune in butcher shops over the past five years."

Although she made a valiant effort, Caroline could not quite hide her grimace of distaste.

Julian blew out a disgusted sigh. "When you women are all swooning over the romance of the vampire, you never stop to think about the little inconveniences like blood breath, do you?"

"Five years," Caroline repeated, her eyes still dazed. "That would have been around the time your mother went abroad and Julian came to stay with you at Oxford."

Adrian nodded. "I told you he fell in with an unsavory pack of young bloods. Unfortunately, they were led by a man who wished to do me grave harm."

"Duvalier," Caroline whispered before either of them could.

The two men exchanged a startled glance before snarling in unison, "*Larkin.*"

"But I thought Duvalier was your friend," Caroline said.

"So did I," Adrian said, feeling his face darken with old memories, old regrets. "I didn't realize until it was too late that he'd always been secretly jealous of me."

"Only because you were stronger, smarter, richer, better looking, a more skillful boxer, more well-respected, and far more popular with the ladies." Julian scowled at him. "Now that I look back on it, you *were* fairly intolerable."

Adrian shot him a quelling glance. "Victor managed to hide his bitterness toward me until I inadvertently stole his most treasured *possession.*"

"That wouldn't have been Eloisa Markham's heart by any chance, would it?" Caroline asked as she gently but firmly extracted herself from his arms.

Although he knew he wasn't being fair, Adrian felt his temper begin to rise. "Is there anything the good constable didn't tell you when he was whispering sweet nothings in your ear?"

Putting a few feet between them, Caroline met his challenging gaze with one of her own. "He didn't tell me what happened to Eloisa."

Adrian turned away from her, resting his hands on the ancient stone parapet that separated the bridge from the night. A cool breeze laced with the aroma of night-blooming jasmine ruffled his hair. "After Eloisa broke his heart, Victor changed. He began to drink to excess and to frequent one of the more sordid clubs in Whitechapel. Larkin and I had no idea it was a gambling *hell* in every sense of the word."

"A nest of vampires," Julian said softly.

Adrian continued. "Since I had taken the one thing he wanted, he decided to seize the one thing he believed I could never have—immortality. He became one of them. He willingly surrendered his soul to those monsters so that he would have the power to destroy me and everyone I loved." Adrian turned back to face Caroline, refusing to shy away from his own complicity in what followed. "When I ordered Julian to stop following me around like a pup, Victor was waiting. He took Julian under his wing and treated him as an equal. He even took him to the gambling club. When Julian came to me and tried to tell me that there were vampires in London and Victor might very well be one of them, I ruffled his hair and accused him of having an overactive imagination."

He could tell from Caroline's almost imperceptible flinch that his words had struck a raw nerve.

"Eloisa and Julian vanished the very next day. I didn't know where to turn, so I went to the club, believing in my naiveté that Victor might be able to help me find them. The club was deserted. He and his *companions* had already fled. But Eloisa . . ." Adrian closed his eyes, still haunted by the sight of that pale, slender throat streaming twin ribbons of red, those beautiful blue eyes frozen forever in a vacant stare. "I never dreamed he would destroy something he had loved so much." He opened his eyes to meet Caroline's stricken gaze. "I was too late to save Eloisa, but I found Julian curled up in the corner, panting and clutching at his throat. When I reached for him, he growled at me like some sort of wild thing. Victor had murdered Eloisa in cold blood, but he had decided it would be a more fitting punishment if he turned my brother into the very thing he knew I would despise the most."

"How?" Caroline asked, looking as heartsick as Adrian had felt in that moment.

Julian gazed at the distant horizon, the moon etching the purity of his profile in its lambent light. "In that very moment when my heart stopped beating, he bit me again. He ripped the soul right out of me. I've often thought that Eloisa was the lucky one. When she died, her soul was set free."

"Why didn't the police ever find her body?"

Adrian stole an awkward look at Julian. "At the time I had no way of knowing if Eloisa was going to *stay* dead or if she was going to turn into . . . something else. So after I confined Julian in the carriage, I went back into the club and torched the drapes." His eyes stung with the ghost of soot and tears. "I stood on the walk and watched the cursed place burn to the ground, not realizing until it was too late that I had just destroyed all evidence of Duvalier's guilt and my own innocence."

Caroline shook her head helplessly. "Why didn't you confide in Larkin? He was your dearest friend. Wouldn't he have helped you?"

"I couldn't risk it. I was terrified that if anyone else found out what had happened to Julian, they would take him away from me . . . or destroy him."

Settling back on the parapet and folding his arms over his chest, Julian surveyed him with wry affection. "I would have destroyed myself in those early days if not for you." He shifted his gaze to Caroline. "He had to keep me locked away and restrained for nearly a month. I fought him. I scratched him. I tried to bite him. I would have ripped his throat out if I could have broken out of my chains. But the stubborn fool refused to give up on me. He brought me the sustenance I needed to survive and spent hours locked in that attic with me, shouting until he was hoarse, reminding me of who I was—*who I had been*—until I could find some slender thread of my humanity to hold on to. And he's been reminding me every day since then without fail."

Adrian glanced down to find Caroline gazing up at him, her gray eyes misty with tears. "Don't look at me that way," he warned. "I may not be the villain you believed me to be, but I can assure you that I'm no hero."

"How can you say that when you've sacrificed so much to save your brother?"

"Because I haven't saved him," he replied grimly. "Not yet."

"Adrian hasn't just been hunting vampires for the past five years," Julian said. "He's been studying their lore as well. He was the one who discovered that there may be a way to restore my soul."

"How is that possible?" Caroline asked.

Julian's eyes glittered with excitement. "If I destroy the vampire who sired me and retrieve what he stole from me, I can live again. We have to find and capture Duvalier, then *I* have to be the one to drain him dry."

"Drain him dry?" Caroline swallowed. "Does that mean what I think it does?"

Julian nodded. "I'm afraid I'll have to give up my fastidious eating habits for at least one meal."

"But what if someone else destroys him first? Will your soul be lost forever?"

Adrian exchanged a look with his brother before saying, "Not necessarily. But it would make things extraordinarily more difficult because Julian's soul and all the souls that Duvalier has stolen in the past five years would revert back to the vampire who sired Duvalier, only making *him* more powerful. And although we have a few prospects, we're not entirely certain who that was."

Caroline gave her head a little shake, plainly still struggling to sift through everything they were telling her. "So vampires aren't just creatures who drink blood to survive. They have no souls of their own, but they hoard the souls of those they convert into their own kind."

"That's right," Adrian confirmed. "They feed on them and grow stronger with every soul they steal."

Wrapping her arms around herself, Caroline hugged back a shiver. "So Duvalier has been growing more powerful all these years."

"More powerful, but not invincible," Adrian said grimly. "We've spent the last five years tracking the bastard all over the world—Rome, Paris, Istanbul, the Carpathians. We've kept him on the run, but he's always managed to stay one step ahead of us. Until now."

"Now?" Caroline echoed. "Why now?"

Adrian reached for Caroline, no longer able to resist putting his hands on her. Especially since it might be for the last time. He cupped her face in his hands, his thumbs tenderly stroking the creamy satin of her cheeks. "Because we finally found something that he couldn't resist."

Julian propped one boot on the wall and began to buff at an invisible scuff with his handkerchief, looking as if he desperately wished he *could* turn into a bat and fly away.

Caroline shook her head in bewilderment. "But what could possibly tempt such a monster to . . . ?"

Adrian could only watch helplessly as her bewilderment began to harden into horror.

"Oh, God," she whispered, the blood visibly draining from her face. "It's Vivienne, isn't it? Aunt Marietta told me that the first time you saw her, you looked as if you'd seen a ghost. Larkin tried to warn me that she bore a striking resemblance to Eloisa, but I wouldn't listen. That's why you were coaching her on how to wear her hair. The cameo . . . the ballgown . . . they belonged to Eloisa, didn't they? Why, I'll wager she even wore white roses in her hair and played the harp, didn't she?"

"Like an angel," Adrian reluctantly confessed.

Clapping a hand over her mouth, Caroline wrenched herself away from him. This time when he reached for her, she recoiled violently from his touch. "Dear Lord," she breathed, backing away from him. "You just wanted to use my sister for bait. You never cared for her at all."

"Of course I care for her! She's a very dear girl!"

"Dear enough to lure that monster out of hiding for you? Dear enough to be led like a lamb to the slaughter?" Caroline's voice rose, cracking on a hoarse note. "You gave her a dead girl's dress! Did you intend for it to become her shroud?"

Adrian shook his head, desperate to erase the anguish from Caroline's eyes. "I swear to you on my life that I would never let any harm come to her. I wouldn't have approached her at all if I didn't believe I was powerful enough to protect her."

"The same way you protected Eloisa?"

Adrian closed his eyes briefly. "I'm much stronger now than I was then. I've spent every day since she died honing my skills, both physical and mental. Even then, if I'd have realized sooner that she was in mortal danger, I might have been able to save her."

"But you didn't save her, did you?"

Adrian had no defense against that blow. Caroline whirled around and started back across the bridge, her fists clenched with determination. This time Julian made no move to stop her.

"Where are you going?" Adrian called after her.

"To tell Vivienne all about your ugly little scheme."

"Are you going to tell her about us as well?"

Caroline froze in mid-stride. If not for the wind stirring the folds of his cloak and sifting its fingers through the moonlit silk of her hair, Adrian might have believed she'd been turned to stone.

She slowly turned to face him. It wasn't the contempt in her eyes that cut the deepest. It was the longing, the regret. Her voice was soft, yet as clear as crystal. "Just when I was starting to believe that you weren't a monster, you had to go and prove me wrong."

Although he wanted nothing more than to go after her, to drag her into his arms and beg her to understand, Adrian could only stand and watch as Caroline walked off the bridge, taking what was left of his battered heart with her.

* * *

Caroline slipped silently into her sisters' chamber. After hours of weeping, her tears had finally dried up, leaving her ravaged face feeling as numb as her heart.

She had expected to find her sisters nestled in their respective bedchambers, but they had both fallen asleep in the sitting room. Portia was curled up in an overstuffed wing chair, her nightcap sliding down over one eye, while Vivienne was sprawled on the chaise in front of the hearth, her cheek pillowed on her folded hands and a faded quilt tucked around her. The waning fire cast a cozy glow over their sleep-flushed faces. Judging from the pair of half-empty tea-cups and the china plate littered with biscuit crumbs resting on the hearth, Portia had made good on her promise to keep Vivienne occupied for the evening.

Caroline was still reeling from learning that Julian was a vampire and Adrian was a vampire hunter. But as shocking as those disclosures had been, they couldn't compare to the most astonishing revelation of all: Adrian didn't want Vivienne—he wanted her.

For years she'd been stuck playing the prince in the theatricals they put on for their parents just because she was older and taller than her sisters. Now she'd finally found a man willing to cast her in the role of princess only to make the bitter discovery that there would be no happy ending for the two of them.

Adrian had proved himself to be as ruthless as Duvalier. Duvalier might steal souls, but Adrian had slipped past all of her well-honed defenses to steal her heart. She had to close her eyes against a wave of yearning as she remembered those moments in his arms, in his bed—the only ones she would ever know.

She drifted deeper into the room, her slippers whispering over the Aubusson carpet. Like an honored guest at a tea party, the box containing the ball gown had been left open and propped in a sitting position on the damask-draped sofa, where it could best be admired. Just a few short hours ago she had been as besotted with its beauty as her sisters. Now the mere thought of it touching Vivienne's skin made her want to shudder. If the dress was no more than a shroud, then the box was a coffin, ready to be nailed shut with all of her dreams inside.

Yet even now, something about the gown's radiance still proved irresistible. Caroline reluctantly trailed her fingertips over the shimmering tulle, wondering about the girl who had once worn it. Had her heartbeat quickened every time Adrian walked into a room? Had she ached with longing every time he gave her one of his lazy smiles? Had she believed he would rush in and rescue her up until that very moment when she met her unthinkable fate at the hands of a man she had once trusted but never loved?

Caroline withdrew her hand from the gown, turning back to her sisters. It seemed only yesterday that they had been little girls, all scraped knees and flyaway curls. Now they teetered on the verge of being women grown, yet still their lush lips curved into wistful half smiles as they dreamed of exquisite gowns and masquerade balls and handsome princes who would rescue them from every peril.

She reached for Vivienne's shoulder, determined to shake her from those dreams and take her away from this place before they turned into nightmares. But something stilled her hand.

She could still see Adrian standing on that bridge, the wind blowing through his hair. Even though he wasn't a man who begged, she had seen the entreaty in his eyes. She thought of the years he'd spent hunting Duvalier and other monsters like him, the enormity of the sacrifices he'd made to protect his brother's secret. While other men of his age and station in life were dancing until dawn, gambling away their fortunes, and seducing married women, he'd spent the last five years exiled from his own kind, living in the shadows just like the beasts he hunted.

What would she do if their situations were reversed? She gazed at Portia as she gently stroked Vivienne's hair. To what lengths would she go to spare her sisters' lives? To save their very souls?

She had believed her tears were all dried up, but she'd been wrong. She could feel them stinging her eyes as she realized exactly what she would do.

Anything.

Anything at all.

Seventeen

 "What do you mean I can't go to the ball? How could you be so cruel?"

Caroline gazed down at Portia, steeling herself against the wounded outrage in her sister's eyes. It felt doubly cruel to deliver this blow while standing in the middle of Portia's bedchamber surrounded by a colorful swirl of petticoats, ribbons, and lace. Garbed only in her chemise and pantalettes, and with her dark hair bound up in curling rags, Portia looked all of twelve years old. The open box of rice powder glimmering on the vanity might have been fairy dust, just waiting to transform an awkward young girl into a lovely young woman on the night of her very first ball.

"I'm not being cruel," Caroline replied. "I'm simply being practical. You've yet to be introduced at court, so you've never had a proper coming out. It simply wouldn't do for you to appear at a ball attended by some of the most illustrious members of the *ton* with your hair up and your hemline down."

"But I'm seventeen years old!" Portia wailed. "If I don't come out soon, it will be time for me to go back in again!" Her eyes narrowed to accusing slits. "And besides, *you've* never had a proper coming out and *you're* going to the ball."

"*I* have no choice. Your sister requires a chaperone."

Portia glanced frantically around the room, casting about

for some new argument to sway her. "You don't have to be afraid that I'll embarrass you. One of the maids helped Vivienne and I cobble together a perfectly respectable ball gown from my old Sunday frock." She swept the familiar blue-striped muslin off the back of a chair and held it against her chest for Caroline to admire, giving her a hopeful smile. "Isn't it lovely? We even stitched on a new sash and an extra layer of flounces to hide how much my bosom has grown in the past year. And just look at this!" She snatched a papier-mâché half-mask decorated with a pert pink nose and long feline whiskers from the vanity and held it up to her face. "Julian found it for me in one of the castle attics."

Caroline stiffened. She desperately wanted to believe that Julian had truly rejected his destiny, but as she remembered the darkness that had conquered his eyes and the glint of the moonlight on his fangs, she felt her trepidation rising.

Plucking the mask from Portia's hand, Caroline tossed it back to the vanity. "It's all quite lovely and I'm sure you'll have the chance to wear it one day very soon. But not tonight."

Her smile shifting to a stormy scowl, Portia pitched the dress on the bed in a careless heap. "I don't understand what's wrong with you. You haven't been yourself since you went looking for Lord Trevelyan yesterday. One minute you're convinced he might be the devil incarnate. The next you're telling me it was all some sort of silly mistake."

Caroline tugged a length of lace from the vanity and twined it around her finger, avoiding Portia's eyes. "What I told you was that the viscount and I had cleared up all of our misunderstandings. He's no vampire and I've decided that he'll make a perfectly fine husband."

"For Vivienne?" Portia folded her arms over her chest. "Or for you?"

Feeling her cheeks flood with color, Caroline jerked up her head to meet her sister's defiant gaze. She should have anticipated this. Despite the difference in their ages, she'd always been closer to Portia than Vivienne. Which made it doubly difficult to lie to her now.

"For Vivienne, of course, you silly little goose! I don't know why you have to indulge your imagination with all of these romantic fantasies when you know nothing of what really goes on between a man and a woman."

"If you don't let me go to the ball, I may never find out! Please, Caroline!" Portia clasped her hands together, her beseeching gaze winsome enough to melt a heart of stone. "When I told Julian how the three of us used to practice our dancing in the parlor at Edgeleaf, he promised to save me a waltz."

As she pictured her sister whirling around the ballroom in Julian's arms, his gleaming teeth only inches from the vulnerable curve of her throat, Caroline's trepidation swelled into full blown panic.

Before she could stop herself, she had grabbed Portia by the arm and given her a sharp shake. "You're not to set foot outside of this room tonight, young lady. If I find out you did, I'll send you back to Edgeleaf in the morning and you'll never lay eyes on Julian Kane again. Or any other man!"

Wrenching herself out of Caroline's grasp, Portia began to back away from her, tears swimming in her eyes. "Why, you're nothing but a selfish, hateful creature! You just want me to be a dried-up old spinster like you so you won't be left all alone when Vivienne marries the man you love!" Turning, she flung herself facedown on the bed and burst into heart-wrenching sobs.

Only yesterday, Portia's words might have cut her heart to the quick. But not today. Caroline knew her sister was as tenderhearted as she was impulsive. Portia would soon regret her unkind words, if she didn't already.

Although she wanted nothing more than to sink down on the bed and rub Portia's shoulders until their violent shuddering subsided, Caroline forced herself to turn and walk away.

"I'm sorry, pet," she whispered, gently drawing the bedchamber door shut behind her. "Perhaps someday you'll understand."

She flinched as something heavy that sounded suspiciously like a boot struck the closed door behind her, warning her that someday might not come as soon as she had hoped.

"A maid brought me your note. You wished to see me?"

Caroline slowly pivoted on the vanity bench to find Vivienne standing in the doorway of the tower, looking absolutely radiant in the viscount's gifts.

The maiden's blush of the ball gown's tulle skirt coaxed out the roses in her cheeks, while the cameo nestled between the swell of her breasts only served to emphasize their own ivory perfection. The everpresent white rose was tucked behind her right ear. On second glance, Caroline decided that her sister looked a bit *too* radiant. Her eyes were too bright, her cheeks too flushed. As Caroline watched, one of Vivienne's pale, slender hands darted nervously to her hair, smoothing the cascade of golden curls that had been gathered at the crown of her head with a pink satin ribbon and adorned with a plume of white ostrich feathers.

"Why aren't you dressed?" Vivienne squinted at Caroline's velvet dressing gown and braids in obvious bewilderment. "It's nearly time to go downstairs for the ball."

Caroline rose from the bench, feeling curiously calm as she glided toward her sister. "Don't worry. There's ample time. Is Portia still sulking?"

Vivienne sighed. "I haven't heard a peep from her room in over an hour. I do wish you'd relent and at least let her come down for one dance."

"Nothing would please me more, but it simply wouldn't be proper." *Or prudent*, Caroline thought grimly, once again picturing her little sister being swept around the ballroom in Julian's embrace. "Portia's young. I'm confident that she'll recover from this dire tragedy. By next week she probably won't even remember why she was so angry at me. Besides, this is supposed to be *your* special night, not hers."

Vivienne pressed a hand to her stomach. "That must be why I feel as if I've swallowed an entire flock of bats."

"I had the feeling you might be a little anxious, so I rang for something to soothe your nerves."

With her back to Vivienne, Caroline poured a cup of tea from the tray on the table next to the bed, her hand perfectly steady. Her fear that Vivienne might refuse her offer vanished as her sister snatched the cup from her hand and downed its contents in three grateful gulps.

"I can't imagine why I'm so jittery." Vivienne held out the cup in a plea for more. "It's not as if I've never attended a masquerade ball before."

"But you've never before received a proposal from a wealthy viscount." Caroline gently removed the cup from her sister's hand and replaced it on the tray next to the open bottle of laudanum.

It took Vivienne less than a minute to sink down on the edge of the bed, a glazed expression slowly replacing the feverish glitter in her eyes.

She startled Caroline by seizing her hand and tugging her down on the bed next to her. "Do you think you'll ever be able to forgive me, Caro?" Her lush lower lip began to tremble as she searched Caroline's face.

"For what?" Caroline asked, baffled by her sister's plea. Especially when she should be the one begging for forgiveness.

"For *this*!" Vivienne's hand fluttered over the shimmering tulle of her skirt. "While I was in London, living the life that should have been yours, you were stuck at Edgeleaf, sneaking extra potatoes onto Portia's plate and trying to squeeze a shilling out of two halfpennies. I stole Aunt Marietta's affection. I stole your debut. I stole all of the pretty gowns and slippers Mama had made for you. Why, if you'd have gone to London in my place, the viscount might be proposing to you tonight!"

For a painful instant Caroline couldn't breathe, much less respond. "There now, dear," she finally managed to murmur. "You needn't trouble your pretty head about any of that right now."

Vivienne rested that head against Caroline's shoulder, her voice fading to a slurred singsong. "Dear, sweet Caroline. I hope you know that there will always be a place for you in my heart and my home." Falling back among the pillows, she smothered a yawn behind her hand. "Once we're wed, perhaps Lord Trevelyan can even find a husband for you." Her eyes fluttered shut. "Some lonely widower with two or . . . three . . . children . . . who . . . need . . . a . . ." She trailed off, a delicate snore escaping her parted lips.

With the golden fans of her lashes resting flush against her cheeks and a drowsy half smile curving her lips, she was once more an enchanted princess, perfectly content to slumber until awakened by her prince's kiss.

"Sleep, darling," Caroline whispered, pressing a kiss to her sister's brow even as she gently plucked the white rose from behind her ear and tugged the cameo's chain over her head. "Dream."

The *ton* loved nothing more than a masquerade. For one magical night they were free to cast off the rigid roles forced on them by society and become anyone—or anything—they wanted to be. Once they donned their elaborate masks, they could be virgin or Viking, lamb or lion, peasant or prince. As they milled through the crush of the castle's great hall, their bawdy good cheer harkened back to the pagan Midsummer Night festivals of old when every man was a pirate and no woman's virtue was safe.

Their host watched from the balcony, his broad fingers curved around the delicate bowl of a champagne flute, as a masked shepherd girl darted through the crowd, pursued by a leering centaur. She shrieked with laughter as he caught her by the crook and dragged her into his arms. Bending her over his arm, he ravished her mouth with a long, deep kiss. The crowd sent up an approving cheer, prompting him to straighten and take a bow while the blushing shepherdess collapsed in a mock swoon. Adrian took a sip of his champagne, envying them their carefree love play.

Aside from a row of chairs that lined the south wall, every stick of furniture had been removed from the great hall, restoring the cavernous chamber to its austere medieval splendor. In accordance with his command, the footmen had rolled up and carted away the heavy Turkish rugs, clearing the flagstone floor for dancing. A full orchestra garbed as Benedictine monks, complete with homespun robes and tonsures, sat on a raised dais in the corner, the exuberant notes of a Mozart concerto wafting from their instruments.

The gentle glow of the Argand lamps had been replaced by pitch-coated torches in iron sconces. Shadows gathered beneath the towering beams of the vaulted ceiling, their roiling masses only adding to the aura of mystery and menace that cloaked the hall.

Adrian searched each mask, each face, for any hint of his prey. The erratic flickering of shadow and torchlight seemed to transform every sparkle of the eye into a predatory gleam, every grin into a sinister leer, every man into a potential monster.

"Oh, dear. I forgot this was supposed to be a masquerade," Julian quipped as he approached. He spread his flowing black cape and did an unsteady turn for Adrian, baring a pair of ivory fangs obviously fashioned from wax.

"I am *not* amused," Adrian bit off, a simple black domino mask his only concession to the occasion. He had defied convention, eschewing the usual jewel-toned coat and buff trousers to wear a black cutaway tailcoat, black lawn shirt, and black trousers, all deliberately designed to help him slip through the shadows without being detected.

As a footman strolled past, Julian swept a brimming champagne flute off of his tray. "And what costume would you have suggested for me? A winged cherub perhaps? The archangel Gabriel?"

Adrian plucked the glass from his hand and returned it to the tray, his glower dark enough to send the footman scurrying for the stairs. "Just in case Duvalier should show up tonight, you might wish to have all your wits about you. Luring him here is only half the battle. We still have to capture him."

"Not to worry. I've been told by the ladies that I'm exceptionally witty after imbibing a bottle of champagne . . . or two." Julian joined him at the balcony railing, surveying the crush below through heavy-lidded eyes. "I doubt we'll have to worry about Duvalier making an appearance. Without Vivienne to coax him out of hiding, he'll probably go crawling right back into the hell that spawned him." He slanted Adrian a glance, a glimmer of hope shining through his cynicism despite his best efforts to disguise it. "I can't help but notice that the Cabot sisters haven't yet fled our nefarious clutches. Do you think there might still be a chance that your Miss Cabot would allow Vivienne to help us?"

"I haven't heard a whisper from her all day," Adrian replied, the champagne tasting exceptionally bitter on his tongue. "And she's not *my* Miss Cabot. After last night she most likely never will be."

"I am sorry for that," Julian said, his glib tone softening on an earnest note.

"Why should you be sorry? I have only myself to blame." Adrian lifted his glass to Julian in a mocking toast. "Even as a vampire, you're a better man than I am. You've managed to rein in your appetites, while I allowed my hunger for one sharp-tongued, gray-eyed girl to endanger everything I've been trying to save for the past five years—including my own brother's soul."

"Ah, but what value is a man's soul when compared to the incomparable riches of a woman's heart?" Stealing the glass from Adrian's hand, Julian tipped it to his lips and drained it dry.

Adrian snorted. "Spoken like a true romantic. You really should stop reading so much bloody Byron. It's rotting your brain."

"Oh, I don't know," Julian murmured, his gaze suddenly transfixed by the double doors at the far end of the great hall, where Wilbury had been given the task of announcing new arrivals. "Wasn't it Byron who wrote:

> *She walks in beauty, like the night*
> *Of cloudless climes and starry skies;*
> *And all that's best of dark and bright*
> *Meet in her aspect and her eyes.*"

Adrian followed his brother's gaze to the doors where a slender vision in a gold loo mask and rose tulle, with a white rose tucked behind her ear, was waiting patiently for Wilbury to shuffle over to her side.

Adrian could only be thankful he was no longer holding the champagne glass because he would have doubtlessly pulverized its fragile stem into powder. His hands curled around the balustrade, gripping it like the rail of a sinking ship.

"What's wrong, brother dear?" Julian asked, amusement rippling through his voice. "You look as if you'd seen a ghost."

But that was precisely the problem. Adrian could have never mistaken the woman in the doorway for some tragic shade from his past. She hadn't come to haunt him, but to taunt him with a future he could never have. She might be wearing a dead woman's dress, but life resonated through every inch of her exquisite flesh, from her low-heeled slippers to the proud set of her shoulders to the determined tilt of her chin. She surveyed the room with the regal grace of a young queen, her gray eyes slanting like a cat's behind the golden shield of her mask.

He and Julian weren't the only ones who had noted the arrival of the enchanting creature. A low murmur had begun to rise from the guests, eclipsing even the last triumphant notes of the concerto.

Due to the roaring in his own ears, it took Adrian a moment to realize his brother was laughing. Laughing with an unrestrained mirth Adrian hadn't heard in over five years.

Nearly livid with fury, Adrian rounded on him. "What in the devil are you chortling about?"

Julian wiped his streaming eyes. "Don't you see what the clever little chit has done? You never once looked at Vivienne the way you're looking at her."

"As if I'd like to throttle her?" Adrian growled.

Julian sobered before saying softly, "As if you'd like to take her into your arms and never let her go as long as there was a single breath left in your body."

Adrian wanted to deny his brother's words, but he couldn't.

"Don't you see?" Julian asked. "Duvalier only wants to destroy what you love. If he's within fifty leagues of this place, he's not going to be able to resist showing himself once he hears about this. Simply by appearing at the ball, Caroline just doubled our chances of capturing him."

Adrian swung back around to the balcony, his anger tinged with swelling panic. If Julian was right, his love could very well cost Caroline her life. Just as it had cost Eloisa hers. He had finally been successful in setting his trap, only to find that its steely jaws had clamped down neatly on his own heart.

He turned on his heel and started down the steps at a brisk clip.

"Where are you going?" Julian called after him.

"To get her out of that damned dress."

"I'll drink to that," Julian muttered, beckoning to a footman with a full tray of champagne flutes.

* * *

"Your name?" Wilbury barked, his scarlet livery and moldering wig making him look as if he'd just recently escaped the guillotine.

"Miss Vivienne Cabot," Caroline replied, staring straight ahead.

Wilbury edged closer, peering into the eyeholes of her mask. "Are you certain about that? I'd almost swear you had the shifty air of an imposter about you."

Caroline turned to glare at him. "Don't you think I know my own name, sir?"

His only response was a skeptical *harrumph*.

When she continued to glare at him, he cleared his throat in a near approximation of a death rattle, snapped to attention and croaked, "Miss Vivienne Cabot!"

Caroline lifted her chin to endure the crowd's avid scrutiny, wishing she felt as cool and composed as she looked. She couldn't help but wonder if Duvalier might not already be among them, his baleful intent masked by some clever disguise. But as she scanned the curious faces, her gaze was caught and held by an all too familiar pair of toffee-brown eyes.

She was confident her costume was convincing enough to fool those who had made her sister's casual acquaintance in London, but she had forgotten that there was one man who would not be so easily duped. Constable Larkin's eyes narrowed, the bewilderment in them hardening into suspicion as he excused himself from his companions and began to wend his way through the crowd.

Caroline darted into the crush, thinking only of escape. As she dodged a gypsy fortuneteller and ducked past a woman carrying Marie Antoinette's head beneath her arm, a stray peacock feather tickled her nose, forcing her to pause long enough to pinch back a sneeze.

Before she could lurch back into motion, Larkin's hand closed around her wrist with the relentless bite of a cold iron manacle.

He tugged her around to face him, his narrow face no less

forbidding for being unmasked. "What do you think you're doing, Miss Cabot? What in the devil have you done with your sister?"

"I haven't done anything with her," Caroline insisted, trying not to stammer with guilt. "She simply wasn't feeling well enough to attend the ball."

"Dear God," he whispered, lowering his gaze from the rose in her hair to her gown. "I know this dress . . . this necklace . . ." He reached out to stroke the cameo, his fingers visibly trembling. "Eloisa was wearing this dress the night we first met her at Almack's. And Adrian gave her the cameo for her eighteenth birthday. She was wearing it the last time I saw her. She never took it off. She swore she would wear it over her heart until the day she . . ." His gaze returned to her face. "How did you get these things? Did *he* give them to you?"

"I can assure you that you're making far too much of an old gown and a handful of trinkets my sister found in the attic."

"Am I also making too much of the way he caressed your cheek the night Vivienne fell ill? The way he looks at you when he thinks no one is watching?" Larkin jerked her closer, the steely resolve in his eyes chilling her to the bone. "If you've been in league with Kane all this time and are plotting to do some harm to Vivienne, I swear I'll see you *both* rotting in Newgate before this is done."

Painfully aware of the rapt interest their little drama was generating, Caroline smiled through gritted teeth. "There's no need to manhandle me, sir. If you wish to dance, you have only to say so."

"Dance?" Larkin hissed. "Have you lost your wits, woman?"

Caroline was fighting to ease her wrist from his implacable grasp when a forbidding shadow fell between them.

"Pardon me, mate," Adrian growled. "I do believe the lady promised this dance to me."

Eighteen

A few soaring notes of a Viennese waltz, a dizzying twirl, and Caroline was swept back into the one place she had feared she would never be again—Adrian's arms. From the corner of her eye she saw Larkin shake his head in disgust before turning and stalking away, his long-limbed stride cutting a broad swath through the crowd.

Her relief was short-lived. When she tipped back her head to meet Adrian's gaze, the look in his eye made the threat of Newgate look like a weekend at a Bath resort.

"Just where is your sister?" he demanded. "Knocked out and tied up in an armoire somewhere?"

"Bite your tongue! I would never stoop to such base treachery." She hesitated a minute before blurting out, "If you must know, I drugged her."

Adrian threw back his head with a bark of laughter, garnering startled stares from a Turkish sultan and a harem girl swirling past them in the waltz. "My darling Miss Cabot, remind me to never underestimate your ruthlessness once you finally decide to cast aside your overzealous scruples and have your own way."

"I'm sure it can't compare to your own, my lord," she replied sweetly. "Duvalier may already be watching us, you know," she pointed out as he guided her through another intricate turn of the dance, his powerful hand splayed over the delicate arch of her back. "You should be looking at me as if you want to make love to me, not strangle me."

"What if I want to do both?" he retorted, his resolute words sending a heated shiver down her spine.

His natural grace served him as well in the dance as when he had disposed of the ruffians at Vauxhall. Even with her hand resting ever so lightly on his shoulder, Caroline could feel the fluid shift of his muscles beneath the kerseymere fabric of his coat.

He scowled down at the spray of golden curls sprouting from the top of the rose satin demi-turban she'd wound around her head. "That's not your hair."

Caroline sniffed primly. "My sister has an abundance of curls. I didn't think she'd mind if I borrowed a few."

His gaze drifted lower, boldly surveying the generous décolletage revealed by the gown's plunging neckline. "And those aren't your—"

"They most certainly are!" Caroline dared an outraged look downward. "You'd be amazed at what can be accomplished simply by asking the maid to tighten up your corset strings. And besides, it wasn't as if I had any choice," she sheepishly admitted. "In case you haven't noticed, I'm rather lacking in that area when compared to my sisters."

"I've done more than notice," he murmured, his possessive gaze reminding her that only last night he had curled his warm fingers around her naked breast, claiming it for his own. "And I can assure you that the only thing you're lacking is a healthy dose of common sense. If you had any, you wouldn't have attempted this dangerous little charade."

"Isn't that the point of a masquerade? To come as someone you're not?" She returned his challenging gaze with one of her own. "I could be Vivienne or Eloisa for you tonight. Who would you prefer to have in your arms? Who would you prefer to make love to if you believed Duvalier was watching us this very moment?"

Without missing a single step of the dance, Adrian leaned close to her ear and whispered, "You."

As Larkin's determined strides carried him out of the great hall and up the stairs, the notes of the waltz faded to a ghostly echo. He was still shaken by the sight of Caroline wearing Eloisa's cameo. He had never quite forgotten how Eloisa's lovely face had lit up on the night of her eighteenth birthday when Adrian had presented it to her. Watching Adrian fasten the chain around her graceful neck, Larkin had slipped his own gift—a well-worn volume of Blake's sonnets—back into the pocket of his coat.

His resolve faltered just outside the door of Vivienne and Portia's sitting room. Now that he'd arrived at his destination, he realized just how improper it was for him to be lurking around the door of a young lady's bedchamber with nary a chaperone or maid in sight.

Clearing his throat awkwardly, he gave the door a forceful rap. "Miss Vivienne?" he called out. "Miss Portia? It's Constable Larkin. I'd like to have a word with you if I may."

Silence greeted his request.

He glanced both ways down the corridor, then tested the knob. The door swung open easily beneath his touch.

The sitting room was deserted, the hearth cold. The door to Portia's bedchamber was closed, but Vivienne's door was cracked open. Unable to resist such a blatant invitation to investigate, Larkin crossed the sitting room and eased the door open a few more inches. Although a candle was still burning on the vanity, an air of abandonment clung to the room.

Larkin knew he had no right to snoop, but the temptation was nearly overpowering. The delicate lilac of Vivienne's perfume lured him into the room like the most potent of aphrodisiacs. Judging from the urgent response of his body, he might have been sneaking into the forbidden realms of a sultan's harem.

The top of the vanity was a charming jumble of powders,

unguents, and other mysterious potions all deemed indis-
pensable when in pursuit of the elusive ideal of feminine
beauty. As far as Larkin was concerned, Vivienne required
none of them. A silk stocking had been slung carelessly
over the back of the vanity's bench. He ran his fingertips
over the gossamer fabric, trying not to imagine Vivienne
sitting on that very bench and drawing the stocking up
over one of her creamy calves. Trying not to imagine his lips
following that same path until they reached the sensitive
dimple behind her knee.

Larkin snatched his hand back, appalled by his lack of
self-restraint. He was turning to go when he spotted the
note lying open on the vanity. A note penned in a precise
yet feminine hand.

This time he took the stairs two at a time, his dread at
what he might find mounting right along with him. Without
bothering to knock, he burst into the north tower.

His steps slowed as he approached Caroline's bed. The
hangings were drawn back like the curtains of a stage ready
to sweep down for the final act. Garbed in a dressing gown
of emerald velvet, Vivienne reclined on her back among the
pillows, the slender fingers of one hand curled like a child's
near her cheek. Larkin's own breathing slowly steadied as
he watched her chest rise and fall in sweet repose.

He slumped against one of the bedposts, running a
shaky hand over his jaw. It seemed he owed Caroline an
apology. Perhaps Vivienne really hadn't felt well enough to
attend the masquerade. Perhaps she had seized upon Caroline's summons to the tower to escape the fuss and noise
emanating from the great hall. She might even have found
the dress and cameo in the attic and insisted that Caroline
wear it, not realizing they had once belonged to another
woman Kane had loved.

Drinking in the angelic purity of her features, he sighed.
He would have been content to stay and guard her slumber
for the rest of the night. But if one of the servants should

stumble upon him, there would be grave consequences to her reputation.

He gently drew the quilt up over her, determined to linger only long enough to add another shovel of coal to the fire.

An empty teacup rested on the table beside the bed, along with an unmarked bottle. His instincts beginning to hum once again, Larkin uncorked the bottle and gave it a suspicious sniff. It took little more than a whiff of the pungent sweetness for him to recognize its contents.

"Damn them," he muttered, slamming the bottle back down on the table. "Damn them both!"

He sank down on the feather mattress beside Vivienne, no longer caring what the servants would think if they were discovered.

Capturing her by the shoulders, he gave her a gentle shake. "Vivienne! Vivienne, darling, you've slept long enough. You need to wake up now!"

She stirred, a sleepy moan escaping her parted lips. Her eyes fluttered open. It was too late for Larkin to school his features into indifference. All he could do was wait for the horrified scream that would doubtlessly come once she realized exactly who was looming over her in the bed, gazing down at her with his heart in his eyes.

It took him a dazed moment to realize she must still be dreaming for she lifted a hand to his cheek, her lips slowly curving in a tender half smile, and whispered, "Portia always told me my prince would come."

Caroline closed her eyes, growing flushed and breathless and dizzy, not from the whirling motion of the waltz, but from the blood rushing from her head to other, far more reckless corners of her body. She almost wished she *would* swoon in Adrian's arms so he could carry her from the hall and do all of the tender, wicked things to her that she secretly desired, but could never be bold enough to demand.

None of her girlhood fantasies had prepared her for this

moment. She was no longer the sensible sister, content to watch wistfully while her sisters joined the dance of life. Instead, she was the one commanding every eye in the hall, the one spinning around the floor in the embrace of this magnificent man.

His hand caressed the small of her back, urging her ever closer, so close that her breasts ached to escape from the torturous confinement of her corset each time they brushed the starched lapels of his tailcoat.

"If you want to put on a show for Duvalier, shall we pretend we're at Vauxhall again?" Adrian whispered, his voice vibrating with urgency. As his thumb stroked the very center of her palm, his lips nuzzled the sensitive shell of her ear, coaxing a shudder of yearning from her womb. "I haven't forgotten what a convincing little actress you can be. I still remember the sound of your sighs, the taste of your lips, the way you clung to me as if you never wanted me to let you go."

The other dancers were beginning to give them a wide berth. Some had stopped waltzing altogether and were craning their necks to openly gawk at their scandalous display. Adrian's guests had come to Trevelyan Castle expecting some sort of show, but not one quite this rousing.

"Your guests..." she finally managed to gasp out, "...they're watching us."

"Wasn't that what you wanted? Didn't you come here tonight so that Duvalier would see you? So you could bait him with your beauty? So you could stir his unholy lust and drive him half mad with wanting you?"

As the heated velvet of Adrian's lips grazed the curve of her throat, she knew instinctively that they were no longer talking about Duvalier. In truth, no vampire, however cunning, could pose as much of a danger to her as this man did. Duvalier could only make her heart stop beating; Adrian possessed the power to shatter it into a thousand pieces, leaving her to walk around for the rest of her days with the broken shards lodged in her breast.

Digging her fingers into his shoulder to keep from melting against him in complete surrender, she said, "I came here tonight to help Julian. To help you."

Adrian drew back to gaze down at her, his eyes burning with both desire and anger. "And just how did you intend to do that? By getting your fool self killed? You're wearing Eloisa's dress. Do you wish to meet her fate as well?"

"Of course not! I knew you would protect me. You swore that you were strong enough to protect Vivienne, didn't you? How can you promise to protect my sister, but not trust yourself to keep me safe?"

The music swelled to a crescendo. Although Adrian kept her imprisoned against the muscular length of his body, he gave up all pretense of dancing. "Because I don't lose my wits every time Vivienne walks into a room. I don't toss and turn in my bed every night dreaming of making love to her. She doesn't drive me to distraction with her endless questions, her incessant snooping, her harebrained schemes." His voice rose. "I can trust myself to protect your sister because I'm not in love with her!"

His words echoed back from the rafters, warning them too late that both the waltz and the music had ended. Caroline stole a sheepish peek at the other dancers, fully expecting to find every gaze in the hall riveted on them. But oddly enough, the guests seemed to have been distracted by a new arrival.

As their shocked murmurs rose to an audible buzz, Caroline followed the direction of their gazes to the door. Her heart sank into her slippers as she recognized the slender figure cradled in the arms of a man whose narrowed eyes promised both justice and retribution.

She caught only the briefest glimpse of her sister's stunned expression before Constable Larkin pressed Vivienne's face to his shoulder, sparing her from witnessing another minute of the sordid spectacle she and Adrian had just made of themselves.

Nineteen

The silence within the castle's library was worse than any sound Caroline had ever heard. She paced back and forth in front of the door, wringing a handkerchief in her numb hands. When Adrian had escorted a white-faced Vivienne into the chamber, Caroline expected to hear brokenhearted sobbing, shouting, and bitter recriminations. But although nearly an hour had passed since their disappearance, not so much as a whimper had escaped the room. Perhaps Vivienne had decided to suffer this betrayal, as she had so many other things, in silence.

"She shouldn't be alone in there with him. They require a chaperone," Larkin muttered, shooting Caroline an accusing glare that reminded her just how miserably she had failed in that regard. Instead of protecting her sister's tender heart, she had been the one to break it.

The constable was slouched against the opposite wall, his casual posture belied by the watchful glitter in his eyes. He and Adrian had nearly come to blows when Adrian had insisted on wresting Vivienne from his arms and whisking her away from the prying eyes of his stunned guests.

"After everything I've told you," Caroline said, "surely you can't still believe he would harm her. He wasn't the one who slipped her those drops of laudanum. I was."

Larkin shook his head. "Am I actually supposed to believe that Victor murdered Eloisa in cold blood, then turned

Julian into some sort of monster? That Kane is a vampire hunter and he and Julian have spent the last five years tracking Victor to the ends of the earth and back? Why, I've never heard such a preposterous tale!"

"I thought the same thing when Adrian first told me, but Julian showed me . . ." Caroline trailed off, twisting her handkerchief into a new knot. She could expect no help from that quarter. Although she'd had the servants searching for him ever since the ball came to such an unceremonious end, Julian was nowhere to be found.

Desperate to convince Larkin that she was telling the truth, as much for Adrian's sake as for hers, she met his eyes squarely. "Weren't you the one who once challenged me to trust in something other than logic?" He gazed down his long nose at her, his stony expression not softening one whit. "Would it be easier for you to believe that I'm the sort of woman who would drug her sister for the sole purpose of stealing her suitor for a torrid interlude?"

He continued to glare at her for a moment before blowing out a reluctant sigh of defeat. "I suppose that's even more preposterous, isn't it?"

Without warning, the library door swung open. Caroline turned as Adrian emerged from the shadows of the room. In some small corner of her heart she had hoped that he would come striding through that door, sweep her into his arms, and kiss every one of her fears and regrets off of her lips.

But that hope died when she saw his face. The passionate lover from the great hall had vanished as surely as if he'd been a figment of her imagination, no more real than one of Portia's mermans or noble princes, leaving behind a forbidding stranger.

"I told her about Duvalier," he said, his inscrutable gaze barely brushing over Caroline. "I told her *everything*."

Although Larkin straightened as if he'd like nothing more than to confront him, Adrian stalked right past him and down the corridor, the staccato click of his booted heels echoing behind him.

Caroline had no time to linger over his deliberate slight, not with the library's open door beckoning to her.

Larkin gave her an uncertain glance. "Would you like me to—"

Before he could finish, Caroline shook her head. The last thing she deserved was the constable's companionship or sympathy. No longer able to delay the moment she had been dreading, she slipped into the library, silently pulling the door shut behind her.

Vivienne was sitting on a leather ottoman in front of the fire, the skirt of Caroline's emerald green dressing gown fanned out around her. She sat utterly still, utterly silent, her face buried in her hands.

Caroline gazed at her sister's shoulders in mute misery, knowing she would feel much better if Vivienne would bawl at the top of her lungs, hurl something breakable at her head, chastise her for being the shameless suitor-stealing trollop that she was.

Creeping as close as she dared, she whispered, "Vivi?"

Vivienne remained huddled in a despondent knot, refusing to acknowledge her presence.

Caroline stretched out a hand toward Vivienne's bowed head, aching to touch the golden silk of her hair. But just as quickly, she withdrew that hand, fearing such a touch might shatter her fragile sister into a thousand pieces.

"I can't imagine what you must think of me," she began, choking out each word around the lump in her throat. "You have to know that I would have given anything within my power to make you happy. I would have cut off my right arm if it would have ensured your happiness and your future." A hot wash of tears filled her eyes. "But he was the one thing I couldn't bear to give you because I . . . I wanted him so badly for myself."

To Caroline's horror, Vivienne's shoulders began to shake.

She had thought it would be a relief if her sister would cry. But it wasn't. Those silent sobs nearly tore Caroline's heart in two.

She went to her knees beside the ottoman, feeling the tears in her own eyes spill down her cheeks in a scalding rush. "I should have left this place the moment I realized I was falling in love with him. I could have begged Aunt Marietta to find me a position as some sort of governess or paid companion and gone so far away that neither one of you would have ever had to see me again. If I had an ounce of decency in my soul, I'd return to Edgeleaf right away and accept Cousin Cecil's proposal. A lifetime of waking up every morning to that odious toad is no more than I deserve for what I've done to you!"

Her voice broke on a ragged sob. No longer able to bear up beneath the weight of her guilt, she dropped her head into Vivienne's lap, clutching at her sister's skirts as she wept out her shame.

The last thing she expected to feel was a hand stroking her head. For just an instant it was almost as if time had gone tumbling backward and it was her mother's gentle touch seeking to soothe away her heartache. Caroline slowly lifted her disbelieving eyes to her sister's face. Vivienne's cheeks were also streaked with tears, but her serene smile was no less loving than before.

"You can't marry Cousin Cecil," Vivienne informed her. "I refuse to play the role of doting aunt for a passel of odious, toad-faced brats."

Caroline blinked up at her sister through a wavery curtain of tears. "Don't you want to see me punished for the terrible thing I've done? How can you forgive me for stealing the man you love?"

Vivienne gave her head another stroke, looking wise beyond her years. "Because I don't love him, Caro. I never did."

Caroline shook her head, her bewilderment growing. "I don't understand. How can you say such a thing? What about that letter you sent us? You went on for pages and pages, detailing his irresistible charms and his manly virtues. For heaven's sake, you even dotted the *i* in his name with a heart!"

Vivienne winced at the memory. "All of the things I said about him were true, but I think I was trying to convince myself that I was falling in love with him. After all, he was exactly the sort of man I was *supposed* to fall in love with— wealthy, titled, powerful. If I could land a gentleman like him, I knew it could be the making of us. I could single-handedly pull our family back from the brink of ruin. I was just trying to look after you and Portia." She seized Caroline's hand, her blue eyes shining with a tenderness Caroline had feared she would never see again. "Especially you, dear Caro, after all you'd sacrificed for us. You didn't always have to be the strong one, you know. Portia and I would have helped you. We *needed* to help you."

Caroline shook her head ruefully, still struggling to absorb her sister's words. "We make a fine pair, don't we? Both trying to sacrifice for the other and making a dreadful muck of it." She gave Vivienne's hand a fierce squeeze. "Even if we were begging on the streets, I never would have forced you to marry a man you didn't love."

"Don't you think I knew that?" Dragging her hand from Caroline's, Vivienne rose to pace in front of the fire. "It wasn't as if becoming the viscount's wife would have been such a terrible ordeal. He's a very kind and handsome man and I admire him more than I can say, even more now that he's told me about poor Julian's . . . affliction." She whirled around to face Caroline, her pretty brow puckered in a tortured frown. "But how could I marry him when my heart belongs to Alastair?"

"Alastair?" Caroline echoed, baffled anew by the passionate declaration. She searched her memory, wondering if there was some village lad or brawny gardener she'd overlooked. "Who on earth is Alastair?"

"Why, Constable Larkin, of course! I've loved him ever

since he spilled sherry on my skirt at Lady Marlybone's afternoon musicale and tried to dab it away with his cravat. But I knew he wouldn't suit. He has no family of any repute and unless there's some major kidnapping or jewel theft among the *ton*, he can barely support himself on his commissions, much less a wife and her family. And besides, he has abominable fashion sense."

"Yes, he does, doesn't he?" Caroline murmured, thinking how very happy the constable was going to be when he discovered that he wasn't going to have to hire that valet to tie his cravat after all.

"And worst of all," Vivienne continued, "I knew he didn't have a single acquaintance that you or Portia could marry. Not a friend, not a brother, not even a second cousin thrice removed!"

"What about a doddering old uncle?" Caroline asked, finding it more and more difficult to suppress her smile.

Vivienne shook her head sadly. "Not even that, I fear. I knew he wasn't a suitable prospect from the beginning so I tried to discourage him by being distant and cruel." Her eyes softened in a look Caroline didn't need a mirror to recognize. "But the more insufferable I became, the more he seemed to adore me."

"That seems to be the curse of true love," Caroline whispered, no longer thinking about the constable. Struck by a sudden thought, she tilted her head to study her sister. "If you weren't distraught because I'd stolen the man you loved, then why on earth were you crying just now?"

"Because I was so very relieved to learn that you were truly in love with him and I hadn't just made a dreadful mistake!" Vivienne beamed at her. "Now that I've fixed everything, you and Portia will always be taken care of and Alastair and I can finally be together."

"Fixed everything?" Caroline climbed to her feet to face her sister, plagued by a sudden tingle of foreboding. If memory served her right, the last time Vivienne had *fixed* something, her own favorite yarn doll had ended up with three legs and no hair.

"I decided it was time to put everything right. You've been looking after me for all of these years. Now it's my turn to look after you."

"Whatever do you mean?"

Vivienne lifted her chin with all the haughtiness of the viscountess she would never become. "I informed Lord Trevelyan that he had behaved in a shameful and disgraceful manner toward the both of us and there was only one way for a true gentleman to make amends."

Caroline could barely choke out the words. "And what was that?"

"He is to marry you as soon as possible."

Caroline collapsed on the ottoman, her knees betraying her. "No wonder he looked as if all the hounds of hell were pursuing him." She blinked up at her sister through a daze of disbelief. "Oh, Vivienne, what have you done?"

Vivienne blinked back at her, still looking unbearably smug. "Isn't it obvious? I made it possible for both of us to marry the men we loved."

"But you know that Constable Lark—*Alastair*—wants to marry you. Did the viscount give you any indication that he feels the same way about me?"

"We-e-e-ell . . ." Vivienne chewed on her lower lip. Unlike Portia, she had never been a particularly accomplished liar. "He didn't seem *completely* resistant to the idea of making you his bride. He might have been a *little* reluctant at first, but once I reminded him of his duty to you, he was quite congenial."

Burying her face in her hands, Caroline groaned.

"Besides," Vivienne continued, "it's not as if he has any choice. He compromised you in the great hall for all the world to see." She pressed a hand to her breast, her voice climbing to a pitch dangerously near Aunt Marietta's. "Personally, I've never witnessed such a shocking display of decadence! One would have thought the two of you were on the Lover's Walk at Vauxhall. Now that he's sent the guests packing without so much as a by-your-leave, the gossip will be all over London by tomorrow."

"And what do you think the gossips will say when the viscount weds the wrong sister? What will they say when they hear whispers that he was forced into wedlock against his will? This may come as a shock to your tender sensibilities, but not all men are as noble as your Alastair. A man like Adrian Kane is perfectly capable of wanting to bed a woman without having any intention of wedding her."

"Not when that woman is *my* sister!"

Caroline blew out an exasperated sigh. "You're missing the point. How can I wed him knowing that he's only marrying me because you're holding a pistol of propriety to his head?"

Vivienne frowned. "I don't think a pistol will be necessary, but I can ask Alastair if you like. I'm sure he has one."

This time it wasn't a sigh, but a shriek of frustration that escaped Caroline's lips. The library door flew open, framing a wild-eyed Larkin. He had obviously expected to find her and Vivienne rolling around on the Turkish carpet, spitting epithets and pulling each other's hair.

As Larkin's gaze caressed Vivienne's face, a flush stained his high cheekbones. "Forgive the intrusion, Miss Vivienne. I was afraid you were in some sort of distress."

Clasping her hands in front of her, Vivienne rewarded him with her most adoring smile. "Not any more, sir, now that *you're* here."

Larkin's mouth fell open. He couldn't have looked any more dumbfounded had she clubbed him over the head with the fire iron.

His baffled gaze traveled between the two of them, finally settling on Caroline. "Are you quite all right, Miss Cabot? You look as if someone just walked over your grave."

"Well, that's fitting, isn't it? Haven't you heard?" Caroline sagged against the hearth, a slightly hysterical laugh bubbling from her throat. "I'm marrying a vampire hunter."

The servants hadn't been able to locate Julian after the ball because he was perched between two merlons on the parapet walk that ringed the highest battlement of the castle. He knew there was only one person who would think to look for him there so he didn't even bother to turn around when he heard a footfall behind him.

He and Adrian had spent hours in this very spot as boys, playing at Vikings and Crusaders and pirates. The meadows and glades surrounding the castle had been both their battlefields and their oceans. In the brash eyes of their imaginations, a farmer's wagon trundling over the rutted road below had become a Saracen's exotic caravan guarded by dark-eyed, saber-wielding warriors while the farmer's swayback nag and flea-bitten old hound were transformed into an Arabian steed and a fierce pack of wolves that would storm the castle, howling for their blood. Back then, their invisible enemies could be vanquished with nothing more than a thunderous war cry and a solid thwack from a wooden stick. Julian tipped the bottle of champagne in his hand to his lips, wishing for those simpler days.

Tonight the rutted road below was dotted with the light of swaying carriage lamps. Their guests were departing one by one, taking the last of Julian's hopes with them.

"I'm sorry," Adrian said softly, stopping just behind him to watch the lights fade into the darkness. "I wanted to let her go through with it, but I just couldn't bring myself to do it. Not even for you."

"If I had even half a soul, I wouldn't have asked you to," Julian said with a shrug.

"I refuse to believe that using Eloisa's ghost to lure him back was our last hope."

Julian snorted. "It might have been our only hope."

"I swear to you that we'll find another way. *I'll* find another way. I just need a little more time."

Julian turned to give his brother a crooked smile. "Time is the one thing I have in abundance. I can give you an eternity if that's what you require."

Even as he said the words, Julian knew he was bluffing. His time had been running out for a very long while now, his humanity trickling out of him like grains of sand from a cracked hourglass.

Adrian touched his shoulder ever so briefly, then turned to go.

"Adrian?"

His brother turned back, and for just an instant Julian saw the ghost of a younger Adrian superimposed over his face.

"If I had a blessing to give the two of you, I would."

Adrian nodded before melting back into the shadows.

Julian turned his face to the wind, welcoming its stinging lash. The night should have been his realm, his kingdom to rule. Yet here he sat, trapped between two worlds, two fates, with only a bottle of flat champagne to ease the hunger gnawing at the place where his soul had once resided.

He was tilting the bottle to his lips when the chain came out of nowhere, snaking around his throat with savage force. The bottle slipped from his fingers, shattering against the stones. Julian clawed at the heavy links, fighting their choking pressure, but his supernatural strength seemed to be waning, slipping away like the petals of a dying rose.

His eyes bulging, he glanced down just in time to see the silver crucifix dangling from the end of the chain burn its way through his shirt and into his chest. The stench of charred flesh flooded his nostrils.

Even as he fought to croak out a bellow of pain and rage, a hoarse whisper filled his ear. "You shouldn't have lied to your brother that way, *mon ami*. Your time just ran out."

As Duvalier yanked him to his knees with brutal efficiency, all Julian could think was that it was a damn shame Adrian might never know that their plot had succeeded.

Twenty

"While I realize that my sister had only my best interests at heart and I appreciate your willingness to conform to the demands of propriety, my lord," Caroline said, her tones both cool and measured, "by outlining each of my arguments in considerable depth, I think I've made it perfectly clear why I have no choice but to refuse your suit." She finished her speech with her head held high and her hands clasped in front of her—the very model of reason and common sense.

At least that's what she hoped. Since she had no one to listen to her well-rehearsed speech and was only able to judge her appearance by the wavering reflection in the French doors of her bedchamber, it was difficult to tell. Although she'd lit every candle in the tower upon her return from the library, the inky blackness of the night beyond the doors leached all of the definition from her image, leaving it as misty as a ghost's.

A sharp gust rattled the doors, making her jump. The wind had risen steadily for the past few hours, sending more clouds scuttling over the luminous face of the moon. The flickering glow of the candles made it impossible to track the shadows flitting across her balcony.

Somewhere deep in the castle a clock began to chime the midnight hour, each hollow bong resonating through Caroline's frayed nerves. She wanted nothing more than to strip off Eloisa's cursed gown, bound into the bed, and draw the blankets up over her head. But she forced herself to move toward her ghostly image in the French doors, to reach down and methodically check to make sure they were unbolted.

As the moments ticked away, fresh doubts began to creep into her consciousness. Perhaps Adrian wasn't coming. Perhaps he blamed her for ruining his plot to trap and destroy Duvalier. Perhaps he was so unhappy at the prospect of being forced to wed her that he was regretting every moment they'd shared—every touch, every kiss.

Caroline began to restlessly pace around the bed. He could hardly blame her for forcing him into marriage when he had been the one to compromise her in front of half of the *ton*. He was the one who had taken her devotion to her sisters and wielded it like a weapon, she thought, growing more incensed by his unfairness with each step.

She had no intention of spending the rest of her life pacing her bedchamber and longing to hear her husband's footstep on the stairs. If he wouldn't come to her, then by God, she would go to him.

She was turning toward the doors when they came flying open. She caught the briefest glimpse of a man silhouetted against the darkness before the wind whipped through the tower, extinguishing all of the candles with a single breath.

She held her own breath, waiting for the clouds to shift again. Waiting for a single bright lance of moonlight to gild his hair and bathe the rugged planes of his face.

It was the face of the warrior in the portrait. And he had come for her. Caroline took an involuntary step backward, her courage deserting her. The uncompromising black of Adrian's shirt and trousers perfectly suited his grim visage. The more distant and unapproachable he appeared, the more her treacherous heart seemed to yearn for him.

"I'm surprised you didn't bolt the doors," he said.

"Would it have kept you out?"

"No," he admitted, taking a single step toward her.

"Then perhaps you have more in common with your ancestors than you realize."

"I tried to warn you that they were all scoundrels and reprobates, didn't I? I'm sure they stole and ravished more than one bride in their day."

Caroline's outrage at his arrogance sent all of her well-rehearsed speeches flying right out of her head. "While you and my sister were deciding my future in such a high-handed manner, did it never occur to either of you that I might wish to be consulted?"

"I don't see that you have any choice in the matter. Your good reputation is in ruins. No decent man will ever offer for your hand."

Caroline wondered why he was so quick to place himself among the ranks of the indecent.

"As I see it," he continued, "you have only two possible futures. You can become my wife." The smoky note in his voice deepened. "Or you can become my mistress . . . with all of the inherent duties that come with the privilege."

Refusing to blush, Caroline lifted her chin. "As I see it, a wife has exactly the same *duties*. She just isn't usually compensated for them with flowers and jewels."

His eyes narrowed. "Is that what you want from me? Roses? Diamonds?"

Caroline bit her lip before she could blurt out what she wanted from him. She wanted him to touch her again with shattering tenderness. She wanted long, melting kisses in the moonlight. She wanted him to press his lips to her hair and call her his darling.

"I don't want anything from you," she lied. "My sister made it abundantly clear that you were only marrying me out of duty. Well, this isn't Vauxhall and I won't have you playing the champion on my behalf. I don't need to be rescued and I won't become just another one of your strays. I have no use for your pity. My reputation may be in ruins, but I still have my pride."

"Your sister was absolutely right," he agreed. "Marrying you is the last thing I want to do."

An unbidden gasp escaped from Caroline's lips. She might have suspected him of many things in the past, but she had never judged him capable of deliberate cruelty.

"I don't want to marry you. I don't want to want you," he added fiercely, taking one measured step toward her, then another. "And I sure as hell don't want to love you. But, God help me, I just can't stop myself." Closing the rest of the distance between them in a single stride, he snatched her up by the shoulders, his burning gaze searching her face as if to sear her features into his memory. "I don't want to marry you because I love you too much to ask you to spend the rest of your life hiding in the shadows."

Her heart brimming over with some new and wondrous emotion, Caroline touched a hand to his cheek. "I'd rather spend the rest of my days living in the shadows with you than walking in the sunlight all alone." As the chains of her pride fell away, Caroline whispered, "Will you marry me?"

Adrian's lips descended on hers, giving her the only answer she would ever need. He caressed the silken corners of her mouth, growing more insistent, more persuasive, with each tender sweep of his tongue. Without breaking the kiss, he swept her up in his arms, cradling her against his chest as if she weighed no more than a child.

As he started for the doors, she murmured against his lips, "Where are you taking me?"

He only tightened his possessive grip. "To my bed. Where you belong."

As Adrian carried her down the steps and across the bridge, his body sheltered her from the battering force of the wind. The windows below were darkened now. There were no prying eyes to witness their journey. Caroline curled her arms around Adrian's neck and buried her face against the warmth of his throat, breathing deeply of his sandalwood and bay rum scent.

She was still shyly nuzzling his neck when he set her on

her feet. She had half expected him to tumble her right into his bed, but she opened her eyes to find herself standing at the foot of it, in front of the tall, silk-draped piece of furniture that had captured her curiosity on her last visit to his chamber.

Adrian strode back over to the French doors to rip down the heavy velvet drapes that veiled them, inviting the moonlight into his lair.

As silent as a shadow, he slipped up behind her. He plucked the rose from behind her ear and crumpled the velvety petals between his fingers, releasing their heady fragrance. As they drifted to the floor, he tugged away the satin demi-turban, freeing her hair to spill around her shoulders in a silken waterfall. Lifting its luxuriant weight from her nape, he pressed his lips there, sending an exquisite shudder of pleasure down her spine. As his arm slipped around her waist to steady her, she could feel the heat from his body radiating through her every pore.

Twining her hair around his hand, he exposed the long, elegant curve of her throat. "You were right about me all along, you know," he said, the smoky whisper of his voice a caress all its own. "From the first moment I laid eyes on you, I wanted nothing more than to devour you where you stood." His lips sought the throbbing pulse at the side of her throat, parting to soothe the very spot he had nipped only the night before. "I wanted to drink from your lips. I wanted to sample the softness of your skin." His mouth moved to her ear, the husky urgency of his voice pouring over her starved senses like molten honey. "I wanted to taste every drop of nectar your sweet flesh has to offer."

His lips traced her ear, lingering against the tender lobe. As the velvet warmth of his tongue plundered the delicate shell, an answering pulse of pleasure between her thighs dampened her drawers and made her knees go weak. Her eyes fluttered shut as she sagged against the hard length of his body, feeling as limp and pliable as a rag doll in his hands.

She felt him reach around her and suddenly knew exactly what was beneath that shroud of silk. She kept her eyes pressed tightly shut, some fanciful corner of her soul still afraid that she would open them and discover that she was cradled in the invisible arms of a demon lover she had neither the strength nor the will to resist.

She heard the ripple of silk as the drape drifted to the floor.

"Look at me, darling," Adrian urged. "Look at us."

Helpless to resist his entreaty, Caroline obeyed, only to find herself gazing into the luminous eyes of the man she loved. Adrian's reflection in the gilded cheval glass was as solid as her own, binding them together with far more than just his tender embrace. For the first time in her life Caroline was shocked by her own reflection. It wasn't the shimmering tulle of her gown or the moonlit curtain of hair flowing over her shoulders that made her beautiful. It was the raw desire in Adrian's eyes.

"Oh my," Caroline breathed, turning in his arms.

Adrian did tumble her into the bed then, groaning her name deep in his throat as they rolled across the silk sheets until she was beneath him and he was looming over her in the darkness. As his mouth came down on hers and her arms went around him, she savored the wonder of being in his arms. He would never belong to Vivienne or to any other woman. From this moment on, he was all hers.

The hypnotic plunge and retreat of his tongue coaxed her own tongue into chasing him with tantalizing little flicks that implored him to take her mouth more fully, more deeply. He eagerly obliged until they were both breathless with want. Her shyness banished, Caroline's hands tore at the thin lawn of his shirt.

Adrian chuckled, delighted by her boldness. Shrugging his way out of the remains of the shirt, he tossed it aside, then divested himself of his trousers, stockings, and boots with equal haste.

He gently tugged Eloisa's gown over Caroline's head, then slipped behind her to unlace her corset.

"Did you love her?" Caroline asked softly, drawing the chain over her head and gazing down at the fragile cameo.

Adrian's grief and guilt and regret were so mingled by now that he could no longer remember. All he could do was plant a tender kiss on her shoulder and tell her, "I thought I did. Until I met you."

The cameo slipped from her fingers. She turned in his arms, her lips melding with his in a fierce kiss. As he tore his lips away from hers just long enough to tug the corset and her worn chemise over her head, the wind drove away the last of the clouds, bathing the tower and their entwined bodies in a silvery mist of moonlight.

"Sweet Lord," he breathed, the words more prayer than oath as he laid her back among the pillows.

His eyes devoured her. She was even more lovely than he'd envisioned—all lithe curves and delicately sketched angles. She gazed up at him with her big gray eyes, her hair flowing in a gossamer curtain across his pillow. She looked as if she should be reclining on a bed of moss in an enchanted forest, waiting for the arrival of a unicorn.

Instead she was waiting for him.

His gaze lingered on the gentle swell of her rose-tipped breasts, on the silky triangle of curls between her thighs. Although he would have sworn it impossible, they were a shade paler than the hair on her head.

"Thank God for the moon," he said. "I was growing ever so weary of the darkness."

"I don't mind it," Caroline whispered, tenderly stroking her fingertips through the crisp whorls of his chest hair, "as long as I can share it with you."

Caroline couldn't believe they were naked in each other's arms, yet she felt no need to blush or hide her face. It astonished her even more that her touch could wreak such havoc on this magnificent male creature. When her hand drifted lower, grazing the taut muscles of Adrian's abdomen, his entire body jerked as if struck by a bolt of lightning.

He caught her hand in his own, gazing deep into her eyes as he urged it lower. As he pressed her open palm to his fully aroused length, Caroline let out a breathy little moan, finally comprehending the full measure of his desire for her. He was a big man—in more ways than one. Her fingers instinctively curved around him, marveling that something so strong and hard could feel like velvet to the touch.

Throwing his head back, Adrian groaned through gritted teeth.

Alarmed, Caroline snatched her hand back. "What is it? Did I do something wrong?"

Lacing his fingers through hers, he brought her palm to his lips and pressed a tender kiss to it. "No, angel, you did something very, very right. But if you do it again, this night is going to be over before it's begun."

He lowered his head, but this time it wasn't her lips he sought, but the rosy peak of one breast. He blew softly, bathing her in the silken mist of his breath, before touching his mouth to her. As his tongue flicked across the turgid bud of her nipple, pleasure purled deep within her, making her whimper and arch against him. Although her breasts still couldn't compare to Portia's, they seemed to grow fuller and heavier beneath his skillful caresses. By the time he shifted his attentions to the other breast, she was writhing with some primitive need too deep to articulate.

Adrian lifted his head to gaze at her over the glistening peaks, his eyes heavy-lidded with a hunger of their own. "When my brother first met you, he insisted that you were full of starch and vinegar."

"Did you agree with him?" she asked, her breath coming in short, shaky pants.

He shook his head, a devilish grin curling one corner of his mouth. "I always knew you were full of honey."

To prove his point, he gently sifted through the curls at the juncture of her thighs, his clever fingers unerringly seeking and finding the thick pool of nectar welling from her inner springs.

Caroline threw back her head, gasping at the bold intimacy of his touch. She was no longer fool enough to believe he had the hands of a workman. They might be broad and powerful, but they were as skilled as any artist's, molding her to his will with each deft brush of his fingertips. He petted and teased and stroked her, parting the delicate petals to expose the extraordinarily sensitive bud nestled between them.

"There now," he whispered in her ear, the callused pad of his thumb circling that sweet nubbin of flesh with exquisite care. "You've taken care of everyone else for so long, my sweet Caroline. Let me take care of you."

It wasn't as if she had any choice. She lay in a near swoon in his embrace, ravished by the waves of sensation fanning out from his touch.

As his thumb continued to work its dark magic, two of his fingers dipped lower—circling, stroking, gently spreading the tight little hollow at her very core, as if to prepare her for some unspeakable delight only he could deliver.

"Please," she choked out, not even knowing what she was begging for, but wanting it more than anything else she had ever sought. She whipped her head back and forth on the pillow, nearly incoherent with need. "Oh, please . . ."

Not even in her wildest dreams had she imagined that her plea would result in Adrian sliding down her body with sensual languor until the delectable heat of his mouth was where his thumb had been.

Although she gasped with mortification, her thighs fell apart, inviting him to have his way with her in any way he chose. She had once accused him of enslaving women with his dark powers of seduction, but in her innocence she had never guessed how eagerly she would go into his chains or how binding they would be.

His tongue flicked over her distended flesh, devouring her as if she was the only sustenance he would never need.

She had no defenses against a hunger this primal, this powerful. As he made good on his vow to taste every drop of nectar her sweet flesh had to offer, all she could do was clutch the rough silk of his hair in her hands and surrender herself to him, body and soul. Only then did his tongue double its rhythm; only then did he slide one broad finger deep inside of her.

A wave of ecstasy, as thick and hot as the sweetest of nectars, surged through her shuddering body. She arched against him, crying out his name. He rose up to catch her broken cry in his mouth, kissing her wildly.

His weight shifted and suddenly it wasn't his thumb nestled in the damp softness of her curls. It wasn't his fingers poised to bury themselves in her yielding softness.

"Caroline," he muttered against her lips. "My sweet, sweet Caroline . . . I don't want to hurt you. I never wanted to hurt you."

"Then don't," she whispered, framing his face in her hands and forcing him to meet her pleading gaze. "Just love me."

She didn't have to ask him twice. He rubbed himself between those tender petals until he was slick with her dew, then positioned himself against the part of her that was aching to receive him. Using exquisite restraint, he penetrated her an inch at a time. Only when her whimpers deepened to moans did he surge against her, shattering the last of her body's resistance and burying himself to the hilt in her welcoming softness.

Adrian felt his entire body shudder as Caroline gloved him in ecstasy. He had mistaken her for moonlight, but she was sunlight, illuminating and warming all of the dark and lonely corners of his soul. Burying his face against her throat, he held himself still for as long as he could, trying to give her untried body time to adjust to his ruthless invasion.

As her pain faded to a dull ache, Caroline's eyes widened at the raw shock of his possession. He was on top of her; he was inside of her; his mastery was complete. Yet she was the one who possessed the power to drive him half mad with nothing more than the restless arch of her hips, the desperate scrape of her fingernails down the small of his back.

Accepting her invitation with a hoarse groan, he began to move deep within her, taking her innocence, but giving her something infinitely more precious. He glided in and out of her like a powerful tide drawn by the will of the moon. This was a different sort of pleasure from the tremors of pure bliss he'd sent spilling through her only minutes before— stronger, more primal. She gave and he took. He gave and she took. He made her a woman while she made him *her* man. She clung to him, murmuring his name in a breathless litany, as his measured strokes gave way to a pounding, relentless rhythm that banished all thought, all reason, leaving only sensation.

Just when she thought she couldn't endure another second of such sweet torture, he angled his hips so that each plunging stroke brought him to bear against that taut nubbin at the crux of her curls.

Caroline cried out as her body exploded in a frenzy of delight. Feeling that irresistible tug, Adrian went crashing against the shore with her, a guttural groan escaping his throat as he surrendered both his seed and his soul into her keeping.

Caroline sat on her knees at the foot of the bed, gazing at her moonlit reflection in Adrian's mirror. Although the woman with the tumbled hair and kiss-swollen lips might have been a stranger, she had seen that look before—in the eyes of the woman on the Lover's Walk at Vauxhall. She now knew the secret that drove lovers to rendezvous on those dark and shadowy walks. She had tasted the pleasures they hungered for and been left thoroughly satisfied, yet longing for more.

As if sensing her wayward thoughts, Adrian rose up behind her.

As his strong, muscular arms enfolded her, she clutched the sheet she'd wrapped around her even more tightly, seized by a belated surge of modesty. "I thought you were sleeping."

"I was," he murmured, nuzzling her neck. "Until you slipped out of my arms and my dreams."

Melting against him, she tilted her head to give his warm lips freer access to the downy skin beneath her ear. "What were you dreaming about?"

"This." He slipped his arms beneath the sheet, filling his hands with her naked breasts.

Caroline gasped as he gave her breasts a gentle squeeze, then began to tease her nipples between his thumbs and forefingers. They ripened beneath his touch, greedily absorbing every ounce of the pleasure he sought to give her. Letting the sheet slide away until she was once more naked in his arms, she reached around to cup the back of his head in her palm and turned her head, desperate to steal a kiss from his questing lips.

"If you must know," he murmured, tasting the corner of her mouth with his tongue, "I was dozing off when it suddenly occurred to me that I forgot to check you for stakes. You could have very well murdered me in my sleep."

Caroline arched against him, feeling the impressive proof of his desire nestled against the softness of her bottom. "As far as I can tell, my lord, you're the only one who's armed around here."

She felt his mouth curve in a wicked smile. "Does that mean I get to stake you?"

"You already have." Dragging her lips away from his, Caroline met his eyes in the mirror. "Right through the heart."

Groaning, he pressed his palm against the very heart of her femininity, claiming it for his own. She watched him in the mirror, mesmerized by the sight of his longest finger disappearing into her nether curls, disappearing into her. Utterly undone by that exquisite pressure, she arched against him, inviting an even deeper invasion. Only too eager to oblige, he rose up on his knees, driving himself deep into her melting softness.

Caroline moaned, the faint soreness from their first encounter only heightening the sensation of being impaled upon some unyielding staff designed solely to pleasure her. The sensual creature in the mirror was even more of a stranger to her now, willing to writhe and claw and beg to get what she needed. Her moist lips were parted, her eyes glazed over with want.

Adrian used the callused pad of his finger to provide an irresistible counterpoint to the commanding thrusts of his hips. Soon she was the one riding him, the one controlling the rhythm of his long, deep strokes. His love had banished the last of her shyness, transformed her into a temptress—a bold enchantress who didn't just beg for satisfaction, but demanded it. Shivering pulses of pleasure fanned out from his touch, building with each deft flick of his fingertip, each sinuous rise and fall of her hips.

"That's it, sweetheart," he panted in her ear. "Take the pleasure and the power. Claim it for your own."

As that pleasure swelled to a crescendo, Adrian's name broke from her lips, half sob, half scream. Filling his hands with the softness of her breasts, he went rigid, his entire body shuddering with the same rapture that wracked her womb.

She collapsed in his arms, so dazed with delight that it took her a long moment to realize his body was no longer shuddering with rapture, but laughter.

"Why are you laughing?" she demanded, not the least bit amused to think she had done something foolish or clumsy enough to provoke his mirth.

He wrapped his arms even more tightly around her, his eyes glowing with tenderness as they met hers in the mirror. "I was just thinking about all of the times Julian berated

me for keeping this mirror because I was too ham-fisted to
tie my cravat without it."

Feeling as contented as a cat, Caroline lay curled up in
Adrian's arms, watching a hazy beam of morning sunlight
creep toward the bed. As he combed his fingers through her
tumbled hair, it was all she could do to keep from purring.
She nestled her cheek against his chest, marveling at the
steady thump of his heart beneath her ear.

His chuckle was a deep rumble. "What is it, sweeting?
Are you listening for a heart you're still not convinced I
have?"

She stroked the golden fleece on his chest, twining one
of the crisp whorls around her finger. "I'm just glad it
wasn't broken when Vivienne threw you over for Constable
Larkin."

He cleared his throat. "Well, I must admit that your sister's devotion to the good constable didn't come as a *complete* surprise."

Caroline sat up on one elbow, gazing at him through narrowed eyes. Although he blinked at her in boyish innocence, he still managed to look like a sleek jungle cat that
had just wolfed down a rather large and bony canary.

"Why, you shameless wretch!" she breathed. "You knew
all along that Vivienne was in love with Larkin, didn't
you?" Thinking of all the guilt she'd suffered on her sister's
account, she wailed, "Why in the name of heaven didn't
you tell me?"

"If I'd have told you before you found out about Julian,
you would have given her and Larkin your blessing and
gone away." He cupped her cheek in his hand, gazing deep
into her eyes. "Not only would I have lost Vivienne, I would
have lost you as well."

She brushed his hand away, refusing to be seduced by his
soulful gaze. "And if you had told me *after* I found out about
Julian and Duvalier, you wouldn't have had any leverage
to keep me from telling Vivienne all about your wicked

scheme." She flopped back onto the pillow and shook her head, torn between outrage and admiration. "You, my lord, are a scoundrel *and* a reprobate!"

Adrian rose up to lean over her, his eyes sparkling with devilment. "You weren't even privy to my most nefarious plot of all."

"And what would that be?" Her stern tone couldn't quite hide her growing breathlessness as he began to lavish feather-soft butterfly kisses along the curve of her jaw.

His lips glided down her throat, punctuating each word with a kiss. "My diabolical plot to get you out of that accursed dress before there was any chance of Duvalier seeing you." He cupped one of her breasts in his hand, molding it into the perfect shape for his tongue to swirl around the quickening bud of her nipple.

Caroline gasped, her temper softened by a melting rush of desire. "I might not approve of your motives," she said breathlessly, twining her fingers through the raw silk of his hair, "but I can't dispute the effectiveness of your methods."

The tantalizing warmth of his lips had just closed around her breast when a sharp rap came on the door.

Caroline groaned. "If Portia has tracked me down here, you have my permission to toss her in the dungeon."

Adrian lifted his head. "What if it's Wilbury? He's a staunch defender of propriety, you know. If he finds out you've compromised me, he'll insist that you make an honest man out of me."

She grinned up at him. "That would be a refreshing change, now wouldn't it?"

"Impertinent miss," Adrian growled, tickling her ribs. Not even her shrieks of laughter could drown out a fresh round of pounding on the door.

Muttering an oath beneath his breath, Adrian rolled off of her and stalked over to the gilded screen in the corner to retrieve his dressing gown.

He swept the ruby velvet garment around him and

knotted the belt, leaving Caroline to sigh over the finely muscled length of his calves.

As she drew the quilt up to her chin and blew a wayward strand of hair out of her eyes, he stalked to the door and swung it open. It wasn't Portia or Wilbury who stood there, but Constable Larkin.

Running a hand through his rumpled hair, Adrian sighed. "If you've come to call me out on Miss Cabot's behalf, Alastair, there's no need. I plan to marry her just as soon as I can procure a special license from the archbishop. I have no intention of my heir being born a mere eight months after our nuptials."

Caroline touched a hand to her stomach beneath the sheet, wondering if Adrian could have already put his babe inside of her. The possibility made her heart soar with joy.

But as he stepped aside and she saw the look on Larkin's face, it went plunging all the way to her toes.

"I haven't come about Caroline, but about Portia," Larkin said, his face gray and drawn. "She's missing. We fear she may have run away."

Twenty-one

Portia's bedchamber was deserted, but the window nearest the bed stood wide open, inviting in a lark's cheery song and a balmy spring breeze. It was too easy for Caroline to imagine the distant strains of a waltz floating through that window, its soaring melody irresistible.

While Larkin hovered by the door, murmuring words of comfort to a white-faced Vivienne, she and Adrian followed the trail of bedsheets knotted around one of the bedposts to the window. The makeshift ladder disappeared over the ledge. Tucking a strand of hair that had escaped her hastily wound chignon behind her ear, Caroline leaned out of the second-story window. The end of the sheet was dangling right over a minty green patch of grass bathed in a bright pool of sunshine. Last night there would have been only shadows waiting to receive whoever was bold enough to shimmy down its length.

"I haven't been able to find any sign of struggle or foul play," Larkin informed them. "All I found on the ledge was this." He held up something that looked like a broom straw.

"It's a whisker from the cat mask Julian gave her," Caroline said, her dismay growing. "She was so excited about wearing it for him."

"It's all my fault," Vivienne said, still clinging to Larkin's arm. "If I had come back to my room before dawn, I might have realized she was missing."

While Caroline's mouth fell open, Adrian swung around to level a piercing look at his old friend. "Am I going to have to call *you* out, Constable?"

Larkin jerked his waistcoat straight, an endearing flush staining his high cheekbones. For the first time, Caroline noticed that although Vivienne was still wearing the green dressing gown, Larkin's cravat was tied in a French knot meticulous enough to make Brummel pale with envy. "I should say not. I can assure you that my intentions toward Miss Cabot's sister are honorable. If I'd have had my way, we would be halfway to Gretna Green right now. But Vivienne refused to elope. She insisted it was only proper that her older sister be the first to wed."

Watching how tenderly he gathered Vivienne in his arms, Adrian said softly, "You'd best get used to it, mate."

"What?" Larkin asked.

"Not having your way."

"I don't understand," Vivienne said as Adrian leaned out the window to study the grounds below. "If Portia simply snuck out to attend the ball against Caroline's wishes, then why hasn't she returned? Alastair has made discreet inquiries throughout the castle, and the servants swear there's been no sign of her since yesterday afternoon."

Caroline shook her head, remembering her last encounter with Portia. "She was terribly angry at me for not allowing her to go to the ball. She may still be sulking somewhere on the grounds, trying to give me a bit of a fright to punish me."

Even as she said the words, Caroline knew how unlikely they were to be true. Portia had never been one to hold a grudge. Her temper usually cooled to a simmer just as quickly as it boiled over. Caroline had lost count of the number of times Portia had charmed her into forgiving some tantrum or cross word simply by throwing her arms around her and blurting out an apology. She would have given almost anything to feel those arms around her now.

She also couldn't help but remember how she had deliberately scoffed at Portia's fears and fancies. How, in a misguided attempt to protect her, she had assured her that there was no real danger. Thanks to her, Portia was the only one of them who didn't know that vampires really did stalk the night.

She tugged at Adrian's sleeve, no longer able to choke back her rising fears. "You don't think it could be Duvalier, do you?"

He drew his head in the window and slowly turned to face her, his jaw set in a grim line. Before spending last night in his arms and his bed and experiencing firsthand the limitless depths of his passion, she might not have recognized the utter absence of emotion in his eyes.

She took a step back and clapped a hand over her mouth, remembering too late that Duvalier wasn't the only monster of their acquaintance.

Caroline followed Adrian past the basement kitchens, taking two steps for every one of his long strides. When he started down the dank, sloping passage that led to the spice cellar, she had to gather up Eloisa's gown in one fist to keep from tripping over its hem. She was beginning to despise the thing even more than before, but there had been no time to return to her chamber and change. Not with Adrian's urgency driving them through the castle like a whip.

She didn't even have time to shudder when a large rat went scurrying out of the path of Adrian's boots, squeaking frantically. Before she could catch her breath, they were standing outside the door of the spice cellar.

Remembering the iron ring of keys Wilbury wore at his waist, she said, "Won't you need a—"

Adrian lifted one powerful leg and kicked the door right off its hinges.

"—key?" she finished weakly, waving away a choking cloud of dust.

He wrested one of the crude tallow candles from the iron sconce just outside of the cellar, then strode over to the shelf on the opposite wall. Before Caroline could catch up with him, his sure fingers had sought and found the smoky glass bottle perched on the back of the shelf's edge.

"What is it?" she asked. "Holy water?"

Instead of replying, he gave the bottle a savage twist. The entire wall of shelves swung inward, revealing a passage that was even danker—and darker—than the one they'd just traversed.

"I knew it!" Caroline exclaimed. "Why, I'll bet Wilbury knew about this all along."

Adrian ducked beneath the sagging door frame. "It was probably one of his ancestors who helped build it. His family has been serving mine for centuries. That's why he was the only one I ever trusted with Julian's secret." He glanced over his shoulder, his eyes warming for an elusive instant. "Until you."

As he disappeared into the shadows, Caroline hastened after him. A narrow set of stone stairs hugged the circular wall, spiraling down into the darkness. As they descended with only the wavering flame of the candle to light their way, Caroline edged closer to Adrian, clutching a fistful of his shirt in her trembling hand. He reached behind him, twining his warm fingers through hers.

They seemed to be descending into a realm of eternal night, some shadowy kingdom banished forever from the sunlight they'd left behind. Caroline could hear water trickling through some subterranean crack and the faint squeaking of something that she fervently hoped was another rat.

When they reached the bottom of the stairs, Adrian touched the wick of the candle to a pitch-soaked torch mounted on the wall. The torch flared to life with a sinister hiss, its hellish glow transforming their shadows into hulking monsters.

"Welcome to my dungeon," Adrian said softly, plucking the torch from its sconce and holding it aloft.

Her fingers slipping from his, Caroline went gliding forward, her fear momentarily supplanted by astonishment. Despite the absence of the village virgins, the dank stone chamber was just as she'd imagined it. Chains and manacles dangled from hooks set at regular intervals in the walls, their iron links rusty from disuse.

Caroline scooped up one of the manacles in her hand, studying it with ill-disguised fascination.

"Perhaps we can try those another time if you're so inclined," Adrian said.

She returned his teasing smirk with one of her own. "Only if *you* agree to wear them."

He arched one eyebrow, the husky note in his voice playing havoc with both her body and her heart. "For you, my love? Gladly."

The manacle slipped from her hand, striking the wall with a musical clank. As she surveyed the gloomy cavern of a chamber, a helpless laugh escaped her.

"What is it?" Adrian asked, his rugged features softened by concern.

"I was just thinking how much Portia would be enjoying all of this. A mysterious disappearance. Secret passages. A genuine dungeon. It's like a scene from one of Dr. Polidori's ridiculous stories." Without warning, hot tears flooded her eyes.

Adrian crossed to her and drew her into a fierce one-armed embrace. "I'll find her," he vowed, pressing his lips to her hair. "I swear it on my life."

Blinking away her tears, Caroline tipped back her head to give him a shaky smile. "We'll make sure this story has a happy ending, won't we?"

Since Adrian was kind enough to nod, she pretended not to see the shadow of doubt in his eyes. He turned, sweeping the torch in front of them. For the first time, Caroline noticed the wooden door set deep into the corner, an iron grate its only window to the world.

Although she half expected Adrian to lift his leg and kick the door down, he simply gave it a gentle push. Caroline gasped, astonished anew.

Instead of a rat-infested cell, the door swung open to reveal a spacious chamber that could have been located anywhere in the castle.

From the cashmere blanket tossed over the scrolled arm of the chaise longue to the walls hung in rich Chinese silk to the marble chess set resting on the Chippendale table with a game still half in play, it was evident that the room was inhabited by a creature who prized his every comfort. It might have been the opulent bedchamber of a young Indian rajah if not for one thing.

There was no bed on the raised dais in the center of the room, only a wooden coffin.

Caroline swallowed, the sight bringing a primal knot of dread to her throat. She stole a glance at Adrian to find his eyes hooded and his jaw clenched. Realizing just how difficult this must be for him, she slipped her arm through his.

He glanced down at her. "I should warn you that my brother's not going to be very happy with me for disturbing him. Even as a boy, he was always a cranky napper."

She edged even closer to him. "If he insists upon sulking, we'll ring for Wilbury to fetch him some biscuits and milk."

His reluctance growing ever more palpable, Adrian slowly moved toward the coffin. Caroline matched him step for step, fighting her own dread.

She held her breath as Adrian reached down and slid aside the heavy lid. As the flickering torchlight played over its interior, she realized that there was something even more terrible than seeing an actual vampire slumbering in his coffin.

Because the coffin was empty. Julian was gone.

* * *

Julian lay huddled on the cold stone floor, his body wracked with spasms of agony. It had been over fifteen hours since he'd had any sustenance. The hunger was devouring him from the inside out, the thirst leaching every last drop of moisture from his veins, leaving them as parched as an endless desert beneath the scorching heat of the sun. Although his skin was icy cold, he burned with fever. If its flames were allowed to rage unchecked, he knew they would sear away the last of his humanity, leaving behind a ravening beast that would devour even those he loved for a chance at survival.

With a growl that was more animal than human, he gave the chains binding his manacled wrists to the wall a savage yank. Only a few hours ago he could have ripped them from the mortar with one hand. But the crucifix Duvalier had left around his neck throughout the long night had doubled the drain on his waning strength. Although Duvalier had come to remove it at dawn, its imprint was still seared into the flesh of his chest. Duvalier's utter depravity had turned a symbol of hope into a weapon of destruction.

A fresh shudder coursed through him, so violent he could almost hear his bones rattle together. He collapsed against the stones, the chains slipping from his fingers.

He was dying. Soon he would no longer be among the unhallowed ranks of the living dead, just the dead. Without his soul, there would be no promise of redemption, no hope of heaven. He would simply dry up and crumble to dust, leaving the gritty ashes of his bones to be scattered on the wind.

He pressed his eyes shut, the light from the single torch too bright for him to bear. The singsong words of a prayer he and Adrian used to repeat at bedtime when they were boys echoed through his mind in a taunting refrain. No prayer could protect him from the bloodlust that was ravaging his sanity and his will. The drive to feed was supplanting every other instinct, every shred of human decency Adrian had fought so hard to preserve.

Groaning, Julian turned his face to the floor. Even if Adrian came for him in time, he didn't know if he could bear for his brother to see him like this again. He almost wished Duvalier had left him chained in some grassy glade where the ruthless rays of the sun could have ended his miserable existence before anyone even realized he was missing.

Portia Cabot's face suddenly rose up before him in the darkness, all impish charm and dewy innocence. He wondered if she would mourn him when he was gone. Would she weep into her pillow and dream of what might have been? He tried to summon up an image of her sitting next to him on the piano bench, but all he could see was the candlelight playing over the graceful curve of her neck, the tantalizing flutter of the pulse at the side of her throat as she tipped back her head to smile at him. He could see himself leaning over her, brushing his lips over the creamy satin of her skin . . . before sinking his fangs deep into her succulent flesh, taking her innocence and her blood with equal ruthlessness.

Howling with denial, Julian lunged to his knees, flinging himself against the weight of his chains again and again until he finally collapsed in an exhausted heap.

He never heard the door creak open. Didn't know he was no longer alone until Duvalier's melodious voice poured over him like honeyed venom. "You disappoint me, Jules. I had expected so much more from you."

Twenty-two

It's the little one who keeps following me around like some sort of lovesick puppy just begging for a morsel of my attention. She's the one who gazes up at me with those lovely blue eyes of hers as if I was the answer to her every prayer. If I was going to slip, don't you think it would be with her?

Adrian checked the charge on his pistol with brisk efficiency before slipping it into the waistband of his trousers, his brother's words haunting him just as much as Caroline's steady gaze.

While she watched from the doorway of his bedchamber, he reached back into the battered chest that had crossed oceans and traveled halfway around the world with him and Julian and drew out a black cloak. He whipped it around his shoulders, securing its voluminous folds with a copper brooch.

Delving back into the chest, he filled the cloak's various inside pockets with half a dozen wooden stakes carved from aspen and wild hawthorn, all honed to a lethal point, several knives of varying shapes and sizes, three bottles of holy water, and a miniature crossbow.

He was sliding a small but deadly silver blade into the inner sheath of his boot when Caroline sidled up next to him, peering into the chest.

"Are you going to find my sister or fight a war?"

Slamming down the lid, Adrian turned to face her. He

was keenly aware of the bed behind her. The sheets were still rumpled from their loving, and he couldn't help but feel that he was somehow profaning this sacred place with his instruments of destruction. Seeing the rusty stains on the sheets—all that was left of Caroline's innocence—almost made him feel like one of the monsters he was preparing to hunt.

"If Duvalier is somehow involved," he said, "then I'm going to do both."

He turned toward the door, but she grabbed his arm before he could escape. "And if it's not Duvalier? What will you do then?"

He tugged his arm out of her grasp, meeting her steely gaze with one of his own. "My job."

He was halfway across the tower when he realized she was right behind him. He wheeled around to face her. "Where in the bloody hell do you think you're going?"

"With you."

"You most certainly are not!"

"I most certainly am. She's my sister."

"And he's my brother!"

They glared at each other, the echo of his roar hanging between them. Caroline finally lifted her chin and said, "You can't tell me what to do. You're not my husband."

Adrian's eyes widened with disbelief. "And I suppose when I am your husband, you're going to obey my every command?"

Caroline opened her mouth, then snapped it shut again.

He snorted. "I didn't think so."

He raked his fingers through his hair, then grabbed her by the hand and dragged her back over to the chest. Still muttering imprecations beneath his breath, he dug out another, slightly shorter, cloak and whisked it around her shoulders. She stood patiently while he crammed weapons of every variety into every conceivable pocket.

As he equipped her with two bottles of holy water, he said, "You must always remember that it's not the blessed items themselves that a vampire fears. It's your faith in those items. Faith is the one enemy they can never fully defeat."

As Caroline nodded obediently, he turned and strode back to the door. It wasn't until she took her first clanking step to follow him that he realized she was so weighted down with weapons she could barely walk.

Sighing, he marched back over to her and began to divest her of the heaviest of them. Avoiding her eyes, he gruffly said, "When I first found Eloisa that day at the gambling hell, I tried to kiss her. I suppose I thought that I could warm her with my flesh, that I could somehow breathe life back into her. But her lips were cold and blue and unyielding." No longer able to resist the temptation, he lifted his fingertips to Caroline's lips, tenderly tracing their velvety contours. "If such a thing should happen to your beautiful mouth . . ."

She caught his hand in hers, pressing it to her cheek. "I may be wearing her dress, Adrian, but I'm not Eloisa. If you had known she was in danger before it was too late, I'm convinced you would have saved her. The same way you're going to save my sister. *And* your brother." She gazed up at him, her lips curving in a tremulous smile. "I believe that with all my heart because I have faith in you."

As Duvalier's shadow fell over him, Julian lunged at it, his teeth bared in a growl.

"Ah, that's more like it!" Duvalier said, his full lips curving in a smile. "I'd rather have you snarling at me like a mad dog than cowering in the corner like a whipped pup."

Clenching his teeth against a fresh round of chills, Julian choked out, "The only one mad around here, Victor, is you."

Duvalier eased back the hood of his cloak to reveal the glossy sweep of his long black hair. Lifting his shoulders in a Gallic shrug, he said, "I fear that madness, like so many things, is in the eye of the beholder." His French accent had only deepened in his years away from England, softening his consonants to a throaty purr. "Some might even consider it a gift, just like immortality."

"I consider both a curse," Julian spat.

"That's why I'm so much stronger than you. So much more powerful. I've spent the last five years embracing what I am while you've spent the last five years running from it."

"From where I stood, the only one running was you."

Duvalier's smile no longer quite reached his eyes. "I have only myself to blame for that. It seems I underestimated your brother's persistence. I thought he would be forced to destroy you and that, in turn, would destroy him."

"What you underestimated was his love for me and his determination to hunt you to the ends of the earth."

"If he truly loved you, he would accept you for what you are, would he not?" Sighing, Duvalier shook his head. "I almost pity you. You're not willing to be a vampire, but you're not a man, either. Tell me, what are you thinking about when you're with a woman? Are you thinking about the scent of her skin, the softness of her breasts, the pleasure she can give you with her hands, her mouth, that sweet little nest between her legs? Or are you listening for the beat of her heart beneath yours as you enter her, the irresistible whisper of her blood rushing through her veins when you make her come?"

Julian groaned as a cramp of raw hunger knifed through him. Doubling over, he crumpled to his side.

Duvalier knelt next to him, his voice soft yet relentless. "You're a man who adores women, are you not? Yet in all these years, you've never allowed yourself a virgin. Why is that? Do you think you're unworthy to defile such a treasure? Or are you afraid the scent of the blood of her innocence might drive you mad? Are you afraid you might awaken bathed in it with no memory of how the girl with the slack mouth and unseeing eyes came to be lying next to you?"

Julian clapped his hands over his ears, biting back a whimper.

Duvalier stroked his hair, his touch almost gentle. "Poor sad boy. I made you, you know. When you were playing at vampire hunter with your brother and his new whore, did it never occur to you that I could break you as well?"

Julian lay utterly still, afraid to think, afraid to feel, afraid to hope, as Duvalier slipped a key into one manacle and then the other. The iron bracelets fell away, freeing his arms from the weight of the chains.

Julian gave Duvalier just enough time to rise to his feet before lunging for his throat, fangs bared. As Duvalier danced easily out of his reach, Julian lurched forward a few steps, then went crashing to one knee. Even without the chains, the burden of the crucifix etched on his chest coupled with starvation had left him too weak to fight. He was too weak to do anything now but feed. And soon he would only have the strength to die.

Duvalier clucked in sympathy. "Perhaps it's time I showed you that even a monster like me is capable of mercy."

Drawing up the hood of his cloak to protect him from the sunlight, he ducked out the door. He reappeared a few seconds later carrying a squirming bundle wrapped in burlap.

Julian licked his parched lips. Perhaps Duvalier had brought him a sheep or some other animal to sustain him. The bastard was just sadistic enough to keep him alive, if only to prolong his torture.

As Duvalier set his burden on its feet and jerked away the burlap, Julian's helpless anticipation turned to horror.

Portia stood there, her hands bound in front of her and a silk gag stuffed between her beautiful lips. Her hair tumbled around her shoulders in wild disarray and grimy tear tracks stained her cheeks. The blue-striped muslin of her gown was ripped and stained in several places, as if she'd put up a valiant struggle against Duvalier's machinations.

When she saw him, she let out a muffled cry, hope flaring in her terrified eyes. She had no way of knowing she was facing her doom.

Although it took the last ounce of his strength, Julian

managed to stagger to his feet. "No!" he rasped. "I won't let you kill her the way you killed Eloisa!"

Duvalier's smile was as tender as a lover's. "Oh, I'm not going to kill her. You are."

Sneering with triumph, Duvalier hurled Portia straight into Julian's arms. With his senses heightened by starvation, he could smell her fear, hear every rhythmic nuance of the blood pumping its way through her racing heart. As she pressed her trembling body against him, his body reacted with a lust as keen as any he had ever known.

"No," he whispered, already feeling his fangs lengthening, sharpening.

"When I caught this *jeune fille* sneaking out of her bedchamber window last night, she begged me to take her to you. So I have. As I said, I am not without mercy." Sweeping his cloak around, Duvalier turned to go.

Swallowing the last bitter dregs of his pride, Julian cried out, "Don't do this, Victor! Please! I'm begging you!"

Duvalier shrugged as if his words were only an afterthought. "If you don't want to kill her, you could always wait until that precious moment when her heart is beating its last and suck the soul right out of her. Then she would be one of us and you could enjoy the pleasure of her company for all eternity." He lingered just long enough to give Julian one last smile. "It's your choice."

Then the door closed, the turn of the key in the padlock echoing with grim finality.

When Adrian and Caroline slipped out one of the French windows in the breakfast room, seeking to avoid the prying eyes of the servants, they found Vivienne and Larkin on the terrace waiting for them.

Vivienne was wearing a pretty little bonnet and a forest green cloak, while Larkin sported a pearl-handled pistol and a resolute expression.

"You *can't* be serious," Adrian said, folding his arms over his chest and surveying them through narrowed eyes.

Caroline stepped in front of him, glaring at her sister. "If you think for one minute that I'm going to allow you to accompany us, young lady, then that silly little bonnet of yours must be constricting your brain."

Vivienne drew herself up with a regal sniff. "And why shouldn't I accompany you? Portia is my sister, too."

Having just been defeated by the same argument, Adrian was enjoying Caroline's discomfiture more than he knew he ought to be. "She has a valid point, darling."

Caroline turned her glare on him. "Who asked you?"

Remembering that she was armed, he lifted his hands in a gesture of surrender and backed away, exchanging a wary look with Larkin.

The two sisters stood toe-to-toe, neither showing any sign of budging.

"Portia may already be in trouble," Caroline said. "I won't stand by and let you put yourself in danger as well. I haven't the time nor the inclination to rescue the both of you."

"I'm not asking for your permission," Vivienne retorted. "You're my sister, not my mother."

Larkin was possessed by a sudden coughing fit, forcing Adrian to clap him on the back.

After a moment of stunned silence, Caroline breathed, "Why, you ungrateful little brat! After everything I've done for you, everything I've sacrificed, how could you—"

Vivienne started talking right over her. "No one ever forced you to play the role of mother or martyr. If you weren't so proud and so pigheaded, you might have been able to ask for a helping hand every now and then. All you had to do was say, 'Vivienne, would you mind putting the bow in Portia's hair today?' or 'Vivienne, why don't you run down to the market and pick us out a nice—"

"—might have but you were probably too busy sitting in front of the mirror combing your long golden curls or practicing dotting your *i*'s with ridiculous little hearts or trying on all the beautiful gowns that Mama had made for *me*!"

Vivienne gasped. "Why, you jealous cow! I might have *borrowed* your gowns for a time, but at least I never accidentally left your favorite doll sitting too close to the fire, singing off all of *her* long golden curls!"

Caroline leaned forward until her nose was almost touching Vivienne's, a nasty smile curving her lips. "Who said it was an accident?"

As they each launched into a new tirade, detailing each other's failings for the past two decades, Adrian tapped Larkin on the shoulder and jerked his head toward the woods.

They had nearly made it to the edge of the underbrush when Caroline's head suddenly whipped around. "Just where do you two think you're going?"

Adrian sighed. "To find Portia and Julian, we hope."

"Not without us you're not!" Grabbing Vivienne by her gloved hand, Caroline dragged her sister off the terrace and toward the woods. "Aren't men the most impossible creatures? You spend one night in their beds and they think that just because they gave you a few hours of unspeakable pleasure, they can spend the rest of their lives deciding what's best for you."

Vivienne nodded in agreement. "They're absolutely insufferable. Why, Alastair refused to let me come today until I agreed to wear a pair of his boots!" She lifted her hem to display the ungainly things. "I had to put on half a dozen pairs of stockings just to keep them on. Now my feet feel like great ugly slabs of ham."

"You poor lamb," Caroline crooned, linking her arm through Vivienne's. "As soon as we find Portia and Julian, we'll give your feet a good soaking in front of the fire."

As they passed the men, still chattering like magpies, Adrian and Larkin exchanged a disbelieving glance.

"It appears they've found a common enemy," Larkin murmured.

"Yes," Adrian agreed, blowing out a beleaguered sigh. "Us."

* * *

As they trudged over hill and dale, waded through chill streams, and ducked beneath the low hanging eaves of shallow caves, searching all of Adrian and Julian's boyhood haunts, Caroline almost wished she had borrowed a pair of Adrian's boots. The soles of her own boots were worn so thin she could feel the bite of every rock and root.

She would have collapsed into an exhausted heap more than once, but each time she stumbled, Adrian's hand was there to bear her up. Each time her strength faltered, the sight of his determined face would goad her into continuing.

He was handing her over a fallen log with a steep and rocky crevasse below it when he murmured, "Unspeakable pleasure, eh?"

Caroline lowered her head to hide her smile. "You needn't look so satisfied with yourself. I suppose it was all rather . . . *tolerable*."

"Only tolerable?" He gave her hand a tug, giving her no choice but to stumble against him. With the softness of her breasts crushed against his chest, he gazed down at her, his eyes smoky with promise. "Then it seems I'll have no choice but to redouble my efforts tonight."

Tonight, when Portia and Julian were safe. Tonight, when they were curled up in Adrian's cozy bed, making plans for their wedding and laughing at the fright their silly siblings had given them. Gazing into his eyes, Caroline could see how badly they both wanted to believe in that future.

But as the day waned, so did their hopes. The sun vanished behind a veil of clouds and a light rain began to fall, hastening the descent of twilight. Vivienne's sprightly little bonnet began to droop. When it collapsed altogether, she tugged it off and tossed it away in disgust, drawing the hood of her cloak up over her hair.

They emerged from the shadows of the forest to find themselves in a large clearing. A squat building sat in the middle of it, its ancient stones weathered and encrusted with lichen. A stone angel stood guard over its entrance, his stern face warning them that this was no haven for the weary traveler.

"What is this place?" Caroline whispered, unsettled by the unnatural hush.

"The Kane family crypt," Adrian murmured in reply.

She shivered, thinking it was no wonder that the voices of the living seemed so unwelcome here.

Adrian picked his way over the blanket of crushed and sodden leaves, cautiously approaching the crypt. The rest of them trailed behind, their reluctance palpable. But once he reached the crypt door, he simply stood gazing down at the ornate iron handle.

"What is it?" Larkin asked, drawing Vivienne closer.

Adrian lifted his head. All Caroline could think was that he must have had that exact same expression when he stood outside that gambling hell with Eloisa's body inside and watched it burn. "The crypt door has never been padlocked from the outside before. You don't usually have to worry about its occupants escaping."

Caroline felt the tiny hairs at her nape prickle with dread.

"Stand back," Adrian commanded, drawing the pistol from the waistband of his trousers.

As he backed away several paces, the rest of them followed suit.

He took aim and pulled the trigger, shattering the padlock with a single shot. The pistol's sharp report echoed through the clearing. As the smoke rising like mist from its barrel slowly cleared, the crypt door came creaking open.

Twenty-three

Julian came staggering through the crypt door, bearing Portia like a child in his arms. Her head hung limp over his arm, her sooty curls spilling nearly to his hip. Her eyes were closed, her skin deathly pale—so pale that there could be no mistaking the twin gashes marring the ashen perfection of her throat.

A broken cry tore from Caroline's lips. As Vivienne's knees buckled, Larkin sank to the leaves with her, wrapping his arms around her to muffle her sobs against his chest.

His face even more beautiful and terrible than the face of the angel guarding the tomb, Adrian reached inside his cloak and drew out a wooden stake.

He started forward, but Caroline grabbed his arm, staying him. "No, Adrian," she whispered fiercely, digging her fingernails into his sleeve. "Look at her chest. She's alive!"

Although the movement was nearly imperceptible, Portia's chest was rising and falling in an even rhythm.

Julian lurched toward them, the tears streaming down his face mingling with the rain. Caroline gasped, not realizing until that moment that he looked even closer to death than Portia. His eyes were hollow, his cheeks sunken, his skin as pale as parchment. His teeth looked ghastly white against the blue of his lips.

His voice was little more than a hoarse croak. "I only took

what I needed to survive." He gazed down into Portia's face with wrenching tenderness. "I wouldn't have done that if the stubborn little fool hadn't insisted. I tried to warn her that it was too dangerous, that I didn't trust myself to stop before it was too late, but she wouldn't listen."

As he stumbled to his knees, still cradling Portia to his chest, they all rushed forward. Larkin gently removed Portia from Julian's arms with Vivienne's help while Adrian lowered Julian across his lap.

"I didn't ever want you to see me like this again," Julian bit off through his chattering teeth. He clutched at Adrian, his body wracked with uncontrollable tremors. "I didn't want anyone to s-s-see what Victor did to me. To know what a terrible m-m-monster I am."

"You're no monster." Adrian gently stroked Julian's sweat-drenched hair away from his face, his own hand trembling. "If you were, Portia would be dead right now."

Julian blinked up at him. "If I'm not a monster, then what am I?"

"You're what you always have been and what you always will be." Adrian rested his brow against Julian's and closed his eyes, but not before Caroline could see the tears shining in them. "My brother."

"How is he?" Caroline whispered, standing in the doorway of the south tower several hours later.

Adrian was sprawled in a chair beside the bed in shirt-sleeves and trousers, his long legs stretched out in front of him and his chin pillowed on his palm. Although his eyes were hooded with exhaustion, the candlelight revealed that they'd lost none of their vigilant glitter.

He had insisted upon carrying Julian up those five flights of stairs himself and installing him in his own bed. Dawn was fast approaching and the tower's heavy velvet drapes had all been drawn to ensure that there would be no risk of a single ray of sunlight stealing into the room.

"He's resting well," Adrian said as Caroline drew near the

bed. He gazed fondly down at his brother's sleeping visage. "He should be back to nagging me about my crooked cravats and beating me at chess in no time at all."

Julian's lips had lost their blue tinge and a hint of color was slowly returning to his cheeks. Caroline averted her eyes from the goblet resting on the table next to the bed, knowing she didn't have to ask if it contained red wine.

"How is Portia?" Adrian asked.

"Positively insufferable," Caroline assured him. "She keeps demanding fresh glasses of water and kidney pie and gloating because she and Dr. Polidori were right all along about the existence of vampires. Vivienne insisted on taking charge of her for a little while, and I didn't *dare* refuse." She grimaced down at the tattered hem of Eloisa's gown. "Besides, I can't wait to get out of this gown and ring for a steaming bath."

"Are you sure you don't want me to summon Dr. Kidwell to examine her? I can deal with a few awkward questions if I have to. Especially with Alastair by my side. The local authorities would probably be quite impressed with a London constable."

"No, thank you," she replied with a shudder. "The doctor would probably just want to bleed her."

Adrian hesitated. "Has Portia talked about what happened in that crypt?"

Caroline shook her head before saying softly, "I don't believe she ever will." She studied Julian's handsome face, thinking how boyish and innocent it looked in repose. "She worships the ground he walks on. She would have done anything for him."

Caroline rested her hand on Adrian's shoulder, remembering that terrible moment when it had looked as if his brother had murdered her sister . . . and any hope of a future they might have shared.

She expected Adrian to cover her hand with his own. But he rose from the chair instead, leaving her hand hanging awkwardly in midair.

He paced over to the French doors and swept aside the heavy drapes, gazing out into the waning night. "What about Duvalier?" he asked, the name a poisonous oath on his lips. "What did Portia tell you about him?"

Caroline felt her features harden. "She told me that he snatched her before she could even reach the ball, that he kept her tied up in some cave all night, that he tossed her into that crypt with Julian as if she was nothing more than a piece of raw meat."

Adrian swore. "Not once since all this began has that bastard dared to confront me face to face. I should have known this time would be no different. He's probably leagues from here by now."

"His day of reckoning will come, Adrian. He'll answer for every life he's destroyed, every precious soul he's stolen, including Julian's. Together, we'll make sure of that."

Adrian continued to gaze out into the night. "As soon as Portia is strong enough to travel, I want you to take her and Vivienne and leave this place."

"I'm sure Constable Larkin would be more than willing to see my sisters safely back to Aunt Marietta's."

"Alastair has already agreed to escort all three of you to London."

Caroline smiled. "So the two of you have been conspiring behind our backs, eh? That's not very sporting of you. You'll simply have to tell the good constable that I'm not going anywhere without you."

"Yes, you are. You're going back to London and you're going to pretend the last fortnight never happened."

Her smile faded. "You can't ask that of me."

"I'm not asking." Adrian turned to face her, his eyes meeting hers for the first time since she'd walked into the tower. What she saw in their bleak depths chilled her to the bone.

Despite her growing apprehension, she managed a shaky laugh. "I thought we'd already determined that you haven't the right to order me about. That can only be purchased with a special license from the archbishop."

He shook his head before saying softly, "I'm afraid I can no longer afford to purchase such a license. Not when it could cost the both of us so dearly."

"It's a price I'm only too willing to pay."

"But I'm not. When Julian came staggering out of that crypt with Portia in his arms, both of them half-dead, I realized that I had been a naive fool to believe I could protect any of you. That's why you have to go now . . . before it's too late."

"How can you admit you love me, then in the next breath ask me to leave you?"

He stabbed a finger toward Julian's motionless form. "Because that could be you lying in that bed right now. Or worse yet, lying in your grave. No one I love will ever be safe until Duvalier is destroyed. And until that day, I can't afford any more distractions."

"Is that all I've been to you?" Caroline whispered. "A distraction?"

He strode toward her, his face taut with anguish. "If I say yes, will you go? What if I tell you that the night we spent together was nothing more than a passably pleasant diversion? That you were more easily seduced than most? That I found your lack of experience tiresome and much prefer the practiced caresses of whores and opera dancers to your clumsy fumblings and overwrought declarations of love?"

Caroline backed away from him, unable to keep from flinching beneath the cruel lash of his words.

He caught her by the shoulders, giving her a rough shake. "Is that what you want to hear from my lips? If I tell you that my only intention from the beginning was to seduce you, then discard you, will it make you hate me enough to leave me?"

"No," she whispered, gazing up at him through a veil of tears. "It would only make me love you more because I would know that you loved me enough to put your own soul in jeopardy by telling such a blatant lie."

Biting off an inarticulate oath, Adrian released her and paced a few feet away. "You might be willing to risk your own life to stay with me, but what if we should bring a child into this madness? Would you be willing to risk his life—his soul—as well?"

Caroline touched a hand to her stomach. "Have you forgotten that I might already be carrying your child?"

Adrian might be able to hide his love for her behind a resolute mask, but he couldn't disguise the hopeless yearning in his gaze as it drifted down to her belly. Only then did she realize that she had made a fatal tactical error.

"All the more reason for you to go," he said softly, slowly raising his eyes to meet hers.

She felt the tears in her eyes spill down her cheeks. "If you do this, Adrian, then Duvalier has already won."

And she had lost. That knowledge tasted as bitter as ashes in Caroline's mouth.

Determined to prove that she could be every bit as ruthless as he could, she crossed to Adrian. "If I were a whore or an opera dancer, you would at least owe me one last kiss." Cupping his face in her hands, she stood on tiptoe and pressed her lips to his, much as she had that magical night at Vauxhall when she had offered him both her kiss and her heart without even realizing it.

He was even more helpless to resist that offer now. As his lips parted to welcome the honeyed sweep of her tongue, his arms went around her, molding her soft curves to the hard planes of his body. When he began to walk backward, tugging her toward the dressing screen on the other side of the room, she willingly joined the dance.

He sank down on the stool behind the screen and drew her into his lap, never once relinquishing his greedy claim on her lips. Caroline recognized the urgency in his kiss because it was the same urgency that was coursing through her own veins, a desperate hunger to celebrate life in the tender swirl of his tongue through her mouth, the heated breath of his sigh, the irresistible pulse that beat where their bodies ached to be joined. It was a rejection of death and darkness and all of the shadowy horrors courted by a monster like Duvalier.

As he tugged down the bodice of her dress with one hand, her mouth flowered against the bold curve of his jaw, savoring the salty sweetness of his skin, the tantalizing scrape of his whiskers against her sensitive lips.

She lifted her head to find the ivory curves of her breasts exposed to his heavy-lidded gaze. Her nipples were already as ripe and rosy as fresh cherries.

"Your brother . . ." she gasped, tangling her fingers in his hair.

"Will be dead to the world for hours," he promised her, dragging her nipple into his mouth and suckling her with a fierce and tender hunger that left her panting with need and clenching her thighs together against a molten rush of desire.

Shifting his position on the stool, he urged one of her legs over both of his so that she was straddling the rigid bulge that strained at the butter-soft doeskin of his trousers.

Caroline bit back a moan, that exquisite pressure alone enough to send tremors of anticipation shivering through her womb. Those tremors deepened to shudders when Adrian's hand disappeared beneath her skirt, his deft fingers gliding up the downy softness of her thigh to seek the narrow slit in her silk drawers. When she had spied on the lovers at Vauxhall, she had wondered what the man's hand could have been doing beneath the woman's skirt to make her writhe and moan so shamelessly. Now she knew.

Since she was already dripping with desire for him, there was no need for Adrian to prepare her for what was to come. Yet his fingers lingered against her eager and quivering flesh, working their skillful magic until he was forced to capture her wild cry of abandon in his mouth.

Still kissing her as if she was the only taste of heaven he

would ever know, he tore open the front flap of his trousers and drove himself through the slit in her drawers and into her.

This time he wasn't content to let her set the pace. Cupping her bottom in his big, strong hands, he lifted her off the stool. She wrapped her legs around his waist, clinging to him helplessly as he braced her weight against the nearest wall and drove up and into her again and again, his long, deep strokes battering the very mouth of her womb as his tongue ravished her mouth with equal ruthlessness.

Just when Caroline didn't think she could bear another second of the mindless pleasure without letting out a scream loud enough to wake the dead, Adrian rocked back up into her for one final thrust that threatened to cleave both her body and her heart in two.

She collapsed against his throat, still impaled by his shuddering length. She wished they could stay this way forever with their hearts beating as one, their bodies joined and throbbing with release. Adrian slowly slid down the wall, still cradling her in his arms.

He could no longer feign indifference. When his voice sounded in her ear, it was rough with both urgency and regret. "Once you're safely back home and we're out of England and back on Duvalier's scent, I'll write you. I'll send money, all that you and Portia could possibly need. You'll never have to rely on anyone else's charity again. I've already hired Alastair to manage some of my affairs in London so Vivienne will never have to worry about where their next meal will come from."

Caroline felt every last drop of warmth in her soul cool to ice. Carefully extracting herself from his lap, she climbed to her feet. With all the dignity she could muster, she pulled up her bodice and adjusted her skirt. She was rather at a loss on how to proceed from there until Adrian reached up to a nearby shelf and handed her one of his cravats. Turning away from him, she performed the necessary ablutions.

When she turned back to him, her face was as composed

as it had been when she had stood in the doorway of the great hall and pretended to be Vivienne. "If you think I'm going to wait for you, then you're wrong," she informed him. "I'm afraid I won't be able to pretend this fortnight never happened. Now that you've given me a taste of the pleasures a woman can find in a man's arms, I doubt that I'll be content to spend the rest of my life in a cold, empty bed. You needn't bother to send money. If I can't find a husband, then perhaps I can find some kind and generous man who would be willing to make me his mistress."

Adrian buttoned the front flap of his trousers, his eyes as stormy and dangerous as she had ever seen them. "Just who's going to hell for lying now?"

Caroline smoothed the rumpled skirt of Eloisa's gown, continuing as if he hadn't spoken. "I'd like nothing more than to throw this gown in the rag bin, but I'll have the servants launder it and return it to you. Perhaps it will bring you comfort when you have only your ghosts to keep you warm at night."

With that, she turned and left him. With Julian sleeping, she didn't even have the satisfaction of slamming the French doors behind her.

Caroline hurried down the stone steps and started across the bridge, swiping hot, furious tears from her cheeks as she walked. The stars were fading and the rain had stopped, leaving the world glistening with the promise of a new dawn. But without Adrian, she knew she would be forever trapped in some dreary night of the soul.

Her steps slowed as she reached the peak of the bridge. She was in no hurry to return to her lonely bedchamber. There was nothing for her to do there but wash Adrian's scent from her skin for the last time and start packing.

"Bullheaded, impossible man," she muttered, turning to rest her hands on the bridge's parapet. She dug her fingernails into the rough stone, welcoming its harsh bite. The wind tugged at her hair, tried to dry her tears before they could fall. "I should have staked him through the heart when I had the chance."

"My my, Adrian likes his women bloodthirsty these days, does he not?"

Caroline whirled around to find a hooded and cloaked figure standing in the middle of the bridge, blocking the path to her bedchamber. She would have sworn he hadn't been there only seconds before.

"How did you get up here?" she asked, her heart lurching into an uneven rhythm.

He drew back his hood to reveal a fall of dark hair and a full-lipped smile that was both cruel and sensual. "Perhaps I flew."

Caroline struggled to swallow her burgeoning terror. "I hope you don't expect me to believe such nonsense, Monsieur Duvalier. Julian already told me that vampires can't turn into bats."

Twenty-four

Dawn was coming, but not for Adrian.

Caroline had taken the last of the light with her, leaving him sitting at his brother's bedside, draped in a shroud of gloom. Without the candlelit brightness of her hair, the tender glow in her eyes, the loving warmth of her smile, he was doomed to dwell in shadow, all but indistinguishable from the creatures he hunted.

Adrian closed his eyes, but all he could see was Caroline waving his handkerchief at him in the drawing room of the town house; rising up on tiptoe to boldly press the enticing softness of her lips against his at Vauxhall; lying back among the pillows of his bed, her ivory skin bathed in moonlight, her arms outstretched to welcome him. Adrian rubbed his aching brow, already coming to realize that she was going to haunt him with a vengeance even Eloisa had never shown.

Julian stirred, giving him an excuse to open his eyes and escape her, if only for a moment.

Julian's eyes had fluttered open. Licking his lips, he croaked, "Still thirsty."

Supporting Julian's head, Adrian tilted the goblet to his lips. Julian swallowed, the muscles of his throat working greedily. Although Adrian's first instinct was to grimace, he'd learned long ago that he couldn't afford to be fastidious when it came to his brother's eating habits. Blood wasn't only sustenance to him, it was life.

When Julian had drunk his fill, Adrian gently settled him back among the pillows.

"Our plan," Julian whispered, blinking up at him. "It worked."

"What do you mean?" he asked, leaning closer to the bed.

"Our plan," Julian repeated. "Eloisa . . . Duvalier knows."

"Knows what?"

"About . . . Caroline. He called her . . ." Julian's lashes drifted back down to his cheeks, his voice fading on a weary sigh ". . . your new whore."

Adrian slowly straightened. He didn't realize the goblet had tilted in his hands until he saw the dark pool of blood spreading around his feet.

"Adrian," Julian said without opening his eyes.

"What?" Adrian snapped, his panic swelling with every breath.

Julian opened his eyes, looking straight at him before whispering, "You need more than your ghosts to keep you warm at night."

"Ah, so no introductions are necessary," Duvalier said, a hint of a French accent burnishing each of his words with a continental flair. He took a step toward Caroline, making the bridge suddenly seem very narrow, if not impassable. "Good. I've always found them tiresome. I can generally learn everything I need to know about a man—or a woman—by listening to the sound of their screams as they beg for my mercy."

"Charming," Caroline said briskly, fighting to hide her fear. She knew he would only feed on it. She desperately wished she was still wearing the cloak loaded with weapons. With her body draped in Eloisa's flimsy concoction of satin and tulle, she felt worse than naked. "So how did you know I was Adrian's woman?"

His aquiline nostrils flared with distaste. "Because I can smell him on you, the same way I could smell him on Eloisa." He caught the shadow that flickered across her face. "Oh, he may have loved her, but they were never lovers, *mon cher*. But that didn't stop him from putting his hands on her, his mouth . . ."

"That must have been very difficult for you."

He shrugged. "More difficult for her, I think. In the end I made sure that she died a virgin. Perhaps that was my greatest revenge of all. That she died never knowing the touch of a man. Never knowing the pleasure he could give her, only the pain."

Caroline began to back away from him, desperate to retrace her steps back to Adrian's bedchamber, Adrian's arms.

Duvalier followed her step for step, the hem of his cloak swaying around his booted ankles. "You can't imagine what it was like to stand there with the taste of her blood in my mouth and watch every longing, every hope, every dream she ever had fade from her eyes as her heart slowed to a sigh, then a whisper, then finally stopped. I was going to have her then, you know, but *he* came and ruined it all."

Caroline shuddered. "How could you even contemplate such an unspeakable thing? I thought you were supposed to love her."

His indifferent façade cracked. "She wasn't worthy of my love! Is that why you're wearing that ridiculous gown? Because Adrian believed that when I saw you, I would clap a hand over my heart and cry out, 'My darling Eloisa, I always knew you'd come back to me.'" He rolled his eyes. "I can't believe he actually thought I'd been mooning over the fickle bitch for all these years. He always was such an incurable romantic."

"Yes, I was," Adrian said, emerging from the foot of the stairs behind Duvalier with a full-sized crossbow braced in his arms. "And I still am. Which is why I'm only going to ask you once to step away from the woman I love."

Caroline let out an involuntary cry, her heart surging with hope. Adrian must have slipped out of the south tower and circled around through her bedchamber.

Duvalier slowly turned to face him, a cold smile chilling his features. *"Bonjour, mon ami.* Or should I call you *mon frère?"*

"You're no friend of mine, you bastard. And you're certainly no brother," Adrian said, his tawny hair blowing in the wind. "You relinquished your right to both of those titles when you embraced a brotherhood of monsters and murderers."

"While you were embracing the woman who was supposed to belong to me."

"That's all Eloisa ever was to you, wasn't it?" Adrian said, his gaze flicking ever so briefly to Caroline's face. "A possession. A pretty trinket to hang on your arm, no different from a shiny new walking stick."

Obeying Adrian's unspoken signal, Caroline turned to flee.

Duvalier's arm snaked around her waist like a band of iron. Jerking her against him, he cupped her chin in his hand, his long nails digging into the tender skin of her throat. Judging by the tensile strength in his hands, he could probably snap her neck with little more than a twitch of his fingers.

"Eloisa was a foolish, empty-headed lamb," he said. "I like this one much better. I wager she'll fight like a tiger when I sink my teeth into her."

"I warned you, Victor," Adrian said softly, taking one step toward them, then another, "that I was only going to ask you to step away from her one time."

"What are you going to do? Put a crossbow bolt through my heart? If you destroy me, your brother may never recover his precious soul, and we all know you won't risk his soul just to save your latest whore. Why don't you beg him for your life, sweeting?" he hissed in Caroline's ear. "I do so love it when a woman begs."

Twisting a fistful of her hair around his hand with enough pressure to nearly tear it from her scalp, Duvalier forced her to her knees. Her eyes smarted with tears of agony; the rough stones bit into her knees through the thin fabric of Eloisa's gown.

"It's probably not the first time you've been on your knees for him," Duvalier crooned. "But I can promise you it will be the last."

Caroline gazed up at Adrian through a veil of tears, knowing that her life was the one thing she couldn't ask of him. Not when he'd already sacrificed so much to try and save his brother's soul. Wishing she could tell him how much she loved him with only a glance, she smiled through her tears. "I chose this fate, Adrian. You're not to blame. No matter what he says or does, always remember that he's the monster, not you!"

Adrian gazed at her with melting tenderness as Duvalier yanked back her head, exposing the vulnerable underside of her throat. As his gleaming fangs descended, Adrian narrowed his eyes and fired.

The lethal bolt came whizzing straight for Duvalier's heart. He cried out in outrage, but there was only enough time to catch a glimpse of his stunned expression before the bolt caught him square in the heart and his body dissolved into a whirling maelstrom of dust.

His cloak collapsed, momentarily blinding Caroline. By the time she could sweep it away, Duvalier was gone, the dust of his bones scattered on the wind. The crossbow bolt kept right on going, striking the wall on the opposite side of the bridge, where it clattered harmlessly to the stones.

Hurling the crossbow aside, Adrian rushed to Caroline and tugged her into his arms. She gazed up at him in disbelief, her shock slowly sharpening into comprehension.

Catching the front of his shirt in her hands, she gave him a harsh shake. "Why in the name of God did you fire? With Duvalier destroyed, how are you ever going to find Julian's soul? After everything you've done, everything you've sacrificed to protect him, how could you choose me over him?"

Adrian cupped her face tenderly in his hand, stroking a fresh tear from her cheek with his thumb. Gazing deep into her misty gray eyes, he said, "As a very wise man once told me, what value is a man's soul when compared with the incomparable riches of a woman's heart?"

As he lowered his lips to hers, Caroline's heart swelled with love and joy. Their lips met just as the first rays of the sun broke over the eastern horizon, bathing them in the holy light of dawn.

"Who on earth ever heard of a midnight wedding?"

Aunt Marietta fanned herself, her shrill voice drawing curious glances from the guests seated around them in the castle's great hall. The same guests who had been summarily dismissed from the great hall only a fortnight ago when the viscount's masquerade ball had erupted in a torrent of gossip and innuendo still being dissected by London's tawdriest newspapers.

No amount of fanning could dry the beads of sweat trickling down Aunt Marietta's throat to disappear between her expansive breasts. They were gathering copious amounts of rice powder as they rolled across her doughy flesh, making her look like a pastry topped with melting marzipan. "Not only a midnight wedding, but a midnight wedding not even being held in a church! I don't know if my own reputation will *ever* recover from the scandal. Everyone knows a proper wedding should be held on a sunny Saturday morning and followed with a hearty breakfast."

Portia sank deeper into her chair, thinking that her aunt was probably much more interested in the hearty breakfast than the wedding. "I've already pointed out that it's Friday night, Auntie. Which means that the minute the clock strikes midnight, it *will* be Saturday morning."

Aunt Marietta snapped her fan closed and whacked Portia on the thigh with it. "Don't be a cheeky chit. You don't want to end up like your sister."

"Ah, yes—poor, unfortunate Caroline." Portia sighed. "Forced to spend the rest of her life married to a handsome, wealthy viscount who adores her. I don't know how she'll ever manage."

"I was speaking of your other sister." Aunt Marietta drew a crumpled handkerchief out of her cleavage and dabbed at her eyes. "My dear, sweet Vivienne. I had such high hopes for the girl. I never dreamed she'd sink so low as to elope to Gretna Green with a *constable*." She spat out the word as if it was the foulest of epithets.

"He's a policeman, Auntie, not an ax murderer. And they wouldn't have eloped if Caroline hadn't given them her blessing. She said she was tired of watching them make calf's eyes at each other over the dinner table." Portia glanced behind them to find Vivienne and her new husband making calf's eyes at each other over an arrangement of fresh cut posies.

"Oh, look, there's your father's cousin!" The handkerchief disappeared back into Aunt Marietta's bodice. "Oh, Cecil! Cecil!" she trilled, wiggling her gloved fingers at the new arrival before leaning over and whispering to Portia, "I've often wondered why such a handsome fellow never took a bride."

Portia craned her neck, unable to bite back an impish grin. "Perhaps that's just what Lord Trevelyan is going over to ask him."

"Ah, you must be Caroline's cousin Cecil!" Adrian exclaimed, his shadow dwarfing the squat man. "She's told me so very much about you."

"She has?" Plainly torn between being flattered and frightened, Cousin Cecil ducked his heavily pomaded head, his beady eyes darting over the crowd as if looking for an escape. "I've always thought very highly of the gel, I have. Not more highly than I should have, mind you," he added, tittering nervously.

Adrian gave him an encouraging smile. "She had much to say about the kindness and generosity you've shown her and her sisters over the years."

"Has she now?" His confidence increasing, Cousin Cecil plumped out his chest like a preening partridge. "I was hoping I might call on you sometime in the near future, m'lord. It has occurred to me that you'll probably be eager to get the youngest Cabot chit off your hands. If the dowry is generous enough, I just might be willing to help. Young Portia has a rather headstrong and impertinent nature, but with a firm hand, I think I can beat that out of the gel."

Adrian's smile never wavered. He simply threw one brawny arm around Cousin Cecil's neck, placing him in an impromptu headlock. "That's a marvelous idea," he said, dragging him toward the door. "Why don't we step out into the garden to discuss it?"

When Adrian returned to the great hall a few minutes later, he was all alone. He dusted off the front of his coat, jerked his waistcoat straight, then ruefully studied his skinned knuckles, hoping his bride wouldn't mind them.

"Surely you can't be planning on getting married with your cravat looking like that," Julian said, appearing out of nowhere to give the crooked scrap of linen a stern tweak.

Adrian jumped. "Bloody hell! I wish you'd stop doing that! You're going to give me an apoplexy."

Julian grinned at him. "I've been practicing. I decided Duvalier was right about one thing. Maybe it is time for me to embrace some of my gifts—at least the more useful ones."

Adrian clapped a hand on his brother's shoulder, giving it an affectionate squeeze. "That suits me just fine as long as I don't catch you turning into a bat and flitting about the chandelier any time soon."

* * *

"Caroline told me you were going away."

The brothers turned as one to find Portia standing just behind them. Her dark curls were piled high on her head and the tall collar of her white dimity gown was not so out of fashion as to generate curiosity or comment among the guests.

Shooting his brother a pointed look, Adrian drew his pocket watch out of his waistcoat and snapped it open. "It's nearly midnight. I should go. I wouldn't want to keep my bride waiting." Giving Portia's cheek a fond tweak, he headed for the huge hearth that was to double as an altar, leaving Julian all alone to face Portia.

She glanced around to make sure no one was eavesdropping before saying, "My sister told me you were going to Paris to search for the vampire who may have sired Duvalier."

Julian nodded. "With Duvalier vanquished for good and Adrian getting married, I thought maybe it was time I started fighting my own battles. I may not be able to grow old, but that doesn't mean I can't grow up. Ah, here comes the vicar," he said, visibly relieved to have found a distraction. "I really should head for the back of the hall. I appreciate Adrian and Caroline not holding their wedding in a church—hallowed ground and all that rot—but all of these robes and candles still make me want to jump right out the nearest window."

He turned to go, then swore softly beneath his breath and turned back. Closing his hands over Portia's upper arms, he drew her close and kissed her gently on the brow, his lips lingering against the warm satin of her skin. "Don't ever forget me, bright eyes," he whispered.

"How could I?" As he drew away from her, Portia touched a hand to her collar, her eyes no longer sparkling with a child's innocence, but a woman's wisdom. "I'll always have the scars to remember you by."

"Portia!" Aunt Marietta barked. "You need to take your seat! It's three minutes until midnight!"

"I'll be right there," Portia called, glancing over her shoulder. When she turned back, Julian was gone. Frowning, she scanned the milling guests, but his lean, elegant form was nowhere to be found.

She sighed wistfully and headed back across the hall, never seeing the shadow flitting around the chandelier that dangled just over her head.

"And which Miss Cabot would you be today?" Wilbury asked dryly as Caroline stepped up to the doorway, preparing to join her groom at the makeshift altar where they were to repeat their vows and begin their life as man and wife.

She slapped the butler on the arm with her bouquet of white roses, releasing a whiff of their heady fragrance. "You needn't tease so, Wilbury. After tonight, you'll be able to address me simply as Lady Trevelyan."

He wheezed out a labored sigh. "I suppose it would behoove me to please you since you'll be mistress of this castle in—" He cleared his throat. "—approximately one minute."

"One minute," Caroline whispered, suffused with both wonder and terror.

But that terror faded when she peeked around the door frame and saw Adrian waiting for her on the other side of the great hall. His hair gleamed in the candlelight while his eyes shone with love and tenderness, the invitation in their luminous blue-green depths impossible to resist.

Caroline plucked one of the blooms from the roses and tucked it behind her ear in a silent tribute to the woman who had brought them all together. As she clutched her bouquet and took her first step toward Adrian's waiting arms, every clock in the castle began to chime at once, heralding the arrival of a brand new day.